The Picasso Scam

STUART PAWSON

Allison & Busby Limited
13 Charlotte Mews
London W1T 4EJ
www.allisonandbusby.com

A CIP catalogue record for this book is available from
the British Library.

This paperback edition first published by
Allison & Busby Ltd in 2004 (ISBN 978-0-7490-8390-8).
Reissued in 2011.

10 9 8 7 6 5 4 3 2 1

ISBN 978-0-7490-0933-5

Typeset in 11.5/16 pt Sabon by
Allison & Busby Ltd.

The paper used for this Allison & Busby publication
has been produced from trees that have been legally sourced
from well-managed and credibly certified forests.

Printed and bound in the UK by
CPI Bookmarque, Croydon, CR0 4TD

The Picasso Scam

CHAPTER ONE

Red was no longer my favourite colour. Suddenly it was the colour of danger. And blood. Is that why it was chosen to represent danger? It seemed the most important question in the world to me. Strange and inconsequential, the thoughts you have when death is only the twitch of a finger away.

The red was mine, my blood, pumping between the fingers I was clutching to my stomach as I staggered towards the doorway from the warehouse. Behind me the shotgun exploded again as I hit the door. I cringed with fear and pain but no fiery blast came, just cold, fresh air as I fell through on to the welcome pavement outside.

Footsteps. I could see feet all around me. And voices: 'He's hurt . . . Call a doctor . . . He's bleeding . . . I heard a shot . . . What's your name?'

'What's your name?'

Somebody was shaking my shoulder: 'What's your name?'

Did they mean me?

Again, gently: 'What are you called, love?'

'Priest,' I said. My face was pressed against the wet pavement. It was cool and friendly, and had a smell that rekindled some way-back memory.

'What did you say, love?'

'Priest,' said a voice in my head, a hundred miles away. If only I could remember . . . 'He wants a priest.'

'We've sent for the police and an ambulance.'

'What are you called?'

'Priest.'

'Don't worry about a priest, love, let's get you to hospital. There'll be a priest there.'

'No! I don't want a priest . . . I *am* a priest.' The voice was a thousand miles away now, or was I just thinking it. 'I am not a priest, I am . . . Priest . . . Charlie Priest. Detective Inspector Charles Priest of the . . .'

That smell. I could remember what it was. When we were kids we played cowboys and Indians. You had to lie on the ground and count to fifty. When you'd been shot. When you were dead.

There are some names you forget instantly and some that you hear once and they are engraved on the inside of your skull for ever. It was three years earlier that I had first come across Aubrey Cakebread, but I knew there was no need to write the name down. Once afflicted there was no cure, like herpes.

We were driving over the Tops from Lancashire back to Yorkshire after interviewing a prisoner being held at Oldfield. I had Nigel Newley with me. Nigel was a graduate recruit seconded to CID as part of his crash course in becoming a wonderful British bobby. He was handsome, athletic, had a decent mind and spoke like a BBC newsreader. He was with me because nobody else at Heckley nick could stand him.

We had been entertained by the Oldfield boys – all part of Nigel's training, of course – and it was late. My ancient Cortina estate was protesting at the gradients. The interior was filled with exhaust fumes and the smell of an abused clutch.

'A Cortina!' exclaimed Nigel. 'How come you drive a clapped-out Cortina?' For a Southerner he didn't mince his words.

'It came cheap,' I said.

'I see. You mean it's all part of your cover so you can bust a gang of fluffy-dice thieves.'

'Don't be insolent. The Cortina is a fine, reliable vehicle. At this very moment there are thousands of housewives snuggling up to their husbands, dreaming about the romantic evenings they used to spend in the back seat of their first company Cortina.'

I crunched it into second for the last hairpin. A few moments later we crested the brow and the car sighed with relief. The fumes cleared and we enjoyed the night air.

'When I say cheap I mean really cheap,' I told him. 'Like free – I had it given.'

'On your pay, and single, I would have thought you'd have something flash,' he replied.

Away to our left were the lights of Heckley and the string of other towns making up what was once called the Heavy Woollen District. Millions of glowing specks: beads of orange streetlights and coloured window lights, like galaxies carelessly flung down to blanket the hills. We used to come up here often, when I was courting Vanessa, just to look at the lights. Well, that wasn't the only reason.

Vanessa had dreams of painting the sight, and one night we brought her paints and a canvas and she worked by the car's interior light. She was going through her Abstract Expressionist phase. The picture had a background of black and Prussian blue stabs of colour, with the lights picked out by splatters of white, yellow and orange. It was good – I liked it – but she made a right Jackson Pollock of the inside of the car.

'The lights look nice,' Nigel confirmed.

'Yes, they do,' I replied eventually.

We were coasting downhill. The Cortina was a lot happier going downhill. I wasn't – the brakes were about as much use as a plough to a fish farmer.

'I had a messy divorce,' I explained. 'Left me cleaned

out, with a big mortgage. A friend gave me this to help out. It's been a godsend.'

'Sorry, boss,' he said. 'I didn't mean to pry.'

'Don't worry about it,' I replied. 'It's over. From now on it can only get better.'

We rolled on in silence for a while. 'Are you in a hurry to get back?' I asked.

Nigel said he wasn't.

'Good. So let's go looking for rustlers. You know all about them, I suppose?' No harm in reminding him of the pecking order. There had been a spate of sheep-stealing lately. Lambs had gone missing, and one had been found staggering around with a crossbow bolt sticking through its neck. Nigel was familiar with the basics of the case. I swung off the main road and followed a much narrower one for about a mile, to the area where the injured lamb had been found. When we reached a crossroads I parked in a gateway, behind a dry-stone wall. In one of the angles made by the roads stood a telephone box. It was the old-fashioned type, and the light was on inside.

I filled Nigel in on the details. The farmer had found the lamb and tyre tracks near the box. It was a slim chance but that was what detective work was all about: put yourself in the right place and then be patient. Besides, I didn't want to go home. A fellow officer is not my first choice for company on a Friday night, but at this hour it was the best I was going to get.

'What the devil is the phone box doing up here?' asked Nigel.

'Saving lives in winter,' I replied, 'and winning a few votes for the councillor who put it there. It's supposed to be the loneliest box in the country.'

We got talking about the job. I told him about the old Heavy Woollen District, and how the low property prices and fine old Victorian houses seemed to be attracting a certain type of criminal who had an eye for privacy. The area had also spawned a disproportionately high number of multiple killers.

'Don't make the mistake of thinking this is the sticks,' I told him. 'Crimewise, this is the land of opportunity. Every one of those lights we could see from up the hill has a story to tell, and plenty of 'em's illegal.'

'Is it true you were the youngest-ever inspector?' he asked.

I laughed. 'Probably not, but I was young. Now I am quite definitely the longest-serving inspector.'

'What went wrong?'

'Who knows?' I said. Apart from me.

Nigel was OK. I decided to expand a little. Maybe it would do me good. 'I started out as an art student but I didn't seem to fit in. When I finished I decided I wanted a complete change, so I came into the family firm. Dad was a Dixon of Dock Green desk sergeant at Heckley for donkey's years. He died of cancer, but I made him happy in the end. I'm glad about that. Now I'm beginning to think that I don't fit in again.

It's only taken me until now to realise it.' This was getting serious. I grinned at him: 'Maybe I'm just shiftless.'

We could see the lights of an occasional vehicle wind up the main road and vanish over the Tops.

'I'd rather be here with the other new starter,' I said. 'No offence, but she's better-looking than you.'

'Helen Chatterton?' said Nigel. 'She is good-looking. Got brilliant marks at college. Pity about the halitosis.'

'You're joking?' I winced at the thought of it.

'No way. She could knock out Schwarzenegger at ten paces, providing the wind was right.'

'Poor kid. Remind me to take her off my Christmas card list.'

A pair of lights was crawling up the hill, brilliant beams sweeping through the cold night air.

'He's taking it a bit steady,' I commented.

'Probably an elderly Cortina,' suggested Nigel.

'Can't be,' I replied. 'They don't have a warm yellow glow like these.'

The lights hesitated at the end of the lane, then swung our way. 'Bingo!' I cried. 'We could be in business.'

The car came slowly towards us, then stopped outside the telephone box and switched off its lights.

'It's a Roller!' exclaimed Nigel under his breath.

A burly figure got out of the Rolls Royce and waddled towards the phone box, barely visible in the meagre illumination it gave off. His silhouette hunched over the coin box and I saw the handset come up to his ear.

After two or three seconds he let it fall from his hand, turned, and walked back to his car.

'What the heck is he playing at?' I wondered softly.

The Rolls Royce did a U-turn, bumping over the verge, and set off back towards the main road.

'Wait there,' I ordered, and jumped out and ran towards the box. The handset was swinging on the end of its wire. I grabbed it and put it to my ear.

'Hello, hello,' a voice was saying. An Asian voice. 'Is anybody there? What do you want?'

'Hello,' I said. 'Who is that, please?'

'This is Hassan's Taxis. Do you want a taxi?'

'Hassan's Taxis,' I repeated. 'Where exactly do you operate from?'

'We are in Welton,' he told me. 'Do you want a taxi?'

'No,' I replied, 'no thanks,' and hung up. I sprinted back to the car and leapt in. 'C'mon,' I said, 'let's get his number.' I gunned the Cortina out of the gateway and down the lane. Nigel was scrambling for his seat belt.

'Oh, no!' he cried. 'Please God, not a chase. Not in a Cortina!'

We rattled and jarred down the bumpy track. 'It's an old trick,' I told him. 'This time of night on a Friday is a busy time for taxis. Find a quiet phone box, dial a rival firm, put a couple of quid in the slot and leave the phone off the hook. It's supposed to keep their line tied up for quite a while.'

'Does it work?' he asked.

'I'm not sure, now. Popular folklore says it does. It

certainly worked in the past, when it was all done by wires.'

We swung on to the main road just in time to see the Rolls's tail-lights vanish over the brow towards Lancashire. The familiar scorching smell stung our nostrils as the Cortina struggled with the gradient. Nigel started making low groaning noises.

'Don't worry about it,' I told him. 'I've seen *Bullitt* three times.'

'*Bullitt?* Was that a talkie?'

'Yes, and in colour.'

'That's right – my dad told me about it. He said Steve McQueen's car had six hubcaps.'

'It probably had brakes, too,' I said. I decided to do some boasting. 'Actually, I've got a Jaguar back home in my mother's garage.'

'Then why aren't we in that?' he moaned, bracing himself against the dashboard as we slid round a right-hander.

'Because it's in a worse state than this. It's in a thousand bits. I'm supposed to be restoring it.'

As we levelled out on to the Tops, the tail-lights came back into view. They were much closer. Mr Rolls was obviously not in a hurry.

'We'll just get his number, then back off,' I said.

We caught him on the downgrade without any heroics.

'Personal number,' commented Nigel, 'ABC, very nice.'

15

'Can't be too many of those about,' I suggested.

Nigel rose to the bait like a hungry trout on the Day of the Mayflies. 'Nine hundred and ninety-nine, I suppose,' he told me, modestly.

We pulled off at the first left turn and as soon as the Rolls had vanished we headed for home.

'We'll check it out Monday morning,' I said, adding: 'That's your job.'

When I arrived at the station on Monday morning, Nigel was hovering around the front desk. I asked him what he was doing there.

'PC Riley has just asked me to watch things, sir, while he goes to the bog. He says he's got a bad stomach.'

'OK, but I want you on parade in five minutes.'

We don't actually have parades in CID, but we still use the term. It just means 'be there', so that we can discuss the previous twenty-four hours' happenings. I sprinted upstairs and stood looking out of the front window. Shortly, a young woman appeared carrying a small parcel in front of her, and walked in through the front entrance of the nick. I could visualise the scene.

'I would like to report some lost property,' she would be saying. Nigel would then make out the proper forms, give the lady a receipt and tell her when she could claim it if the rightful owner didn't. As soon as she had gone Riley would reappear.

After parade and the subdivisional Officers'

management meeting, better known as morning assembly, I asked Nigel what had been in the parcel.

'I was a bit surprised when PC Riley opened it,' he told me. 'It contained a packet of six Lyons individual chocolate Swiss rolls.'

'What did he do with them?' I asked.

'He ate one. That really shook me.'

'Only one?' I enquired.

Nigel looked sheepish. 'He gave me one. I ate one, too.'

'You ate some evidence,' I stated.

'Lost property, not evidence, sir.'

He looked uncomfortable, as if his entire future had been blighted by a wayward Swiss roll.

'Never mind that for now. Have that Rolls Royce checked out.'

I settled down at the small mountain of paper on my desk. I thumbed my way through the pile, looking for money, offers of bribes or letters from pining young ladies. None. It was one of those Mondays. Nigel was back before I had done anything constructive.

'How about this?' he said, looking a little brighter. 'ABC belongs to one Aubrey Bingham Cakebread, of The Ponderosa, Welton.'

Welton was on the outskirts of Oldfield, on the posh side. It was also the home of Hassan's Taxis. I thought about things for a while. 'Ring your new-found friends in Oldfield,' I told him. 'Thank them for their hospitality and then ask them if they have anything on Mr Breadcake.'

'Cakebread, sir,' interrupted Nigel.

'Tell them about the phone box. Don't expect much back, it's just background information. It may help them – they're having near gang warfare between the taxi companies.'

Nigel turned to go back to his desk, then changed his mind. 'Mr Priest, er, do you think I ought to do anything about the chocolate rolls? Maybe buy a new box?'

I hated being called sir and Mr Priest. It made me feel old. Worse, it made me feel my age. We were expected to stick to the formalities, though, when we were in the station. I rocked back in my chair and put one foot on the desk. If I'd been a hat man I would have pushed it to the back of my head with a forefinger. I smiled at him and told him he had been set up.

'The woman is Riley's sister,' I said. 'She's the manageress of the confectionery shop on the corner. The chocolate rolls weren't lost. I have every confidence that she put the money for them in the till. Sometime this morning Sergeant Jenks will request an audience with you and give you a bollocking. Tell him to get stuffed, but politely, of course.'

When Nigel was summoned to Sergeant Jenks's office he was met by a tableau reminiscent of curtain rise on the second act of one of Agatha Christie's lesser works. Jenks was standing with a small carton containing four chocolate rolls held in front of him. Riley was standing to attention with his nose up at a ridiculous angle.

'Come in, Newley,' said Jenks. 'Riley was just telling me about this lost property. Now then, Riley, what 'append to the other two chocolate rolls?'

Riley stood stock-still and silent.

'I demand an answer, Constable Riley!' shouted Jenks.

'Constable Newley ate them both,' he blurted out.

'Is that so?' hissed Jenks, turning to Nigel.

It was cruel, it was vicious. Lifetime enmities could be created by this well-rehearsed scenario, but he would meet a lot worse on the streets.

'Yessir!' said Nigel, without hesitation. 'I ate them both.' He couldn't resist adding, 'They were excellent.'

Jenks tried valiantly to rescue the situation. 'Then what do you suggest we do when somebody comes in to claim them?'

'Two possible approaches occur to me, sir. We can either nip out and buy a new packet, or alternatively deny all knowledge and tell them to piss off.'

Jenks paused for a second as the feeling of defeat registered, then said: 'In that case we may as well eat the rest. Have a chocolate roll.'

Meanwhile Helen Chatterton was having her initiation ceremony in the town mortuary, where she had been taken on the pretext of an identification. When a white-sheeted corpse sat up she collapsed in a gibbering heap. Halitosis that can move the dead is not to be sniffed at.

Eventually Nigel returned to the office and filled me in on the Cakebread saga. Cakebread was now a pillar of Oldfield society, after a shaky start involving a GBH and extortion charge. Now heavily into property and road haulage. Seen at all the posh charity dos. Married to an ex-beauty queen. His pride and joy, though, was his taxi firm, ABC Taxis. He had started out with them – they were his ticket to legitimacy. In return, I told Nigel that as long as he was with me he was a detective. He didn't take orders from uniformed constables, no matter how senior, unless I okayed it. He was as green as a seasick tree frog, but he'd learn if the sadists didn't get to him first. He seemed grateful for the clarification.

Just before lunchtime I received a call from the DI at Oldfield. 'We decided to lean on Mr Cakebread a little,' he told me, 'let him know we have long memories. He took great pleasure in telling us his exact whereabouts on Friday evening. He and his lady wife were slumming it on your side of the continental divide, at a charity bash in the Heckley Dining Club, as the personal guests of Chief Constable Ernest Hilditch and his delightful wife, Nora.'

'Bloody Nora!' I said.

'Shit!' said Nigel when I told him. After a while he asked: 'Why does a successful businessman like him prat about making stupid phone calls in the middle of the night? There's no sense to it.'

'He's a crook,' I answered, 'a bovver boy who never grew up. He has a criminal mind. Can't get it out of his system. Hassan's are an irritation and he wants rid of them. We'll get him one day, as sure as God made little, nasty French apples.'

'What do we do with it?' he asked.

'Nothing. Just put it in a box at the back of your mind, marked For Future Reference. That's where I'm putting it.'

And that's where it stayed for the next three years.

CHAPTER TWO

The Cortina is long gone but unlamented, replaced by one of General Motors' later models. Not one that Nigel would regard as flash, though. Financially I was on an even keel, but if I'd been able to turn the clock back to the days when I was broke, I would have done. My mother had died, and I had inherited the family house. I guess she had missed Dad more than I realised, and I hadn't spent as much time with her as I ought. More guilt to put on the not inconsiderable pile that was there already. Having two policemen in her life caused her more worry than I knew. Before I was married, when I came home in the middle of the night after a long stint on duty, I would hear the bed creak as she relaxed and finally dropped off to sleep.

My modest semi had been sold and I was now master

of the house I had grown up in. No mortgage to pay, so I could afford a reasonable car. I'd spent a small fortune on restoring the Jaguar that my father had bought to keep him busy during his retirement. He had died before he could finish it. It had always been his ambition to own a Jag. I like to think that just seeing it in his garage and working on it and sitting in the leather seats was the realisation of that ambition, even though he never did get to drive it. That was going to be my pleasure, in the near future, when the wheels came back from the specialist who was rebuilding them. It was a relief, though, to be out of the woods money-wise. A police officer with financial problems is open to suspicion. And temptation.

Meanwhile, I had just taken the workaday car into the garage for its first annual service. It was a pleasant spring Monday morning. I had worked most of the weekend and the sun was shining. I left the car at nine a.m., as arranged, and started the leisurely stroll to the police station about a mile away. Sod 'em, I thought – if anybody wanted me they would just have to wait.

Through the town centre I studied the faces on the businessmen and office girls hurrying to their posts. I studied the legs on the office girls, too. I occasionally cast an appraising glance at the fronts of their blouses. It was that time of year when they were beginning to discard their coats. The experience made me feel slightly faint. The old worry came back – that I was turning into a dirty old man. Fortunately I had discussed it with

Gilbert Wood and he said it was perfectly natural – he had always felt this way. I confessed that I had, too. It just seemed worse these days. Walking across town made a pleasant start to the week, even if it did upset my emotional equilibrium. Don't think I could stand it every day, though.

Going up the hill out of the centre I remembered I needed some postage stamps. The post office was in a parade of shops on the other side of the road. A wide grass verge graced the front of it, and three youths were riding round in circles on mountain bikes. There was something aimless, unnatural, about their restless motion. Why didn't they stop and talk, or ride with some purpose? What were they doing up at this ungodly hour? Any self-respecting layabout should still be in bed after watching snuff videos until five o' clock.

There was just one other customer in the shop: a small Chinese man. He kept me waiting quite a long time. The postmaster was counting a pile of money the Chinaman had brought in, ticking off the amounts against the entries in his paying-in book. There were neat bundles of fivers, tenners and twenties, plus bags of coins. We were talking about thousands rather than hundreds. When he left I followed him to the door and noted which car he got into. A shiny new BMW. He drove off and the youths on the bikes meandered off in the same direction. I went back to the counter and showed the postmaster my ID card.

'How often does he come in with money like that?' I asked him.

'Every morning, but on Mondays he has all the weekend's takings.'

'I think we ought to have a word with him, he's asking for trouble.' I bought my stamps and thanked him.

When I walked into the office Dave 'Sparky' Sparkington was sitting at the typewriter desk. He was studying a well-thumbed dictionary.

'Ask me,' I challenged him.

'Morning, boss. How many gs in exaggerate?

'Er, six. Any messages?'

'Thank you. On your pad.'

'You're welcome.'

There were three names on the pad. One was a DI in another force. I knew what that was about. The other two were Wilf Trumble and Rudi Truscott.

'What does old Wilf want?' I asked. He was a retired PC who had been a contemporary of my father's. I had known him all my life, and for a long time, when I was a kid, had called him 'Uncle'.

'Grumpy old sod wouldn't say,' answered Sparky. 'Said it was for your ears only.'

'And Truscott?'

'Wouldn't say, either. Or leave a number. Didn't want anybody else, so I told him you'd be in about ten. He said he'd ring then. Do you know him?'

'Yes, I know him.' I certainly did know him.

I made us both some tea. No point in diverting your DC off police work just to make the tea. Besides, he made it too strong. I rang old Wilf. I had a faint hope about what it might be.

'Hello, Charlie,' he said. 'What time are you supposed to start these days?'

'We've got it sussed, Wilf. Mondays I start about ten, other days I come late. What can I do for you?'

'A lady friend of ours is worried about the security of her home. She's a friend of Betty's from church. I said I would arrange for someone to pop up and give her some advice, if you know what I mean.'

'No problem, Wilf. I'll pass it on to the crime prevention officer.'

'Anybody can ring the crime prevention officer,' he replied testily. 'I told her that I would put one of my best men on to it.' His voice dropped to a whisper. 'Charlie, this is one that I think you should, er, handle yourself.'

I could almost feel and see the nudge-nudge, wink-wink. 'Well, thank you for that information, Officer Trumble,' I said in a loud voice. 'I'll attend to it personally, as soon as possible.'

'The address is the Old Vicarage, on the Top Road. Near St Bidulph's. It's Mrs Wilberforce, she's a widow. Don't dash off, Betty wants a word.'

'Hello, Charlie. How are you keeping?' she asked.

I had to put my hand over the mouthpiece for a

moment. Sparky was comparing his tea unfavourably with sheep's urine. 'Oh, you know, a policeman's lot is not a happy one. Listen, Betty, are you up to your old tricks again?'

It was Betty's vocation in life to see every single man, and me in particular, happily married. 'Don't know what you're talking about,' she laughed, then added: 'I've just made a casserole and there looks to be rather a lot. I don't suppose you are eating properly, so would you like to come for your tea?'

That was the hope I'd been holding.

I checked out the BMW number with the police national computer. It belonged to a man with a very Chinese-sounding name who lived in Heckley.

'If that can wait half an hour I've got somewhere for us to go,' I said to Sparky.

'What about that call at ten?' he asked. It was nearly ten now.

'I don't want to talk to him. If we go now we'll miss him.'

In the car I told Sparky about the youths on the bikes. I felt certain they were watching the Chinaman. We went to the address for the BMW. It was a Chinese restaurant and takeaway, more or less what I had expected.

'He takes his money to the post office every day. But on a Monday morning he has all Saturday's and Sunday's takings to check in. A nice little haul for someone.'

'Are you going to alert him?' asked Sparky.

I thought for a few seconds.

'No,' I decided, 'let's stick our necks out.'

'What about his neck?'

'His neck is already stuck out.'

When we arrived back at the station Detective Sergeant Tony Willis was in. 'Bloke called Truscott been after you, Charlie. Said it was personal. He sounded frantic. I told him to ring back at two.'

'Well, if he rings again tell him I'm not in, even if I am. I don't want to talk to him.'

'It sounded important to him that he spoke to you,' he said.

'It's important to me that I don't,' I snapped.

I was angry and it showed. The two of them were quiet for a while, then Sparky chipped in: 'You sound upset, boss. It's not like you to give someone the runaround.'

He was right. I give the impression of being easy-going, but I set standards. I hadn't a clue what the man could want, I only knew that he had come close to ruining my life. I was with friends, so I said quietly: 'When my wife left me she went off with someone called Rudi Truscott. He was a lecturer at the art college. I assume it's the same one. I don't know what he wants and I don't want to know.'

It had been eight years, and I'd thought the hurt had gone, but it hadn't. It just lurked in the undergrowth, waiting for something to come along and disturb it. I tried to make light of it. 'He probably wants me to get him off a parking rap,' I said.

It was later that afternoon when he caught me. Tony answered the phone. 'I'll put him on,' he said, and passed me the handset. He looked uncomfortable that he had refused to lie for me. Not a bad quality in a policeman, I suppose.

'Hello, Rudolph, what do you want?' He hated being called Rudolph. He liked to be Rudi to everyone, just as I liked to be Charlie, good old Charlie, everybody's friend.

'Charlie, thank God I've caught you, I've got to see you.' He really did sound frantic.

'Why?' I asked.

'I think someone wants to kill me.'

'In that case, I'm on their side.'

'When can I see you, Charlie?'

'I work long hours. But you know that, don't you?'

He ignored the jibe. 'I don't want to come to Heckley. Can you meet me halfway? Say you will, please, Charlie, I don't know who else to turn to.'

I've always been a sucker for a sob story. But maybe I just wanted to see him squirm. He certainly sounded scared. 'Where are you?' I asked.

'Scotland.'

'Scotland! You want me to come halfway to Scotland?'

'Do you know the museum at Beamish?'

I'd heard of it, but never been.

'There's a pub near the entrance called The Shepherd and Shepherdess. Will you meet me there?'

'OK, I suppose so,' I told him.

'Tomorrow?'

'No chance, make it Wednesday, for lunch. Your treat.' He expressed his eternal gratitude and rang off.

'Bad news?' enquired Tony.

'No, just the opposite,' I said, faking a grin. 'He reckons someone's trying to kill him.' I jumped to my feet. 'I'm off to fetch my car. Then I've got places to go and deeds to do. Make sure somebody watches the Chinaman in the morning.'

'Do you want a lift?'

'No thanks, I'll walk.'

As I strode through the yard a patrol car was just leaving, driven by WPC Kim Limbert. The chance of a ride with Kim was more than I could resist, so I waved her down. Kim came to Britain from Guyana as a very small child. Her parents believed she was gifted and wanted to give her the chance to realise her potential. She didn't disappoint them, doing well at school and going on to pick up a degree in law. Then she ruined it by joining the Force, but now she was on the promotion ladder. She was also six feet tall, and could have graced the catwalk of any fashion house she chose, had that been her inclination. I asked her to take me to the garage, then said: 'Looking forward to leaving us, Kim?'

'No, not really, sir. I've enjoyed being at Heckley, it's a good crew. But I'm in the job for promotion, so I'll have to move around.'

Sir. There it was again. It was even more hurtful when a beautiful young woman used it. Why couldn't she call me Charlie, or . . . Snufflebum? I said: 'You'll be OK. There's some mean hombres in the city, but you'll deal with them.'

'No doubt my fellow officers will look after me.'

I smiled wistfully. 'It's your fellow officers I'm talking about. You know where your Uncle Charlie is if you have any problems. Just drop me off on the corner.'

The car was ready for collection so I found myself way ahead of schedule. Ah, well, a faint heart never fondled a fair maiden. Besides, if I called on Mrs Wilberforce it would give me something to tell Wilf and Betty over dinner. I pointed the bonnet up the hill towards the Top Road and the ancient buttresses of St Bidulph's.

Mrs Wilberforce was in the garden. She was going on for my age and almost as tall as me. Her hair was fair and a line of curls fell across her forehead, like you see on Roman statues. The word Junoesque seemed appropriate. I could imagine her in her youth, leading the Cheltenham Ladies' College hockey team on to the field, and being chaired off shoulder-high after scoring the winning goal in the final chukka. She might have been dressed to talk to the WI at the Albert Hall if it hadn't been for the gardening gloves. I showed her my card the way I'd seen Philip Marlow do it.

'Inspector Priest,' I told her. 'I believe you'd like some advice about the security of your home?'

'Annabelle Wilberforce.' She pulled off a glove and held out her hand, looking straight into my face and smiling. Her nose wrinkled when she smiled. I was suddenly struck by an osmosis problem: my throat felt dry but my knees had turned to water.

'I didn't expect an inspector to call . . .' She paused and laughed.

I picked up the drift. 'There's the makings of a play in there somewhere,' I said. I went on: 'Wilf Trumble asked me to come, and when Wilf says jump, we jump.'

'Did you work with Wilf?' she asked.

'We overlapped careers for a while, but he's always been a friend of the family.'

'He and Betty worship at St Bidulph's. They are a lovely couple.'

I asked her to take me round the exterior of the house. It was a fine building and had been extensively modernised. I bet the current vicar would have preferred it to the tacky little box they'd put him in.

'Do you do all the gardening yourself, Mrs Wilberforce?' I asked.

'Please, call me Annabelle,' she said. 'An old gentleman from up the road does most of it. He says I undo all his work.'

A few window locks and perhaps a burglar alarm were all that was required. I gave the speech about it being impossible to keep out a really determined thief but most were easily deterred by a few simple precautions. She didn't want to invest in a Rottweiler, thank God. I gave her a rough idea of what it would cost and recommended a couple of people who would do a good job.

'That's a relief,' she said. 'I'd heard some rather extravagant prices being quoted. Can I offer you a cup of tea, Inspector Priest? I assume you can drink tea when on duty. Or would you prefer coffee?'

'I'm probably off duty by now,' I answered, 'in which case I would love a cup of tea. And it's Charles or Charlie, I answer to either.'

The tea came in a delicate china service, with homemade fruit cake. I restrained myself and used just the tip of the spoon in the sugar, instead of my normal four big ones. When Annabelle noticed that I drank it black she asked if I would like lemon. Conversation was awkward and aimless for a while, then she referred back to our opening remarks.

'Do you go to the theatre at all, Charles?'

I did, although it was a year or three since my last visit. I told her why I hadn't been for a while. I noticed a Mahler CD on the player, so we talked about plays and music for a few minutes. I heard myself confessing to being addicted to art galleries, no need to mention pubs with sawdust on the floor and transport cafes. After the second cup I reluctantly stood up to leave. Annabelle thanked me for coming and said she had enjoyed our chat.

At the door I turned to her and said: 'Annabelle,

I hope you don't mind me saying this, but I can sometimes obtain tickets for concerts at the town hall. Cancellations. Normally they are booked up a year in advance. Would you like me to give you a ring the next time any are available?'

She opened her mouth in mock horror and said: 'Inspector Priest! I hope they don't fall off the back of a lorry!'

This woman could make me laugh. It was getting better all the time. "Fraid not,' I said. 'I ring my opposite number at the town hall and he nips down the corridor to the booking office. Then I have to send him a fat cheque. Shall I see what he can do?'

She leant on the edge of the door for a long while before she answered. Then she shook her head slowly. 'I think you're very kind for asking, Charles, and I'm grateful. But I don't think I want to just yet. Do you mind if we leave it for a while?'

Ah well. Good old flat-footed Inspector Plod had cocked it up again. I gave her a tight-lipped smile and said: 'That's OK. I believe that's what our American cousins call taking a raincheck.'

'Yes,' she said. 'Let's just say we are taking a raincheck.' She said it kindly, as if she meant it.

Wilf Trumble let me in and poured me a beer. Betty went into the kitchen to serve the casserole.

'What have you been up to?' Wilf asked. 'You're grinning like a butcher's terrier.'

I had a sip of beer and grinned some more. After a while I said: 'I've just seen a friend of yours.'

'Who might that be?'

'A certain Mrs Wilberforce,' I told him.

His eyes lit up: 'What do you think of her?

'I think she's a bit of all right.'

'She is, isn't she? Are you seeing her again?'

'What do you mean?' I protested. 'I saw her on a professional basis to give her some crime prevention advice. I don't chat up every woman I meet. I can be civilised when I try.' Then I asked him how long her husband had been dead.

'Peter? About a year, no, maybe going on for two. He was a smashing bloke. It was a great loss to us all when he went. No edge to him at all. You'd never believe he was a bishop. Not like some of the daydreamers we get.'

It was slow to register. It crept over me like a shadow creeping up an ivy-clad wall. 'Did you say he was . . . a bishop?'

'Yes. Didn't I tell you? Annabelle's husband was Peter Wilberforce, Bishop of Leeds. You must have heard of him.'

'Jesus Christ!' I exploded. 'I just asked the Bishop's wife for a date!'

Wilf nearly choked on his beer. 'I hope you didn't blaspheme,' he spluttered.

Betty invited us to go through and eat. Her famous casserole was well up to standard. Wilf took great pleasure in telling his wife what he knew, so out of politeness I filled them in on more or less what had happened.

Betty said, 'I know Wilf thinks I'm an old busybody, but I think you and Annabelle are made for each other. You liked her, didn't you? Help yourself to some more.'

I helped myself. I tried to sound uninvolved but appreciative. 'I think she's an extremely attractive lady, but I suspect she's just a teeny bit out of my league.'

'Nonsense!' snapped Betty. 'She's flesh and blood like everybody else. And she's been mourning for far too long. It's unhealthy.'

'I agree,' said Wilf. 'A fortnight should be plenty long enough.'

Betty glared at him. 'If you go first, I'll be eyeing up all the widowers at the ham tea,' she declared.

I changed my mind about the casserole. It wasn't just up to standard, it was exceptional.

CHAPTER THREE

Gilbert Wood is my superintendent. Our careers can be compared to the early American rocket experiments. His kept going up, but mine just cleared the launch tower before toppling over and flying horizontally. A few people thought I ought to be in his seat, but I wasn't one of them. We got on well together, worked as a team, with lots of mutual trust. It was more than that, though, we were good friends. I called into his office to tell him about the Chinaman and that I wanted Wednesday off.

'Another day off, Charlie? You had one two years ago. You realise you've only five months and twenty-nine days' holiday left now?'

'And a half. I only had half a day off two years ago. And if it turns out to be business on Wednesday I'll be putting in for expenses.'

Gilbert looked interested. 'Might it be business?' he asked.

I told him about the Rudi Truscott call.

'Mmm,' he said. 'Sounds promising. Beamish is a super place. Doesn't half take you back. The kids couldn't believe we lived like that. God, there's a dentist's surgery just like the school dentist had. Scares you silly.' He gave a shudder at the memory of it. 'What does this Truscott do?' he asked.

'He was a lecturer at the art school. He taught me when I was there. And Vanessa a few years later; but then he started making a reputation as a faker of old masters.'

Gilbert was about to speak but I held up a hand to stop him.

'I said he was a faker, not a forger. Legally, there is a difference.'

'Is he any good?' Gilbert asked.

'He will be,' I told him. 'He sells to dealers. What they do with them is their business, but there's probably a few Rudi Truscotts hanging in the galleries of Europe that are attributed to more famous names.'

'Sounds right up your street. Let me know what happens.'

'What about the Chinaman?' I asked him.

He thought for a second, then said: 'I'm not happy.'

'I didn't think you would be, but we've no information that they will try it on, just my instinct. If we grab them before they get near him there should be no danger.'

'Then it will be a lesser charge and it might not stick.'

'Does it matter?' I argued. 'They're only nematodes. It'll be a shock to their systems to get arrested before they do the job.'

'That's true.' Gilbert laughed at the thought of it. 'Scare the shit out of them – and we are supposed to be in the crime prevention business. But don't let them get near the Chinaman.'

I took the A61 through Leeds and then Harrogate and Ripon to avoid some of the tedium of the motorway. It's a rich, pastoral landscape up there; a different climatic zone to what I was used to. The scenery was fashioned by the meanderings of lazy rivers and the action of the plough, not gouged and bulldozed by glaciers. The people are different too, old money and new money, rubbing uneasily shoulder to shoulder. This is Yorkshire's Cocktail Belt, and you can keep it.

Eventually I had to join the A1, that conveyor of salesmen's cars on their ceaseless, brainless dash to the next appointment. I made it to mine. I wonder how many didn't.

The Shepherd and Shepherdess was easy to find. It's a big pub but standards, thankfully, have not been diluted too much. Rudi was already there, sitting in a comer, facing into the room. He is a small man, with a tidy little beard. He was a lot greyer than when I last saw him. So was I. I bought myself an orange juice and lemonade and joined him.

'Hello, Rudi. You brought me a long way.'

'Thanks for coming. I'm grateful. I didn't know who else to turn to.'

The sentiment was the same but he didn't seem as distressed as he had done on the phone. I had a feeling that I was being set up. Before we talked about his problems there was something I needed to know: 'Have you heard from Vanessa lately? Any idea how she is?'

He shook his head. 'No. She left me for some sort of property developer. Pots of money. They got married.'

That was about as much as I already knew. 'Sounds like her type,' I said, as if I couldn't care less. Rudi didn't want to eat but I did, and I enjoyed making him wait and pay. I had a chicken and sweetcorn pie with a salad. It was acceptable. Rudi wouldn't talk in the pub.

'Don't you think you are being just a little melodramatic?' I asked him. He didn't think he was, and insisted on us going into the open-air museum before he would talk. We rode on an old tram just like the ones I used to go to school on when Dad was stationed in Leeds. I stood and hung on a strap, even though we were the only two on it, because I'd always wanted to, but couldn't reach them when I was a kid.

'OK, Rudi,' I told him, 'the tram's not bugged, so let's have it.'

He thought for a while, as if he didn't know

where to begin. Then he said: 'You know the Art Aid exhibition?'

I knew it. It was the latest of a plethora of fundraising events held on behalf of the Third World. Ten paintings by some of the greatest artists who ever lived were travelling the globe. They had toured the USA for a year and were now in Britain. They had just had a week in Leeds and had moved on to Newcastle. Shortly they would be heading for Europe. The art world was showing that anything rock music could do, it could do better. It was five quid a time and punters were queuing round the block to see them.

'Yes,' I said, 'I saw them three times. Mind you, I only paid twice – the third visit was a perk of the job. I fiddled an invite to a private showing. That visit cost me half a week's wage.'

Another long pause. Then he went on: 'At the beginning of the American tour I received a commission to copy four of the pictures. They're not my normal school, but I accepted. I had to go out there, all expenses paid. They had to be perfect, not just the brush strokes and the canvas, the underpainting and the composition of the paints had to be exact.' He looked at me and his face glowed with pride. 'Charlie, they were the best work I ever did.'

'They were copies, Rudi.'

'They were exact copies. Don't you remember what you once wrote when you were a student of mine? You said that every hundred years all works of art should be destroyed, so that the new generations of artists could recreate them, instead of constantly striving for new styles.'

'Bollocks! I said no such thing.'

'Yes, you did. And you were so right.'

'Then I was being controversial. I was struggling to be a clever sod like all the other students.'

'No, Charlie, you were better than most of them would ever be.'

'So what's the problem? Didn't you get paid?'

'The problem is I did get paid,' he said. 'Normally I make about a thousand pounds a picture. They paid me forty thousand, plus expenses. The extra money was for my silence, or else.'

I whistled through my teeth. 'What are you trying to tell me, Rudi?'

'I'm trying to tell you that my pictures are touring the world raising money for charity.'

I thought about it for a while, then I said: 'Are you sure? Have you checked them?'

'No,' he replied, 'I daren't go near them.'

We got off the tram and strolled towards the reconstructed miners' cottages. They had peggy tubs and mangles. The doorsteps were sandstoned and the fire grates black-leaded.

'So what's the problem?' I repeated. 'You got your money and they got the copies. How do you know you weren't commissioned by the legitimate owners?'

'Because . . . because I deal with galleries all the time.

We talk the same language. These people were different. It started out OK, but when the pictures were done they changed. They sounded . . . threatening . . . violent. They scared me.'

'If they paid you they must have been satisfied with the goods. If the silly pillocks who own the originals can't tell the difference, why worry? Let's all just live happily ever after.'

'I don't think they'll let me live happily ever after. I think they'll want me out of the way. I know too much.'

'Do you know who they are?'

He shook his head. 'No, it was all arranged over the phone.'

'Accent?'

He shrugged: 'Sounded North of England to me.'

'Did you paint them in America?'

'No, Britain. I just did the research there.'

'Which four paintings did you copy?' I asked.

'The Van Gogh, the Gauguin and the Monet. I did the Picasso, too, but it got damaged. I don't think that will have been switched.'

'*Portrait of Isobelle Maillot.*' I smiled at the thought of her. 'One of my favourites.'

'Yes,' said Rudi, 'I remembered you when I painted her. You had a thing about Picasso's women.'

'I still have,' I told him. 'And his genius. To paint faces like he does and still make them look incredibly beautiful is amazing.'

And then a pleasant thought struck me. Was it my imagination, or did Isobelle Maillol bear a resemblance to Annabelle Wilberforce? Apart from having an extra eye, of course.

'What do you want me to do?' I asked him.

'I'm not sure. Get the paintings authenticated, or find where the originals are. Preferably put somebody behind bars for a long time. I don't think you can do much, really.'

'I can get the experts to look at them,' I said, 'but we both know what they'll say. They won't admit to losing enough paintings to pay off half the national debt.'

'No, they won't,' said Rudi, eyes blazing with indignation. 'And then the world will be looking at Rudi Truscott's paintings, but he won't get the recognition.'

'Is there anything else you can tell me?' I asked.

He shook his head. I thought about what he'd said so far. It didn't amount to much.

'How did you deliver the paintings and how were you paid?'

'I received a phone call. I'd to leave my studio unlocked and get lost for four hours. When I returned the paintings were gone and the money was there.'

'Forty thousand pounds cash?'

'Yes, plus a couple of grand expenses. Then I received another call telling me to keep my mouth shut. He said he might have more work for me in the future.'

'Where is your studio?'

'Just half of the kitchen in my cottage.'

I sighed and rolled my eyes heavenwards. 'You're not being very helpful, Rudi. Do you have an address?'

'I . . . I'd rather not say. And I'm thinking of moving.'

'Have it your own way. So where can I get in touch with you?'

'You can't. I'll ring you.'

'OK. Give me a month. Ring me a month today. Don't expect too much, though. Now I'm off to look at the rest of this museum.'

He hesitated, then he said: 'Charlie, I'm sorry about Vanessa. I did love her, you know.'

'So did I, Rudi. So did I.'

I watched him wander up the hill towards the exit, then I strolled towards the gift shop to see if I could find something really tacky for the office.

'How many fs in peace and quiet?'

'There's no f in peace and quiet.'

'That's what I keep telling the wife.'

Sparky and Tony were in a good mood. I'd have to take a day off more often. When Gilbert Wood was free we all trooped up to see him. I didn't want to tell the story twice. When he'd heard what I had to say he was silent for a while. Then he said: 'Will the experts be able to tell if the pictures are the real ones?'

'It's a grey area,' I told him. 'They can do forensic tests, same as us, but the real picture is the one they say it is, irrespective of who painted it. They'll never admit that theirs is a copy.'

'Well, it proves one thing,' said Gilbert. 'Anyone can produce this modern rubbish. What about Truscott? Do you think his life is in danger?'

'I don't know, but he might be worth taking out a policy on.'

'So if they were switched, it was done in England,' said Sparky. 'Yes,' I replied.

'They were guarded like the Crown Jewels,' said Gilbert. 'There were more people with guns than we had at D-Day.' He thought for a while, then went on: 'Our only involvement was the Traffic boys. They escorted the convoy through our patch and handed over to the city police. They were in a sealed van, so at least we would appear to be in the clear.'

'Where did the pictures come from?' asked Tony.

'I'm not sure,' I said. 'There were two shows in the north prior to Leeds, at Liverpool and, Oldfield, but I don't know which way round.'

'And the helicopter,' remembered Gilbert. 'We had the chopper watching over them. First time we'd been able to get the bloody thing for weeks. Will you tell the organisers that their paintings are crap, Charlie?'

'Ooh, yes please, that should be fun,' I said.

The Museum of Modern Art in New York jetted Dale T. Schweckert over by Concorde. He leapt straight into a taxi at Heathrow and asked to be taken to the Laing Art Gallery in Newcastle. Louis Vouillarde flew over directly from Paris in a private plane. Bunty I'Anson-

Piggot, from the Tate Gallery, drove up in her Austin Metro. She was the last to arrive. I had hoped that I might gain an insight into the working techniques of an art expert, so I did the long drive north again. Unfortunately they all insisted on working in private, so we didn't see how thorough they were. Their conclusions were as predicted: the paintings were genuine and we had put them to a great deal of expense and inconvenience. They graciously accepted that we had acted with the best of motives.

Afterwards I collared Schweckert. I envisaged a language problem with Vouillarde and I feared Ms I'Anson-Piggot might kick me to death with her Doc Martens. Schweckert wouldn't budge in his judgement. It was evident that the Monet was a Monet because he said it was, not because it was painted by a man called Monet. I pointed him in the direction of the taxi rank and drove home.

There was a message waiting for me from Tony Willis. The Mountain Bike Gang had showed up on Saturday morning. We had been looking for them every day through the week without any luck, but now we were barbecuing with charcoal again. I phoned him and got the lowdown. They were outside the post office at nine a.m. when the takings were checked in. They just pedalled around in circles on their bikes and rode away afterwards. Tony had been there himself and it looked suspicious to him. We both agreed that

Monday morning was highly likely for a snatch. He had followed them for a while but lost them when they took to the old railway track. All the arrangements for surveillance and arrest had been made. Tony had decided to go to town with the planning and turn the event into a training exercise. He saw a low probability of things getting nasty, and it would be experience for the younger troops. It would also get everybody on the job early on a Monday morning.

'Tell me the worst,' I said. 'What are we called?'

On a previous occasion Tony had organised an operation in my absence. It involved an architect who was making illegal payments to the head of the council planning department. We caught him handing over a large sum of money in a supermarket car park. Tony's imagination had developed some sort of blockage, and he had called it Operation Freemason. I was the Grand Wizard. It had a few of the top brass looking over their shoulders, and the judge reaching for his bismuth tablets. It also delayed Tony's promotion by a couple of years. Since then we had compiled a list of names from nursery rhymes and children's stories, which we chose from at random.

'Operation Glass Slipper,' he told me. 'You're Rumpelstiltskin.'

We nearly blew it. No cyclists wearing balaclavas and carrying violin cases were on the streets on Monday morning. We had units outside the restaurant and the post office, in various states of disguise and concealment. Sparky and I were in his car, liaising between the two. We did a cruise round the block and that's when we saw them. Three youths were parked up in an XR2 just round the corner from the post office. I checked the number. It had been stolen in Halifax on Saturday night. Rumpelstiltskin alerted all Glass Slipper units.

At three minutes to nine two of the youths left the car and walked round the corner towards the post office.

'These kids know what they are doing,' said Sparky. 'They're not your average toe-rags.'

I had been thinking the same thing. We told the others to move in. Sparky and I got out and walked towards the back of the XR2 as if in the middle of an animated conversation. He was waving his arms about and telling me about a row, real or imaginary, with his wife. The XR2's engine was running and I saw the driver clock us in his mirror. I joined Sparky in a few gestures. The kid at the wheel probably thought we were a couple of deaf Italians as we windmilled towards him. When we got to the rear of the car we separated and went down each side of it. As Sparky reached the driver's door he wrenched it open and yanked the youth on to the pavement. He was standing with his hands on the roof before he could say: 'I want my brief.'

Sparky poked a finger in the back of his head and drawled: 'One move, Blue-eyes, and I'll cure your acne for ever.'

* * *

Crime has no closed season, no bank holidays, no days off. We are busy round the clock. My job is to manage the troops, make sure the paperwork gets done properly and liaise in every direction at once. Meantime I like to get out on the streets as much as possible, which usually means in my own time. We all have our pet priorities, and mine, next to putting crooks behind bars, is looking after, developing and encouraging the lowly constables in my charge.

The PC, whether in uniform or plain clothes, is the backbone of the Force. He is in the front line for all the danger, all the abuse. He or she. Call me old-fashioned, but somehow it seems even worse for the women. I had been on the point of quitting when my first promotion came through. Some good arrests had come my way, but my overriding feeling was of being scared. I never actually wet myself, but I was grateful for the dark trousers. The thought of going out every day or night for the rest of my life not knowing if I would come back in one piece did not appeal to me.

One Saturday afternoon I was parked near the municipal football pitches when I saw a commotion on one of them. I'd turned out for a local side a couple of times, but couldn't keep my place because of the shifts I was required to work. I got out of the car, and when they saw me some of the spectators came running over. Would I radio for an ambulance, someone was in a bad way? I didn't radio; I dashed over to see what the trouble was. A player was laid on the ground. He'd stopped breathing and his face was turning blue. When I tried to clear his airway I found he'd swallowed his tongue. I fished it out of his throat with my fingers and tipped him on his side, but he still wasn't breathing. I put him on his back again and forced a couple of breaths into him. That did the trick. He was conscious when the ambulance arrived.

The following Saturday should have been my day off, but I was asked to work again. I wasn't happy about it, and grumbled loudly to anybody who would listen. At about two thirty I received a message to go to the Poste Chase Hotel. There'd been a fracas in the restaurant – would I investigate and see if anybody wanted to make a complaint? It was all a bit odd. For a start, the Poste Chase wasn't even on our patch. When I walked into the restaurant a big cheer went up. A young man came up to me and introduced himself as the footballer whose life I'd helped to save the week before. This was his wedding reception and I was to be guest of honour; they'd fixed it all with my super. I sat at the top table, next to the groom's parents. Everybody said nice things about me in their speeches, and my photo, with the happy couple, made the front page of the *Evening News*.

After that I decided to give it another try. I was young and skinny and not very streetwise. But I learnt quickly and I toughened up and found that I could handle myself in a roughhouse. I started to enjoy more and more of the job. Nowadays there is more danger than ever facing the PC. I send them out and breathe a sigh of relief when they all come back, and generally fuss over them like a stupid old hen. I get one of the sergeants to do all the dirty work, like handing out bollockings. The constables appreciate it, and the unintentional result is that the police force is infiltrated at all ranks by officers who came through the Charlie Priest training school. Christ, I sound like Jean Brodie.

I didn't give Truscott a very high priority. Every day I am handed a print-out of outstanding crimes, against which I write high and low values of importance. Truscott didn't even appear on the print-out; I just pencilled him on the end. Fraud Squad have a so-called expert to deal with art frauds and we sent him copies of the file. He made nationwide enquiries but didn't come up with anything. The underworld had no knowledge of any big deals in the offing. He did tell me that there was a ready market among the mega-wealthy for great works. The ultimate in one-upmanship for a certain type of billionaire would be to have the *Mona Lisa* hanging behind the toilet door. I'd have preferred a neverending toilet roll.

Truscott had told me that he would be in contact in one month. It was with relief, not concern, that I saw the month marker in my diary pass by with no word from him. I neither liked nor trusted him, and I wasn't convinced that he was on the level. We had checked with Traffic, and the transport of the paintings had passed off reasonably well. Our boys had taken over on the Yorkshire/Lancashire border and seen them right to the art gallery in Leeds. The only hiccup had occurred when the security van carrying the paintings had broken down. After a delay of nearly two hours the convoy restarted with the security van being towed to its destination by a breakdown truck. Everyone was adamant that the van holding the pictures stayed sealed throughout, and was only opened at the end of its journey. The bonnet had been lifted, briefly, to ascertain the trouble, and then the tow vehicle sent for. It had been quite a convoy, and the cargo had been safer than a nun's virtue on Christmas Eve. If I had been worrying about Truscott, I stopped when two months passed without a word.

It was towards the end of the fourth month that I received the letter from his solicitor saying that they were holding a bequest he had made me in his will. He was dead.

CHAPTER FOUR

McNaughtie, McNaughtie and Niece (Solicitors), of Edinburgh, begged to inform me that subsequent to reading the will after the untimely death of their client, they were holding a parcel for me which had been in their safety depository for some time. Would I please be kind enough to contact them with a view to arranging its collection?

I rang them immediately but they weren't open yet. The Presbyterian work ethic didn't extend to starting before nine of the a.m. I took the letter to the office, skipped morning parade and sent Tony Willis up to the Super's prayer meeting.

I got straight on the blower. It was cheaper to use the firm's phone, and it could be police business. A soft Edinburgh brogue answered immediately, but I didn't catch a word she said.

'Could I speak to one of the partners, please?'

'Yes, they're all here, which one would you be liking?'

'Er, Mr McNaughtie, please.' Except that I pronounced it McNorty.

'It's pronounced Nochty, McNochty,' she told me, 'and both Mr McNaughties passed on many years ago. Miss McNaughtie is in, would you care to speak with her?'

The niece? 'Oh, sorry. Yes, Miss McNaughtie will be fine, thank you.'

Sparky had pricked up his ears in disbelief when I had asked for Mr McNorty, and now his shoulders were bobbing up and down as he hid his face behind a sheaf of court papers.

'Pillock,' I hissed at him with my hand over the mouthpiece.

After I'd introduced myself, Miss McNaughtie started to tell me about my bequest, but I cut her short and asked her how Truscott had died. The poor sod had burnt to death when his cottage caught fire. The verdict had been accidental death, possibly brought about by falling asleep in a highly inflammable armchair whilst smoking. She couldn't tell me anything further, so I asked her what he'd left me.

'It's probably a painting. Mr Truscott was a very eminent artist, you know. It is well wrapped up and has been in our depository for several weeks, along with one or two others. Mr Truscott specialised in copying old masters, but his paintings are very valuable in their own right. Would you like us to arrange delivery by Housecarl, or will you come to collect it?'

Housecarl were the biggest security company in the country. It crossed my mind that they had probably managed the transport of the Art Aid paintings, something we hadn't looked into. Maybe we should start looking again.

'Yes, I'd be grateful if you could send it to me,' I told her, 'but first of all could you possibly open it up and tell me what it is?'

This prospect delighted Miss McNaughtie, and she promised to ring me back as soon as the wrappings were off. She kept her word.

'It's a copy of a Picasso. I didn't think I liked Picasso, but this one is charming.'

'Is it a portrait of a lady?' I asked.

'Yes.'

'Facing left, hair piled on top of her head, lots of blue and yellow, holding a magnolia blossom?'

'That's it, Mr Priest. You obviously know the painting.'

'Yes, I've seen the original. She's called Isobelle Maillol. Rumour has it that she was Picasso's mistress. Can you see if the painting is damaged in any way, probably very slightly?'

She was quiet for a couple of minutes, then she came back to the phone and told me: 'Yes, but it is very slight. There's a scratch, only about an inch long, near the top left-hand corner. It's hardly noticeable.'

'Thank you. Well spotted. Mr Truscott told me that it had been damaged. Is it possible for you to tell me who he left the rest of his estate to?'

'It's public knowledge, Mr Priest. Everything went to his two ex-wives. Not that it amounts to much. As far as we have been able to ascertain, his estate is somewhat smaller than we had expected.'

'How small?'

'Oh, about fifteen thousand pounds, plus a few paintings.'

I'd have put him easily into the half-millionaire bracket. Miss McNaughtie gave me the address of the burnt-out cottage and I confirmed my address with her. Before I put the instrument down I told her it had been a pleasure talking to her, but it hadn't. As I trudged up the stairs to Gilbert Wood's office I wondered if this elderly Edinburgh spinster was gazing upon that beautiful three-eyed lady in a new light in the knowledge that she had been Picasso's mistress. I was also wondering what the hell to do next.

The black economy was booming. How we envy those TV detectives who work on one crime at a time; swanning about with their able assistant until the culprit is firmly behind bars before moving on to the next juicy piece of villainy. It would have been nice to have been able to follow my whim and investigate Truscott's lifestyle, but we had a business to run.

There had been another ram-raid in Heckley over the weekend: a Lada estate had been driven through the shutters of Bink's Hi-Fi and Video, and four youths had made off in a stolen Sierra with eight thousand pounds' worth of goodies. It was the tenth similar raid we'd had in as many weeks. In addition, a gang of pickpockets and bag-snatchers was operating in the New Mall, with apparent impunity from the law. The Super was catching flack from the Chamber of Commerce, the Retailers' Association and the Watch Committee. I was catching flack, with interest, from the Super.

Truscott wouldn't go away, though. We didn't have a crime or a complainant; but dead men don't complain, they just stink, and I could feel it in my nostrils. Eventually I tracked down the officer who had investigated the fire at Truscott's cottage.

'Aye, we're happy that it was an accident,' he told me when I got him to the phone, 'and the Procurator Fiscal agrees. There was nothing left of the body, just a pile of ashes. He used the place as an artist's studio, so there was lots of paint and spirit and stuff lying around. Went up like a bonfire.'

'How was he identified?'

'Personal effects. Signet ring, wristwatch. Decent watch, a Rolex. It'd stopped, though. His ex-wife was the only next of kin we could trace. She recognised them.'

Vanessa? 'Did you meet the ex-wife?'

'No, one of my constables dealt with it.' I told the

sergeant why I was so interested, and about Truscott's claim that his life was in danger. 'Just out of interest, Sergeant,' I chose my words carefully, 'you wouldn't happen to know of any missing persons locally, would you?'

He realised what I was getting at. 'Are you implying that the body wasn't this Truscott fellow?' A note of aggression had crept into his voice.

'It's a remote possibility.'

He was silent for a long while. I'd have thought we'd been cut off except that I could hear him breathing. Then he said: 'Aye, old Jamie.'

'Old Jamie, who's he?'

'He's a vagrant, wanders from village to village. He vanishes into Edinburgh when the weather turns, then comes back in the spring, sure as the swallows.'

'But he's disappeared?'

'Aye. A few people have commented that he hasn't been seen around. We've been half expecting to find him lying in a burn somewhere.'

I could feel the poor sergeant growing agitated. One accidental death and one missing person to deal with, and some Sassenach was accusing him of getting them the wrong way round.

'Accidental death,' he told me with an air of finality, 'that's what the Procurator Fiscal said it was. If you think any different you'd best take it up with him.'

'I'm sure you're right,' I agreed, trying to get him back on my side. 'But I would be interested if old Jamie turns up.' He promised to let me know. As an afterthought I said: 'Oh, by the way, who is the Procurator Fiscal these days?'

He gave me a name that sounded like a chord on the bagpipes. I asked him to spell it. We rang off on reasonable terms, but I couldn't help thinking that they were looking for Auld Jamie in the wrong sort of burn. I'm Gilbert Wood's greatest fan. He actually volunteered to ring the Procurator Fiscal. I was causing him a lot of hassle that he could do without, but deep down he was beguiled by the thought of cracking a multi-million-pound art scam. Especially one that nobody knew had happened.

'OK, Charlie, OK! I'll bloody well ring him, if only to get you off my back.' He was pacing back and forth like a tiger in a cage, except he looked more like a panda. The mood, though, was definitely tigerish. 'But not just yet. Where do we stand with the ram-raiders? The only people who aren't on to me are the bloody glass merchants and the suppliers of eight-by-four sheets of plywood. What are your boys coming up with?'

'You're going to give yourself a coronary,' I stated. 'You've forgotten how to enjoy yourself. Sit down, calm down, and I'll tell you all about it.'

Gilbert sat down. Two young constables were trying to penetrate the gangs on the estates where we thought the ram-raiders came from. It was a risky situation and we were all uneasy about it. They appeared to revel in the job, though.

'Martin Makinson seems to be coming up with the goods,' I told him. 'He's well in with a receiver and is bulk-buying off him. We sell the goods back to the insurance companies. They pay upfront.'

'Bulk-buying! Is he creating the demand that they're trying to fill? This could work wonders for the economy.'

'No, that was just a figure of speech. He just buys enough to keep his credibility high. He's worked himself into a good bargaining position; now he's talking about dealing directly with Mr Big. There is a Mr Big. These people are organised.'

'How safe is he? What have you told him?'

'Maz has been given strict . . .'

'Who's Maz?' Gilbert interrupted.

'Martin,' I answered. 'He calls himself Maz now, it goes with his new haircut. And the tattoos. And the nose-ring. He really takes his work seriously. I've given him strict instructions that if he gets the faintest inkling of being rumbled he's to cut and run. I've also warned him that he might be dealing with dumbos at present, but the next tier will be a different league, they'll have brains. Just a name, that's all I've told him to get.'

Gilbert was calm now. He shook his head slowly. 'Rather him than me,' he said, then asked: 'Do you worry about them, Charlie?'

'Mmm, I worry myself sick. They seem to lap it up, though.'

'And what about John Rose?'

'John is cultivating a couple of contacts in a gang who call themselves the Fusiliers. Plenty going off but all small stuff. Thieving, some drugs, a bit of football hooliganism, racist overtones. Nothing organised, though.'

'God, what a healthy environment to put our best recruits into. What would his mother think? Call him off if he's wasting his time.'

'I'll leave him a bit longer, if you don't mind. No doubt we'll get something out of it. I'm having to be flexible with them both, though, because they're supposed to be unemployed. That's leaving me short in other areas.'

'OK,' agreed Gilbert, 'do what you think is best. How are you getting on with your dad's Jaguar? Is it nearly ready?'

'It's going well. The wheels have just been done up and now they're back at Jimmy Hoyle's for new tyres and balancing. All we need then is an MOT and we're away.'

I stood up to leave. 'Don't forget the Procurator Fiscal,' I reminded him. His reply tripped off the tongue with similar ease.

Nigel Newley was back with us. He'd shown a definite aptitude for detective work and started to fit in when he realised that we weren't complete barbarians north of Hemel Hempstead. We just like to pretend we are. He'd even acquired a taste for the beer, and no longer diluted it with brown ale. I'd had him in, together with another DC, Jeff Caton, to give them a grilling in preparation for their promotion panels. When we'd finished I asked Jeff to find the names of the Traffic boys who had escorted the Art Aid convoy, and to check which security company was involved.

'A fart to a Ferrari it was Housecarl, but check anyway,' I told him.

Nigel had a report to type. He'd caught a pickpocket in the New Mall. She was a sixty-seven-year-old alcoholic. We both agreed that this burst of success was unlikely to get the Super off our necks, but we'd go through the motions by giving her a caution and alerting the Social Services. Tony Willis was busy at the typewriter keys, too, preparing some court reports. Tony's typing has all the intermittency of some dastardly Chinese water torture. After a longer than average pause he asked: 'Does buggery have a g-g in it?'

'A gee-gee, a moo cow, usually something like that,' I told him.

'Thanks, boss. We'd be lost without you.'

'Any time, Anthony.'

Nigel was gazing at us both with a vacant expression when Gilbert Wood burst in. 'Haven't you got anything to do?' he demanded of Nigel. Without waiting for a reply he hurled a screwed-up ball of paper at me and sat down. I smoothed out the sheet and saw it was the Procurator Fiscal's name and number that I had given him. He took a few deep breaths before he spoke. 'I just rang your friend Jock McPillock. Made me feel like a bloody schoolboy. How dare I have the temerity to ring him on the electric telephone? Any second I expected him to call me "wee laddie".'

I waited until Gilbert had calmed down. 'Do I get the impression he's not willing to cooperate?' I asked, stifling a laugh.

'Him and me also. Not without hard evidence. A crime would be a good starting point. My advice is drop it, Charlie, we've enough on our plates chasing real villains without inventing them.'

'OK, boss, but thanks for ringing him. I'll cross it off my list of Jobs I Must Do. Kettle's just boiled if you want a coffee.'

'No thanks. Wife's got me on decaffeinated. Tastes just the same to me.' He stumped off back to his office.

Nigel recovered his voice. 'Could be the perfect crime,' he said. 'The one nobody believes has been committed. Are you going to drop it, boss?'

'Is he chuff,' said DS Willis.

Next morning Jeff Caton presented me with a list of the Traffic officers that I'd asked for, with their current shifts. 'The security company situation is a bit odd,' he told me. 'Housecarl had the main contract to transport the Art Aid paintings, but apparently a firm called ABC Security have a contract with West Pennine County Council to do all their security work. They insisted it was their job and threatened to sue for breach of contract. Eventually a compromise was agreed to by the insurers, whereby Housecarl subcontracted this one journey to ABC.'

'ABC Security, well done.' I'd seen their vans occasionally. They seemed to have sprung up in the last couple of years. I didn't attach any significance to the name: every category in the Yellow Pages has somebody called ABC listed. A part of me was also beginning to think that perhaps Gilbert Wood was right. I could do without all this. I'd have one last throw, though.

'Get some background on ABC,' I told him. 'Find out what sort of company it is and who the registered owners are. But don't let them know we are asking. And if the Super asks what you're doing, tell him you're looking for a lost gerbil.'

It was decision time. What to have for lunch. I didn't fancy the canteen and I could use some fresh air, so I decided to wander down to the New Mall and eat there. The opening of the New Mall had been a bit of a renaissance for the centre of Heckley. We'd gone through the black-hole-in-the-middle period and, hopefully, were now entering a new, more prosperous phase for the town's traders. It was a rather grand place, and had been well accepted after many early misgivings. It had a posher name, but all and sundry referred to it as the New Mall. Unfortunately it had become a happy hunting ground for petty thieves. Today the local radio station was holding some sort of fundraising event there that would provide riveting listening for its countless dozens of fans. For some strange reason this was expected to attract people to the mall, not drive them away, so it could be a good day for picking a pocket or two. We'd got everybody available mingling with the throng of happy teeny-boppers.

Normally, I wouldn't become involved at this level, but the council elections were imminent, and one of the candidates was floating his campaign on the crime wave in there. My plan was simple – I'd eat, look at the girls, nab a couple of villains, then come back to the office. When the others returned empty-handed I'd give them hell and go home with a nice self-satisfied feeling.

The multi-choice, serve-yourself restaurant is on the third floor of the mall. The disc jockey was strutting his stuff on the ground floor, but it was still too close. I was tucking into my pizza when Sparky joined me. One-up to him: he'd found me before I found him.

'Any action?' I asked.

'A definite possible,' he told me. 'Mad Maggie has her eye on three girls who are acting a bit strange. At least three of the women who lost handbags were sitting over in that far left-hand corner when they realised their bags had gone. It's a bit more secluded there, lots of plastic palm trees. These girls keep returning to the spot, looking for a vacant table. Done it about six times so far. Why are you eating pizza? You always say you don't like it when we send out for some.'

'Good for Maggie,' I said. 'Set a woman to catch

a woman. We've too many old-fashioned ideas about villains; we'd have been watching the blokes. I don't like pizza – the girl behind the counter looks like Steffi Graf.'

'Speak for yourself, I'm younger than you. How long have you been a Steffi Graf fan?'

'About half an hour.'

'You should try the roast beef stall, I always go there.'

'What's the waitress like?'

'Henry Cooper, but the beef's good.'

Sparky took me to where DC Margaret Madison was looking at a closed-circuit television monitor, focused down on to the corner of the restaurant where the action was.

'Hi, boss,' she whispered, somewhat unnecessarily, and gestured with an inclination of her head. 'They're back, and they're sitting behind that woman who's put her handbag on the floor.'

The three girls were at a table in the corner, facing outwards. They had a commanding view of the immediate vicinity, but could not be observed themselves. Except by us.

'Can you record this?' I asked Maggie.

'It's in the can, sweetie. Sorry, boss – film producers' jargon.'

A middle-aged woman was at the next table to the girls, with her back to them. Maggie juggled with the camera's remote control and showed me the woman's handbag on the floor. As we watched, the bent end of an umbrella came into view and slowly hooked itself through the strap of the bag. Maggie pulled the camera back into wide angle. The girl on the left gently drew the bag towards her. When it was within reach she picked it up and put it over her shoulder and all three of them stood up and calmly walked away.

'Dave, you go up and collar the woman, and radio the others to join us at the ground-floor exits.' I was speaking as we dashed out of the monitor room. We were already on the ground floor. A couple of the mall's own security people were with us. I told them to get to the Ladies' toilets in case the girls went there with their spoils. Maggie and I stood at the foot of the staircase, from where we could also watch the escalator. We tried to look natural.

'God, you've got beautiful eyes,' I told her. 'Why don't you let me take you away from all this?'

'You say the nicest things, Charlie. What will we do about Robin?'

'There's always a snag. We could poison him, does he like mushrooms? Don't answer that, they're coming down the escalator.'

We walked to the foot of the escalator and it delivered the three girls, as pretty as a postcard, right on to our doormat. 'Police,' I said. 'You're under arrest for sus—'

The front one's face registered horror for a split second, then she burst between us and fled. The second girl tried to follow but I grabbed the sleeve of her baseball jacket. The other one turned back up the escalator with Maggie in hot pursuit. The girl I'd grabbed tried to slip out of her jacket and run, but I managed to hold her arm. She started to thump me with her free hand and kick me.

'Help!' she yelled. 'Help me! He's attacking me! Rape!'

I managed to get her in a bear hug. She was kicking and spitting and still shouting for help. From up the escalator I could hear her pal yelling: 'Get off me, you cow. Let me go!' A crowd started to gather. It looked as if they might join in – on the girls' side.

'I'm a police officer,' I shouted above her screams. 'She's under arrest for suspicion of theft.'

'Do you have to be so rough with her?'

'Bastard pigs, that's all you're fit for.'

Maggie appeared with her girl in handcuffs, closely followed by Sparky and the lady with no handbag. We got the cuffs on my girl, but not without a struggle.

'Take them in,' I told Maggie and Sparky, loosening my tie and brushing the hair from my eyes. 'I'll try for some Brownie points in PR.' I turned to face the crowd and held up my hands. A big youth with a beer gut testing the tensile strength of his T-shirt stood at the front of the crowd, together with a young woman wearing a baby round her neck in a sling, as if it were the latest fashion accessory. They'd done most of the protesting, so I addressed them directly.

'Look, I'm sorry if we appeared rough, but the girls were given plenty of opportunity to come quietly. The third one did escape. There's been a spate of handbag-stealing in the mall recently, and we have good reason to believe that those girls were involved. Now will you please all go back to what you were doing.'

Most of them started to melt, away. Some of the troops had been mixed in with them, keeping an eye on things, and they drifted off. The woman with the baby held back.

'Typical police bullshit,' she snorted. 'Your behaviour was disgraceful. I'm going to take this further. I demand to know your name.'

'Priest,' I answered wearily. 'Inspector. Try to have a nice rest of the day.'

Another woman, a little older, appeared in front of me. She was offering me a tissue. 'She scratched you, Inspector. Your cheek's bleeding slightly.'

I took the tissue and wiped my cheek. 'Thank you,' I said, smiling so wide it hurt my face. 'You're very kind. Could I possibly repay you by buying you a coffee?'

'I'd prefer tea,' replied Annabelle Wilberforce.

CHAPTER FIVE

We went back upstairs to the restaurant and had a pot of Earl Grey and a Danish pastry each. It was unreal after the unpleasantness of a few minutes earlier. 'Did you see it all?' I asked.

'Yes. I'd just popped in to buy a few things and I walked straight into it. Do you often have to put up with such abuse?'

'Oh, now and again.'

'Will that woman really report you? It's people like her who give the left a bad name.'

'I doubt it, but it will be tricky if she does. Manhandling a sixteen-year-old girl could be construed to my disadvantage.'

Annabelle looked grave. 'Oh dear. I hope you are not going to be in trouble. I saw it all – I could make a statement on your behalf.'

I laughed. 'Thanks for the offer, but don't worry about it. She said her piece in front of an audience, that's probably all she wanted.'

Annabelle went off to do her shopping and I scrounged a lift back to the station. It had been a mixed sort of an afternoon, and it wasn't over yet. My reputation had preceded me.

'Hey, who's the stunner you were seen with? You've been keeping her under wraps, you crafty so-and-so,' were DS Willis's opening words.

'Oh, just a friend, Tony. Any messages?'

'Only a note from Jeff Caton for you. It's on your desk somewhere.'

I found the note. It read: 'ABC Security is a privately owned company, founded four years ago. Head office at ABC House, Welton, Lancs. Managing Director named Miss Eunice Grimes.'

Big bells were ringing in my head. I was riding on a lucky streak. Time to spin the wheel once again, but this time we'd do it the easy way. I rang Oldfield CID. There was nobody in that I knew. Eventually I persuaded a young DC to make some enquiries for me. He rang me back, true to his word.

'ABC Security is owned by Eunice Grimes, as you said, but her married name is Cakebread. She's just a front for her husband. He has his finger in all sorts of pies, but he's got a record, so that would rule him out of owning a security company.'

'Aubrey Bingham Cakebread?'

'That's the man. His wife's supposed to be an ex-beauty queen, and she breeds dogs as a pastime.'

'Dogs? What sort of dogs?'

'Some fancy little foreign things. Shites-something-or-other.'

'Shites-on-the-carpet?'

'Not quite, sir, but something like that,' he chuckled. 'How about shih-tzu?'

'That's it, sir! Shih-tzu.'

'Thanks, pal, you've been a big help. I'll keep you informed.'

I went home. The reasonable day had turned into a good one, and I had discovered that wrestling with a nubile schoolgirl was no big turn-on. I was pleased about that, too.

Mad Maggie announced that she had a copy of the incriminating video set up in the conference room, and would show it to us if we cared to proceed there forthwith. I was delayed on the telephone, and when I reached the conference room it was heaving with bodies. I was amazed by the interest she had drummed up. Everybody, from the canteen ladies to the SDO, seemed eager to view the evidence.

It was a superb piece of camera work. First there were wide-angle shots, showing the overall scene, then close-ups of each of the three girls' faces. I'd seen the next bit, where the umbrella neatly hooked the handbag. It was all done without breaks, joints or patches; as evidence it couldn't be faulted. When I thought it had ended I stood up to leave, but somebody said: 'Wait, there's some more.' After a few seconds of snow-storm an overall view of the restaurant came into view. A couple were just taking their places at a table in the middle. The male was being very attentive. The hairs on the back of my neck were already prickling like a bilious porcupine when the camera zoomed in.

'It's Mr Priest!' somebody exclaimed.

A cheer went up all round the room as they recognised me, followed by wolf whistles when they saw Annabelle. 'Never mind him! Who's she?'

'The jammy sod, nabs the villains and gets the woman!'

I was due in court at ten o'clock, but before that I had arranged for one of the Traffic drivers who had been on the Art Aid convoy to come to see me. I knew him reasonably well, and he had a reputation as a no-nonsense officer.

'Cast your mind back about six months,' I asked him, after I'd given him his compulsory mug of coffee, 'to the time you escorted the paintings for the Art Aid exhibition. What can you tell me about the job?'

He thought for a moment, then said: 'Not much to tell, really. It started out pretty routine; we thought there was a touch of overkill, but I suppose you can't be too careful with money like that involved. We waited in the big lay-by on the Lancashire side of the border and took over from the West Pennine boys. Then, coming down this side, the armoured van broke down. We were suspicious, but not worried enough to sign out the gun we were carrying. The chopper had been standing by, so we whistled it up for extra cover. We hung around for two hours until a breakdown truck arrived, then towed the lot straight to the Leeds Art Gallery. It was a bit ball-aching: we were only doing twenty miles per hour, and trying to watch every which way at once. The pictures weren't transferred to another vehicle or anything like that. They stayed in the armoured van throughout.'

'This was an ABC Security armoured van?'

'That's right,' he replied. 'Up to breaking down they'd been very impressive. Well drilled – everybody seemed to know what they were doing. The breakdown cocked it up, though. We were about three hours late when we finally arrived.'

'Did anybody try to find what the trouble was?'

'Yeah, I'd forgotten that. The driver had a look under the bonnet. The oil filter had fallen off and wrecked the engine. He was well watched. I can guarantee that he didn't squirm down the prop shaft, up through a hole in the van floor and swipe a couple of paintings. He just pronounced the vehicle unrepairable and radioed for help.' He shrugged his shoulders as if he had nothing further to offer. 'What's the problem, Mr Priest? Has a picture gone missing?'

'I'm not sure,' I replied. 'I think there may have been a switch, but so far I'm crying in the wilderness. I take it someone rode in the back of the armoured van.'

'That's right. Two ABC guards. I saw them when they unloaded.'

'Can you remember what they looked like?'

'No. They were wearing helmets and visors. One was fairly small, though, and the other was about my size. We were keeping our eyes on the cargo.'

'Mmm. Well, thanks for what you've told me. Sorry to keep you away from swanning up and down the motorway. If you think of anything else I'd be glad if you'd let me know.'

He thought for a few seconds. 'Just one small point,' he said. 'The two in the back liked country and western music. Played loud. All the time we were waiting it was coming out through the ventilators. Nearly sent me barmy.'

I drove down to the courthouse and parked in the reserved parking. I was early, but I'd wanted to escape the distractions of the office. I sat in the car and took stock of what I knew so far. It didn't amount to a shoe box full of polystyrene beads. Truscott was linked to the paintings, and ABC had moved them. I'd always imagined Truscott to be a non-smoker, he was so fastidious in other ways, but he'd had a small cigar when I saw him at Beamish, so he could have set fire to his own armchair. True, he was small, like the security guard, but lots of men were small. Small people weren't usually attracted into the security industry, though. He definitely wasn't a country and western lover: he probably thought the term referred to Cornish folk dances. String quartets were more his style. I thought about our meeting at Beamish and went through it, step by step, word by word. Something didn't gel, and eventually I thought I knew what it was.

I'd left the rest of the day free for the trial, but I'd been given an inkling that it wouldn't take long. At the last minute the accused changed his plea to guilty, so there was no need for me to tell the court how I'd arrested him with the left halves of ninety-six pairs of expensive training shoes in his car boot. I came out and gunned my car over the hill into Lancashire. It was time to have a look at Mr Breadcake on his own territory.

Forty minutes later I was sitting outside ABC House, nerve centre of the Cakebread empire. The building was an old warehouse, the side of which gave directly on to the pavement of a narrow cobbled alley. There was a big sliding door, with a small door let into it, otherwise it was just a huge, blank brick wall. The small door had a Yale lock and a deadlock. Round the front it was much more open. The building was set well back from the main road, with a tall mesh fence enclosing the area to the front and other side. At the side were parked several security vans with the ABC logo on them. In front were presumably the staff's cars. The entrance to the compound was protected by a lowered barrier controlled by a gatehouse. Prominently situated, as close to the door as it was possible to park, was the familiar Rolls Royce with the personal registration number.

I'd no plan. I just wanted to get the feel of the place, so that if I ever came back it wouldn't be a surprise to me. I'd hang around a while, then maybe look for his home, The Ponderosa. What other names could he have chosen for his mansion, I wondered? A combination of their respective monickers would be about right. Eunaub had a certain style to it. Or maybe they'd prefer something a little more up-market, like . . . The Summer Palace.

Suddenly he was there, getting into the Roller. He was even fatter than I remembered him. The gate man came out of his little office and raised the barrier and the Rolls swept imperiously through, the way that Rollses do.

He could have forgotten his cigar clipper and come back for it, so I waited ten minutes before driving up to the little gatehouse that stood between me and the secrets of the Cakebread empire.

'I've come to see Mr Cakebread; he is expecting me,' I told the gateman.

'I'm afraid you've just missed him, sir, he left a few minutes ago.'

'Oh dear. I've a rather important message for him.' I

tried to look suitably downcast and waved my ID card in his direction. 'Do you think I could have a word with his secretary?

'Certainly, sir. Do you know where to find her?

'Yes, I think so, thanks.'

He raised the barrier and I was through. I tried to watch him in the rear-view mirror but didn't see anything. He hadn't had the opportunity to read the name on my ID, but it was a fair bet that he wrote my registration number in his log book.

What the hell, I thought, no point in letting it grow cold, and parked in the spot marked ABC, so recently vacated by the man himself. Just inside the front entrance was a receptionist's desk, combined with a switchboard. I gazed at the blonde sitting behind it with awe. Geological forces were at work underneath her blouse. The thin material was struggling to conceal a demonstration of plate tectonics. Continents were in collision.

'Can I help you?' she asked with a brassy smile, as she looked up from her *True Romances*.

'Er, yes,' I stumbled out, endeavouring to hold her gaze. Oh, to have the eyes of a chameleon, one to look here, the other to look there. 'I, er, was hoping to see Mr Cakebread.'

'Oh! you've just missed him. He left about five minutes ago, for the airport. He's flying to Spain. He has his own plane, you know, flies himself all over the place. I think it's ever so exciting.' She went glassy-eyed with the romance of travel, then the receptionist training resurfaced: 'Would you like to speak to anybody else, Mr . . . ?'

'No, it had to be Aubrey. I'm a policeman, and I needed a word with him. Any idea when he'll be back?'

A look of shock spread across her face, and she exclaimed: 'Oh my God! The policeman, where did I put it?' and started rummaging frantically in her desk. 'Here it is!' she cried triumphantly, holding aloft a manila envelope. She looked at the front of it and read: 'Mr Hilditch, is that you?'

'Yes, that's me,' I lied, taking the envelope and putting it in my pocket. 'Now you know my name, you have to tell me yours.'

She gave me the warm, confident smile of someone who has narrowly missed making a cock-up and doesn't yet know they have made an even bigger one. 'Gloria,' she told me, coyly.

'It suits you,' I said. 'How long have you worked for Aubrey?' We were interrupted by the telephone. While she tried to connect somebody I had a glance round. No Van Goghs or Monets were hanging on the walls, dammit.

'Only about a month, well, this is my third week. I started in the office, then he made me his receptionist.'

'Do you like working for him?'

'Ooh yes, ever so much. Did you know he's a multimillionaire? He's got a plane and a boat, and flats all over the place. Says he'll take me on his boat one day.' She was looking dreamy again.

'Whereabouts in Spain has he gone? Do you know, Gloria?'

'Marbella, I think. He's got a boat there. Don't know where it is but I've heard of it. Sounds ever so romantic. Do you ever go to any of his parties, Mr Hilditch?'

'It's Ernest, you can call me Ernie. Yes, I've been to a couple at The Ponderosa. Old Aubrey certainly knows how to throw a party.'

'Oh, I'd love to go to The Ponderosa. I meant the parties he holds here, in his suite upstairs.'

'No. To tell the truth, I didn't know he had a suite here. Crafty so-and-so's kept it a secret from me. Probably scared I'll pinch all the girls.'

'It's fabulous,' she gushed, 'carpets up to your knees, and the colours are gorgeous – everything matches. He showed me round it once. Says he'll invite me to the next party.'

'I might see you there, then.' The clock behind her head showed a quarter to twelve. 'How about letting me take you for a bite of lunch? What time are you free?'

Her smile looked almost demure. 'That will be lovely,' she cooed. 'About half past twelve; is that all right?'

'That's fine. Where shall I pick you up? Can you get out of the door at the side?'

'No, I don't think so. I'll meet you just outside the gatehouse, if that's OK.'

'Perfect. So I'll see you in three-quarters of an hour; it's a long time to wait.'

I drove away feeling like a prospector who isn't sure if he's struck gold or diamonds. I headed out of town until I found a suitable pub that served food, so that it looked as if I knew my way around. I parked and took the lumpy envelope from my inside pocket. It contained three keys and a note. One, a nondescript doorkey, was on its own; the other two, a Yale and a Chubb, were on a keyring. The note read:

Ernest,
PH Tue. PM Thur. Alarm 4297

It was signed with a stylised ABC, similar to the logo on the vans. He'd obviously spent many hours practising it.

When I arrived back at ABC House I parked just outside the side door. Looking as if I had every right to be there I tried the Yale key in the lock. It turned. Then I tried the Chubb and that fitted, too. I left the door as I'd found it and set off round to the gatehouse to wait for Gloria. That's when the diamond mine fell in.

As I stopped in the road just short of the entrance, a maroon Daimler did a right turn across the front of me. It was driven by the one and only, the inimitable, appearing for the first time in person, Ernest Hilditch,

Chief Constable of the East Pennine force. After a brief word the barrier was raised, and soon he was, no doubt, addressing the considerable charms of Gloria. After a couple of minutes he came storming out and slammed the Daimler's door behind him. As he tore towards the exit the barrier was raised, but he screeched to a halt and leapt out to accost the gateman.

After a few violent gestures they went into his office. Chief Constable Hilditch was playing at being a policeman, collecting car numbers. Somebody was up Shit Creek with a duff outboard, and it looked like me.

My appetite had gone, so I went straight back to the office. Nigel and Tony Willis were in, going through some cases, solved and unsolved, looking for common denominators.

I gave them a terse 'Any messages?' as I hung up my jacket. It was my I Mean Business entrance.

'Two,' Nigel told me. 'Your friend at the Fraud Squad said to tell you that rumour has it that the American private eye firm, Winkler's, are over here and asking a lot of questions in the shady market. He thinks you may be on to something.'

'Good, and the other?'

'Limbo said be sure not to miss her promotion do tomorrow night.'

I caught Tony's gaze and flashed a glance up at a

poster on the wall. It was headed: 'Racism and Sexism', and went on to say that these would not be tolerated, and any officer hearing racist or sexist language should address it immediately.

'Who's Limbo?' I asked him.

'WPC Limbert, Kim Limbert. She moves to the city on the first, as sergeant.'

We sat in silence for a few moments, then I asked: 'Have you ever thought that she might find being called Limbo offensive?'

'Gosh, no,' he confessed, 'it never occurred to me. Everybody calls her Limbo.'

'Not everybody,' I stated.

Nigel was embarrassed at being caught out, and fell silent. I wouldn't have let him off the hook, but Tony was working with him, so after a while he threw out a lifeline. 'Do you still fancy Kim, Charlie?'

I thought about it, leaning back in my chair and looking up at the ceiling. 'Yes, I think I do, but I've stopped dreaming about her. Unless I dream about her and forget.'

'Not enough meat on her for me. I prefer something you can dig your fingers into.'

Nigel was looking from one of us to the other, growing visibly agitated.

'Naw,' I disagreed, 'I like them tall and skinny. It's like wrestling with a boa constrictor, lots of points of contact and intertwining limbs.'

Nigel could contain himself no longer. 'What about

sexism?' he demanded, 'When are you going to start addressing sexism?'

'Good point, boss,' Tony admitted. 'When do we start addressing sexism?'

I thought about it for ten seconds before making my pronouncement: *'Mariana,'* I said.

CHAPTER SIX

Nobody told me I was sacked, so I carried on as normal. We had a murder during the night and I was called from my bed. That's fairly normal. Neighbours had heard a couple having a violent fight and the husband had stormed off in his car. Definitely normal. Four hours later, when the eighth playing of Barry Manilow's *Greatest Hits* was still keeping them awake, the neighbours called the police. Playing Barry Manilow's *Greatest Hits* eight times on the trot is definitely abnormal behaviour – our boys were there in minutes. They pulled the plug on the CD player, then looked for the wife.

He'd made a good job of her. In the kitchen there was a rack with enough chef's knives on it to equip the Catering Corps. I'd seen them advertised in the colour supplements. He'd found a novel use for the cleaver on the end. I drew on my years of police training and told Command and Control to find the husband's car. A bright constable recognised the number as being involved in an accident he had attended at the beginning of his shift. Our man had gone off the road two miles from home, and was now in the General, waiting to have his broken thigh placed in traction.

'He's all yours,' I told DS Willis, 'and if he won't confess, swing on his wires. But make sure his solicitor is looking the other way.'

There was no point in going home, so I hung around the station until the canteen opened. I was snoozing in the office when I received a call from a probation officer called Gav Smith. Could he come round to see me sometime?'

'Come round now and I'll treat you to a bacon sandwich,' I said. My stomach hadn't seen food for twelve hours and was considering suing my mouth for desertion. The popular conception is that we catch criminals and the Probation Service try to get them off. It sometimes seems that way to me, too, but they have an important and difficult job to do. Well, they say they have. I'd met Gavin professionally plenty of times, mainly at various committee meetings, but never socially. I was intrigued to know what he wanted: probation officers have a befriending role with their clients, and no doubt learn lots of stuff we'd find useful.

I met him at the desk and took him to the canteen. 'Two bacon sandwiches, please. One with all the fat cut off and cooked till it frizzles, in a toasted bun; the other as it comes. And two teas: one weak, no milk and three sugars; the other as it comes.'

I joined him at the table. 'What's it all about, Gavin?' I asked. I refused to join the Gav conspiracy.

'I had a client die of a heroin OD at the weekend. There's aspects of the case that I think the police ought to know.'

'Go on.'

'He was a pleasant lad, only seventeen. Brighter than most of our customers; very bright, in fact. He was in trouble for stealing to pay for his habit. An older man, about thirty, had made friends with him and took him to parties and discos. He introduced him to Ecstacy, said he could pay for it later. Jason got hooked on it. We think it must have been laced with something else; you don't get hooked on E like he was. Then they started chasing the dragon; it still seemed like good fun. Next he was having to inject, but by now he owed several hundred pounds to the pusher. He was caught robbing an old lady who had just collected her pension. In his right mind he wouldn't have dreamt of doing anything like that. That's when we got him. I tried to persuade him to grass on the pusher, but he wouldn't. Then during one of our talks, he let a name slip. Parker, that's all. He begged me to keep it to myself, and I had to, to maintain my credibility.

I was working on ways of letting you know, but on Sunday he died. Massive overdose of uncut heroin. Somebody's poisoning our kids, Charlie. The streets are flooded with the stuff.'

The sandwiches arrived; they were both As They Come. Gavin was visibly distressed, but he wolfed his sandwich down; he seemed hungrier than I was. I thought about what he had told me.

'Parker, just Parker?'

'Afraid so. Doesn't narrow it down much, does it?'

'That's OK, it's a starting point.' Providing it's not just his pen name. I wrestled with my sandwich and sipped my tea.

'A couple of weeks ago we caught three youths trying to rob the owner of a Chinese restaurant,' I told him. 'They were all first-offenders and they all had syringe marks on their arms. They're doing cold turkey on remand now. Last week we caught three schoolgirls stealing handbags. When their rooms were searched no drugs were found, but they had all the paraphernalia associated with the scene: posters, weird records, that sort of stuff. Plus their parents and teachers were alarmed at the deterioration in the girls' behaviour recently. You're right, we're just seeing the tip of the iceberg.'

The other reason for talking in the canteen was to escape the constant interruptions of the telephone. It didn't work. 'It's for you, Mr Priest,' the manageress called out. I went behind the counter to take it.

'Is that Inspector Priest?' asked the voice, flatly. Male, northern accent, unemotional.

'Yes, who's that, please?'

'Never mind. I've some information for you, and for you only. Meet me at the Coiners Arms, tonight, seven o'clock.' And he was gone. Today was turning into Let's Tell Charlie Day.

'I'll have to go, Gavin. Thanks for the information, I'll let you know if we make anything of it.'

'I just hope you can catch whoever's pushing this stuff,' he answered. 'Do you think they'll let me have another bacon sandwich?'

I granted him the Freedom of the Canteen and went up to the office. Mike Freer is an old boozing pal from the days before I found out that a crutch made out of liquid is about as useful as a blancmange stepladder. He's also an inspector on the city Drug Squad. His office told me he wasn't in, but they'd get him to ring me as soon as possible, night or day.

DS Willis obtained a confession from the husband, and statements from acquaintances and the neighbours. Our man had been thumping his wife for years, usually when he came home from the pub heavily under the influence. Last night one of his drinking companions had let it slip that the wife was having an affair with a workmate. He'd drowned his sorrows, then taken his vengeance. On the wife, of course. That type has a strong opinion of where blame lies.

'Did you have to twang his wires?' I asked.

'No,' Tony answered, 'I just hung my jacket on the weights.'

'What about his solicitor?'

'No, just my jacket.'

I'd obtained copies of the depositions for the three youths we'd called the Mountain Bike Gang. These are the statements that are presented to court. I read the names out loud, then asked: 'Which of them would you say was the best-looking?'

'Lee Ziolkowski,' Sparky replied. 'He's the fair-haired one, a bonny lad. I've always wanted fair hair.' He looked wistful. 'Or dark hair. Any sort of friggin' hair, actually.'

I set to work on Lee's depositions with white paper and scissors and gum. Then, after a visit to the photocopier, I placed the results of my handiwork in the typewriter and let my imagination plummet. Sometimes I can be so mean I frighten myself.

The Coiners is one of the oldest pubs in the area. There's never been much mining for minerals in the southern Pennines; all the lead and stuff was to the north. But there's supposed to be plenty of gold waiting to be found. The pub gets its name from a neat little scam that was carried out in these hills at the beginning of the nineteenth century.

The Industrial Revolution was giving local businessmen more money than they knew what to do with, but, true to form, they were ever on the lookout for opportunities to increase that wealth. Legally or illegally.

A gang living in the hills developed an ingenious technique for putting a gold sovereign in a mould and then bleeding off a couple of drops of the precious stuff. A fifteen percent profit, overnight, minus commission, had half of Yorkshire, Lancashire and Derbyshire beating a path to their cave. It all came to an end when they were hanged on York Knavesmire, as a prelude to the day's racing, but legend has it that there is still a million pounds worth of gold hidden somewhere in them thar hills.

None of this was on my mind as I drove towards the Coiners after leaving the office. My main concern was whether they served food, closely followed by wondering what my mystery caller had for me.

Hallelujah! There was a big sign outside that read 'Home of Peggy Watt's Famous Yorkshire Puddings'. Wild Bill Hickok sat with his back to the door and paid for it with his life, so I sat in a corner where I could view the entire room. There was nobody else in, apart from the landlord, who seemed to resent my intrusion. I drank four orange juices with lemonade as slowly as I could, and ate one of Peggy Watt's puddings as rapidly as I was able. Two other men, apparently regulars, came in and had a serious discourse on tupping while sipping halves. The Yorkshire pudding had the consistency of a marathon runner's insole. Peggy would have been better employed helping their Jimmy with his steam engine; or perhaps he had to invent the steam engine to stir the bloody stuff.

It was dark when I left. Maybe Sparky and Nigel Newley were having better luck. I'd left them watching over my house – it could all have been a ploy to get me out of the way. I was manoeuvring in the car park just as another vehicle came in, carrying a young couple. We got in each other's way for a few seconds, then the driver wound down his window and shouted to me: 'Watch how you go, mate, there's some rozzers parked down the lane and you've a back light out.'

I waved a thank you and parked up again. The offside rear light was deader than last night's promises. I tapped the lens a few times in an attempt to resuscitate it, then tried to open the boot lid to have a closer look. The key jammed in the lock at first, but with some extra persuasion I managed to force it open. Once I'd figured how it was done I flicked out the offending bulb holder. Surprise, surprise, there was no bulb there; it must have fallen out into the light fitting.

All good cops carry a flashlight with a five-hundred-foot beam. By some chance I happened to have one with me. I didn't find the bulb, but I did discover a white package tucked in the recess where the window-washer bottle was situated. It weighed about half a pound and was neatly done-up with polythene and Sellotape. It could have been special flour for Mrs Watt's Yorkshire puddings, or it could have been something else.

Watching in the rear-view mirror for the blue light to come on was like waiting for the sun to rise: dazzling and inevitable. I pulled over, they got out. It was a textbook exercise in courtesy and Proper Police Procedure. Nobody had been slipping double tequilas into my orange juice, and vitamin C is non-intoxicating, so I passed the breath test as easily as a Charolais heifer passes wind.

'Do you mind if we look in your boot, sir?

'Yes.'

'It'll be easier all round if you cooperate, sir.'

'One of you can look; I want the other to stand well back.'

The lock operated more easily this time. He flashed his light round inside, then asked to look in the car. I watched him like a weasel watches a rabbit, or was it like a rabbit watches a weasel?'

'Everything seems to be in order, sir. You will get that light fixed, won't you? Which station would you like to present your documents at?'

'St Pancras. You're on the wrong side of the hill, Sergeant. Who sent you over here?' It was my turn to ask questions.

'We had a tip-off, sir. Can't say any more than that.'

'Stop calling me sir. An anonymous tip-off?'

'Er . . . I understand it was.'

'Then make sure it was logged, 'cos I'll be checking.'

* * *

The gate to Bentley Prison could have been the prototype for the Great Gate at Kiev. The whole edifice was constructed during Queen Victoria's reign, in a burst of enlightenment and compassion, and an earnest desire to be constructive in the treatment of the criminal classes. Now it was overcrowded, understaffed, and held regular degree ceremonies for those who passed through its courses in advanced criminality. They don't open the Great Gate to let visitors in – there's a normal-sized, but metal, door just to the side of it.

I'd arranged my visit to see Lee Ziolkowski the previous afternoon. The visiting room is like a large canteen, with formica tables and tubular chairs; none of this talking through a screen that you see in the films. Down the side there are small cubicles for special visitors, such as solicitors or policemen. I was told which cubicle to use, and someone went to fetch Lee. I bought a couple of teas and chocolate biscuits from the lady at the WRVS counter and waited. It was normal visiting hours, and the place was noisy with young women with toddlers, come to see daddy doing his bird. At the table just outside my cubicle a tattooed hero was trying to swallow his leather-clad visitor. She wore a mini-skirt and thigh boots, and the gap between displayed enough fishnet to equip a small trawler. Just the thing to raise the morale when you measure the passing of time in Christmas dinners.

Lee appeared a lot healthier than when I last saw him. He'd lost his pallor and gained a pound or two in weight. He still looked at me nervously, though.

'Hello, Lee. Remember me, Charlie Priest? I interviewed you in Heckley nick. I got you one with milk and two sugars; hope that's how you like it.' It's how they always like it.

He sat down opposite me. 'Yeah, thanks,' he said.

'I have to tell you, Lee, that you've no need to talk to me if you don't want to. You can get up and leave right now, or you can insist on your solicitor being present. I hope you won't, though, because I think you should hear what I have to say.'

Legally he was a man, but inside he was just a scared little boy, struggling to survive in a world he couldn't comprehend. He would put up a tough show for my benefit, but was out of his depth, and now had to either grab the lifeline or go under, maybe for ever. He didn't say anything, just stayed where he was and unwrapped his biscuit.

'You and your pals have been used, Lee,' I told him, 'by evil people who don't care if you live or die. They feed you shit drugs and shit friendship, but all they want is for you to get hooked. Then they start bleeding you. You don't belong in here, this place is a dustbin, it's full of garbage. A young kid died over the weekend from a heroin overdose. The stuff he was using was too strong, he was just guessing at the dose. He's the latest in a long line. It could have been you if you hadn't been in here. I know it's not the done thing, Lee, but you could help me stamp it out. You could save lives, including your own. I want you to tell me who you got your works from.' Longest speech I ever made, and he wasn't impressed.

'You mean grass? You want me to grass?'

Sometimes I think they absorb the prison culture with the food. 'The rubbish in here call it grassing, Lee, I call it curing a disease. A few years ago there was a disease called smallpox; killed millions. Then they found a cure for it and thought they'd stamped it out. A couple of years later somebody in Africa said: "Hey! There's a feller in our village still got it." So the doctors moved in and cured him. Now he can't give it to anyone else. The man who spoke out wasn't grassing – he did a public service. You could do the same.'

'They'd kill me.' He looked scared.

'No they wouldn't,' I assured him, without conviction. 'They wouldn't know where the information came from. Besides, I thought the younger generation wanted some excitement in their lives. They've wanted to kill me for years, I can live with it.'

He could have stood up and walked out. An old lag would have done, but he still had a residue of polite behaviour in him, and I hadn't said he could go.

'What's the grub like?' I asked.

He almost smiled; either with relief at the change of subject or at the thought of the next culinary extravaganza. 'Rubbish,' he answered.

I small-talked with him for twenty minutes, asking him about how he was finding it inside, his family, how he'd done at school, anything I could think of. He opened up a little about playing football, but most of the time it was a questions-and-answers session. It usually is with teenagers. After a while I took a long look at my watch.

'Well, I'll have to go, Lee. It's been nice talking to you. I have to ask you once again, though, do you want to become a crime-fighter, or would you rather play all your football against a twenty-foot wall?'

He stared at me across the table with something like contempt in his gaze. 'You don't understand, do you?' he declared.

'Understand what?' I replied, quizzically.

'Drugs,' he answered. 'Drugs are all right. As soon as I get out I'll start taking them again. What else is there?'

'I'm sorry you feel that way, Lee. Drugs are a one-way ride to an early grave or the mental hospital, and it's all downhill.'

I stood up to leave, but as I reached the door of our little cubicle I turned back to him. 'Oh, I forgot to give you these; you have to have a copy.' I reached into my inside pocket for the two sheets of foolscap and laid them on the table in front of him.

He gazed at them for a few seconds, then up at me. 'What are they?' he demanded.

'Your new deps,' I told him.

'I've got my deps.'

'You're not listening, Lee. I said your new deps.'

He looked bewildered, so I spelt it out for him: 'We've got you down as a nonce now, Lee, with a special liking for small boys. Should make a good-looking lad like you very popular in here. I'll organise you some new room-mates on my way out.'

The newly acquired colour drained from his face and he swayed in his chair. I re-took my seat opposite him.

'You couldn't do it,' he said defiantly.

I pointed at the papers. 'Read 'em. Do you want to risk it?' I placed my ball-pen across the sheets in front of him. 'All I'm asking you to do, Lee,' I said softly, 'is turn the sheet over and write a name on the back. I guarantee that nobody will ever know where it came from.' A white-knuckled fist moved a couple of inches towards the pen, hesitated, and then withdrew. His eyes were glistening with tears. He sniffed and shook his head.

'No. I can't,' he mumbled.

'A name, Lee.'

'No.'

'One little name, and I'll go away and take the deps with me and no one will ever know I've been.'

He shook his head. I reached across and turned the top sheet over. Across the middle it said 'Parker'. The effect was electric.

'I didn't write that!' he exclaimed.

'Thanks, Lee, that should do nicely.' I took the fake depositions back and put them in my pocket. 'You won't be needing these any more,' I explained.

'I didn't write it, I didn't write anything.' He wiped his nose on his sleeve.

'Of course you didn't, but your face told me what I wanted to know. Don't worry about it, Lee, we've had his name from several sources, I just wanted confirmation.'

His agitation died down when he realised that we already knew the name. What he didn't know was how useless that piece of information was to us.

'This Parker . . .' I tossed the question in as casually as tossing a cigarette butt into a fire, 'is he black or white?'

No harm in answering that; it only narrows the field down to half of the world's population.

'White,' he said, gazing at the table like a shell-shocked survivor. The dam was cracking. Some judicious leverage could give us a torrent.

'Do you fancy another tea?'

He nodded. I fetched the same again and we sipped and munched in silence for a while. 'Big money in dealing,' I stated. 'What's he drive – BMW? Merc? Porsche?'

'A Porsche.'

'Fabulous. A black one, no doubt.'

'Yeah, how did you know?'

'Just a guess, black ones look best.'

If it really was a black Porsche we probably had enough to pin him down; on the other hand Lee could be smarter than the average junky. Might as well go for gold. 'Where does he hang out, Lee?'

'All over. Sometimes in the Penalty Spot, sometimes in the Fireplace.' The Penalty Spot was the pub outside the football ground, the Fireplace was a nightclub of some repute.

'On match days?' I asked.

'I think so.'

'You think so. Don't you deal with him?'

'No.'

'Then who do you get your works from?' He looked down at the table. He'd clammed up again.

'Lee, look at me. Are you telling me that Parker is the big fish, the pusher who supplies your dealer.' He lifted his head and nodded. 'Any idea where he comes from?'

'Manchester, I think.'

'Thanks, Lee. I'll see what I can do for you.'

The drug network is long and tortuous. Between the hill farmers and chemists who produce the stuff and the street-corner dealers who peddle it are chains of middlemen, each raking off a percentage of the final price. What starts out measured in tons, selling for peanuts, finally lands on the streets in twists of foil selling at twenty-five pounds a go. At each transaction the quantities are divided into smaller units, and the price increases by two or three hundred percent.

A heroin junky needs between one and two hundred pounds every day to pay for his habit. The easiest way to get this sort of money is to become a dealer. He'll buy an ounce at a time and sell individual doses of half a gram, probably diluted with something like baking soda. He's a victim, dealing to pay for the crocodile in his head that needs constant feeding. The people he buys from don't touch the stuff. They haven't got long hair; they wear blue suits, not Funky Junky T-shirts, and do their deals via mobile telephones in their upmarket cars. The more middlemen they can bypass, the bigger the profit. But that makes the risks greater, too.

Where Parker fitted in I didn't know, but I was sure of one thing – he'd been very careless.

CHAPTER SEVEN

I was struggling to write a letter to the Crown Prosecution Service in an attempt to obtain light sentences for the Mountain Bike Gang, on the grounds that they had proffered valuable information, but I kept being interrupted. First it was Sparky.

'Are there two ns in fornication?'

'Only if they're lesbian 'ens, usually it's just one 'en and a cockerel.'

'Cheers.'

'You're welcome.'

Then it was Mike Freer, at last, on the telephone. 'Shagnasty! How y'doin'?' he boomed in my ear. There was a ritual to be gone through before we got down to business.

'Not bad, Fungus Features, how're you?' I replied.

'Oh, fare to Midlands. Listen, Super Sleuth, I want you to know that we're ignoring the rumours and we're all standing by you in spite of everything.'

'Gee, I'm . . . I'm really choked. I don't deserve friends like you.'

'Just tell me one thing,' he went on, 'was it a very old man?'

'It wasn't an old man,' I replied. 'It was an old English Sheepdog.'

'Ah! Then that explains why you were in the City Square toilets.'

'Precisely. Is somebody trying to sully my reputation?'

'Don't worry about it. In twenty years it will be considered perfectly normal behaviour. You're just ahead of your time.'

He could go on for ever; I'd had enough. 'Listen, Fungus, I need your help. When can I see you?'

'Soon as you like.'

'Tonight?'

'Sure, where?'

'My place, about seven. You know I'm back at my mother's house now?'

'Yes, I'm sorry about her. She was a grand lady, I thought a lot of her.'

'Thanks,' I said, 'and now I've got some information for you.' I told him all about Parker.

'Parker? It could be his pen name,' he suggested. He was stealing my material.

'In that case, he's a penpusher,' I countered.

'Well let's see if we can pension him off.'

'To the penitentiary?'

'Pentonville, of course.'

'Let's make that the penultimate comment.'

'Thank God for that. Will your boy give evidence?'

'No way, Pedro!'

'Have you been bending the rules, Charlie?'

'Mmm, massaging them, a little.'

'Listen, Charlie; listen to Uncle Mike. It's not worth it, there's too much at stake. The days have gone when you could give them a clip round the ear and they'd say, "Thank you sir, I deserved that," and send you a Christmas card.'

'Ah, those were the days. You're right, but it's good info. However, whatever you do, keep it to yourself as much as possible – somebody in the Force is involved.' No need to tell him just yet that it's only our Chief Constable.

Mike's voice fell an octave. 'Oh dear, are you sure?'

'That's why I want to see you tonight. Then, when we've sorted that lot out, I'll take you to Kim Limbert's promotion bash. She's coming to the city.'

'So I've heard. Actually I'm supposed to be going to a do over here. One of our number has just become a dad after trying for fifteen years, so we're wetting the baby's head.'

'Lovely. What did they do, change their milkman?'

'Probably,' Mike replied. 'I've only to throw my shirt

on the bed and the wife's pregnant. He's got a little girl, so they're calling her Mira.'

'Myra? After the Pontefract Poisoner?'

'No, after the electric shower manufacturers. Apparently she was conceived under one of their products.'

We drove up towards the Coiners in my car, out of the decent weather into the perpetual rain of the high moorlands. Every schoolboy learns that Lancashire got the cotton because of the damp atmosphere on their side of the hill, whilst we got the wool due to the softness of the water in our streams. Nobody mentions the slave trade, of course. We weren't taught about the merchants from Liverpool and Manchester who financed slave ships to plunder Africa. They carried their wretched cargo to America and returned laden with cotton for their almost-as-wretched mills. The merchants grew fat and wealthy, gave their names to various philanthropic projects and bought respectability.

'We could have a pudding while we're here,' said Mike, with the enthusiasm of the ill-fed, when he saw the sign.

'No way,' I stated.

I led him through a stile in the dry-stone wall at the back of the car park, and paced out twenty-five steps along the wall side. 'There it is,' I told him, pointing at the white package, still wedged between the stones where I had concealed it the night before. Mike fished it out, holding a corner between finger and thumb, and dropped it into a plastic bag.

"Fraid I handled it quite a bit,' I confessed, then asked: 'Any guesses what it is?'

'No, not yet, but it looks interesting. I'll have it analysed in the morning.'

We drove down the hill in silence for a while. Eventually Mike said: 'How do you want us to play this, Charlie?'

I'd filled him in on the background on the way up. 'Softly-softly, if possible. Somebody's out to nail me, so I'd like to keep it under wraps. Let them have to try again. If that stuff's self-raising flour there's no harm done. If it's something else, we've a problem.'

'Thanks for the "we". I think we can both kiss goodbye to our night on the tiles. I'll go straight in with this, see if I can raise a friendly expert; and I don't want it hanging around me for too long. You'd better get something down on paper: if we're keeping quiet we'd best cover our backs.'

I'd been looking forward to seeing Kim again, but never mind – it gave me an excuse to call her sometime in the future. I set to work on the word processor in the spare bedroom-cum-office and put down for posterity the events subsequent to the mysterious phone call. Then, because I felt wide awake, I typed out the story of my trip to ABC House, and the visitation of Chief Constable Hilditch. I ran off three

107

copies and sealed them in separate envelopes.

Seven a.m. the phone rang. It was Mike Freer. I'd forgotten that the Drug Squad are night owls. He sounded agitated. 'It's heroin. I had half a gram analysed. The Professor said it's the purest he's ever seen.'

'So where does that leave us?'

'Easy on the "us", Super Sleuth. It leaves you with half a kilogram of Bogota's best; street value about two hundred thousand quid.'

'Jesus! I'll take it. Where is it now?'

'It's sealed in a jiffy bag with my name on it and in our safe. It should be OK there. Trouble is, your story is that it was planted on you to incriminate you; our story, if we tell it, is that it's the biggest individual haul we've ever had. Over the top's hardly the word.'

'You mean nobody would believe me.'

'Somebody decided to make you a rich man, because they had a grudge against you? Would you believe it?'

'No. They must be swimming in the stuff, whoever they are.'

'And they're clever. What's your next move?'

'I've written three reports,' I told him. 'I'll lodge one with Gilbert Wood this morning. Hopefully that will keep us in the clear. I don't want to go public yet, if that's OK with you. Somebody's invested a lot in me, let's see what their next move is.'

'Anything you say, Sheepshagger. Are you sending me a copy?'

'In the post this morning. Thanks for your help, Mike, I appreciate it.'

'No problem. Meanwhile, we'll have a look for your Parker friend. Who knows, you could qualify for a transfer to the Drug Squad yet.'

As soon as the morning's formalities were over I collared Gilbert Wood in his office. I asked him to sign and date one of the envelopes across the flap, and gave it to him for safekeeping. Next, when he was sitting comfortably, cup of decaffeinated in hand, I told him the full story.

Gilbert looked grave and thoughtful. 'Jesus Christ, Charlie, you've poked a gorilla in the arse with a sharp stick this time. When do you get your twenty-six and a half years in? Is it before me?'

'We don't qualify for good behaviour or ill-health, Gilbert, we're both full-termers.'

'I'm working on it. We've probably enough to bring Cakebread in and spin his premises. It's not very satisfactory, though, and we'd not root out the Force connection. Let's just clarify what we've got so far.'

Gilbert pulled an easel out of the corner of his office, with a large flip-chart on it. The first pen he tried didn't work. He put it back on the ledge and selected one that did. He wrote:

TRUSCOTT DID SOME PAINTINGS

Then he added:

CAKEBREAD (ABC) MOVED THE PAINTINGS

'Hilditch knows Cakebread,' I suggested. Gilbert
wrote:

CHIEF CONST. FRIENDS WITH CAKEBREAD

'What next?' he asked.
   'Why do you save the pens that don't work? Why
not sling them in the bin?'
   'It might start working again. What next?'
   'CC knows Charlie's on his tail,' I told him. He
put:

CHIEF CONST. FINDS OUT CP IS SUSPICIOUS

I wasn't happy about the ambiguity, but I let it go. In a
sudden burst of inspiration Gilbert added:

DRUGS PLANTED ON CP
WERE THE PAINTINGS SWITCHED?
IS TRUSCOTT DEAD?

We stood back and admired his handiwork. Gilbert
selected a different-coloured pen and drew arrows

on the chart. 'We've established links there, there and there,' he said, indicating the top four lines, 'but we've nothing to show that, the drugs are part of the same scam. They might be totally unrelated. I hate to be the one to tell you this, Charlie, but there's other people around who don't like you.'

'Mmm, I know, that's what I've been thinking. Heroin is a highly marketable commodity, though. Which is easier to get rid of: three paintings or fifty million quid's worth of smack?'

'You mean they stole the paintings and traded them for the drugs.'

'That's the theory,' I stated, 'except that maybe they didn't steal the paintings. Maybe they just traded the forgeries.'

'Jesus Christ, no wonder Truscott sounded scared when you talked to him. Drug barons are not the people to meddle with.'

I gazed at Gilbert with my brow furrowed and a deadpan expression on my face, trying hard not to smile. 'Gilbert,' I said, 'do you have to keep using our Saviour's name as an expletive? Some people might find it offensive. In fact, I believe I do. Why can't you just use plain old Anglo-Saxon like everybody else?'

'Oh no!' He put his hands to his head in exasperation. 'Don't tell me: my DI's found God!'

'No I haven't!' I declared.

'Then it's a woman,' he stated triumphantly, stabbing

a forefinger at me. 'You've found a woman and she's found God.'

'Rubbish. Anyway there's something else to add to the chart.'

'You're blushing! I've never seen you blush before.'

'No I'm not. Truscott . . .'

'Yes you are. Hey! It's the lady in the video, isn't it? She looked all right, definitely too good for you. What about Truscott?'

I was relieved to get back to business. I had a feeling that I'd lost that little skirmish. 'The conversation I had with him at Beamish,' I began. 'I've been over and over it in my mind, and I'm certain he said that the Picasso was damaged and he didn't think it had been switched. He pretended he didn't know, as if the pictures had passed on from him. But then he bequeaths me the Picasso, real or forged, in his will.'

Gilbert thought about it. 'Which proves what?' he asked.

'Just that Truscott is a liar,' I stated. 'He knew all along where the Picasso was. He had it himself.'

TRUSCOTT IS A LIAR

Gilbert added to the chart.

'And there's another thing you ought to know,' I said.

'Too late, the sheet's full.' He pulled it off the pad

and started to tear it into shreds which fell into his bin.

'Cakebread's just flown off on his hols in his own plane.'

'Where to?' Gilbert asked wearily.

'The Costa del Crime,' I answered.

His eyebrows popped up. 'Think he might be collecting another payment?'

'Who knows?' I watched the last few strips fall into the bin. 'I'd like to leave things a while, see what their next move is, if that's all right with you.'

'There's not much else we can do,' he stated, stroking his chin, 'but it could be dangerous. They may not be so subtle next time.'

'If I broke my legs tonight, would you manage without me?'

'It would be a struggle at first,' he admitted, 'but by ten o'clock we'd be saying, "Charlie who?"'

'Well in that case, can I have the next two weeks off on leave?'

Gilbert gave one of his all-the-cares-of-the-world sighs. After considering for a few seconds what I'd asked he said: 'If you want to take your lady friend studying ecclesiastical architecture in the Cotswolds – yes. If you're thinking of buggering off to Spain looking for Cakebread – no.'

I didn't say anything, just thought about the options he'd given, and a wave of melancholy swept over me. I could immerse myself in police work and enjoy the banter and the adventure of it; I even enjoyed the long, boring shifts waiting in the car in some alley, watching for something to happen. But the endless shifts always did come to an end. Gilbert had been dismissive of the holiday in the Cotswolds, with 'your lady friend', but his throwaway line expressed an unattainable dream for me. I must be growing sensitive.

The office felt claustrophobic, I needed some fresh air. I delegated a few jobs, then told Tony and Dave that I was going to sort out a few things for the Jaguar. I paused in the exit from the car park. Turning right would take me up towards the moors, past St Bidulph's and the Old Vicarage. 'Not just yet,' she had told me, but when was 'yet', and how would I know? I drummed my fingers on the steering wheel, consumed with doubt and indecision. A patrol car waiting behind me gave a gentle toot on its horn. I waved an apology, signalled left and started down the hill into town.

I'd had a message from Jimmy Hoyle, the mechanic, that the wheels were ready, so I thought I would collect them and fit them in the evening. On the way, as an afterthought, I called in to a travel agency that most of the troops used because it gave a discount to Federation members. There were three girls in varying degrees of desirability behind the counter, and a youth with a ponytail and earrings.

'Can I help you, sir?' enquired the youth.

'I don't know.' I sighed with resignation. 'Have you anything left in or near Marbella, for next week?'

'Doubt it, sir. It's school holidays and the companies have drastically cut down on flights to Spain this year. Everybody wants to go to the States.'

He rattled the keys on his terminal with great fluidity, shook his head and rattled them some more.

'Must it be Marbella?' he asked.

'Well, within driving distance.'

'Sorry, Tenerife and Portugal's the nearest we can do, and they're hardly a drive away.'

'What about accommodation? If I drove down would I find somewhere to stay?'

'Absolutely no problem, sir. There's lots of spare capacity in the area. We could fix you up, but you'd be better having a look round when you got there. You'd probably find a nice villa for next to nothing if you fancied self-catering.'

Self-catering didn't appeal to me, I had enough of that normally, but I was warming to the youth. He knew his job and was trying to be helpful. 'What's the best way of taking a car across the Channel?' I asked.

'There's usually a few spare places on the ferries these days. I'd recommend the hovercraft from Dover. It's busy, but we could book you on from here. When would you be travelling?'

'I can't be certain,' I said. 'What's the chances if you just turn up?'

'You might have a long wait, but they'd fit you on eventually. You'd best be there very early. Here, I'll give you a timetable.'

'Thank you, you've been very helpful. I promise to book my next holiday with you.'

'You're welcome,' he said, with a smile.

Suddenly I was filled with new enthusiasm. I called in at the AA shop and had the Jag put on my policy. I took out their five-star touring service, and the price of it caused my enthusiasm to waver somewhat, but an international driving permit cost me next to nothing. Then I called at Jimmy Hoyle's.

'You'll never fit five wheels in the back of the Cavalier,' he told me. 'I've got them in the van, I was going to bring 'em round. Come on, I'll show you.'

He opened the back of his little van. It was stuffed solid with Jaguar wheels and smelt of new rubber. Jimmy pulled the nearest wheel towards him, and turned it to show off the gleaming chrome spokes.

'Don't they look fabulous,' he enthused. 'I think I'd keep the spare one over the mantelpiece.'

I had to agree with him. They looked a lot bigger than I remembered, and exuded style and excellence. And this was only the wheels.

'Jimmy, do you think I'll be able to take a long trip in it at the weekend?' I asked.

'Course you can,' he said. 'That's what it's meant for. I'll give you an MOT certificate now and you can send off for the tax. As long as you backdate it you'll be OK.

Then it just needs setting up. I'll do that for you. No problem. Where are you going?'

I'd wanted to keep it secret. 'I'm thinking about the South of France,' I said.

'Smashing. Anywhere in particular?'

'Yeah, Spain. But don't tell anyone.'

'I'll make a deal with you,' he said, giving me his lopsided grin. 'Leave the keys with me and I'll pop up this afternoon and put the wheels on. Then I can give it a going-over. That way I get to have the first ride in it. OK?'

It was definitely OK by me. 'Great,' I said, 'but what about this place? Can you leave it?'

'No problem. I'll soon have the wheels on, then I can bring it down here to set up. Do you want me to call round at the station with it?'

'No. Er, definitely not. And make sure you put your time on the bill.' Jimmy's bills were about a third of what other garages charged, which was just as well, otherwise I'd never have been able to have all the work done. He'd done the paintwork and the technical jobs, and had the expert stuff done at cost price for me. It was Jimmy who'd given me the Cortina several years previously, and I still felt indebted to him.

'Don't worry, I will. C'mon, I'll give you an MOT certificate and a tax form.' We went into his little office, where he rummaged among an untidy jumble of papers.

'How can you give it an MOT certificate when it hasn't any wheels on?' I asked.

'Here they are.' He retrieved the pad of certificates and ran his finger down the conditions of issue. He shook his head. 'Doesn't say anything about having to have wheels here.'

CHAPTER EIGHT

There's a photocopying machine in the main post office, so I took copies of the documents before posting them off to the Vehicle Registration Centre at Swansea. Next I called at the bank and cleaned them out of francs and pesetas. They didn't have many, and weren't pleased because I hadn't ordered them, but they paid up without being reminded that it was, after all, my money. Then, because I couldn't think of anything better, I drove back to the office.

Only Nigel was in, immersed in a long report. He told me where everybody else was and gave me a couple of messages. There was nothing that couldn't wait. I sat at my desk and pretended to be busy. I was still feeling restless, impatient, wondering what the next move would be.

The only relief came just before official knocking-off time. I answered the phone to hear a familiar voice whisper: 'Hi, boss, it's me, Maggie. Is Nigel in?' She wasn't called Mad Maggie for nothing.

'Yes,' I stated, flatly.

'Can he see you?'

'No.' Nigel had recently turned his desk round to catch the light from outside, which meant he now had his back to the windows of my little office.

'Then dial him on the party-line number and keep listening.'

I did as I was told, and was rewarded by the trill of Nigel's phone.

'Heckley Police, DC Newley speaking, can I help you?'

The next voice was that of a downtrodden female. 'I'd like to speak to a policeman,' it whined.

'Detective Constable Newley here, ma'am, how can I help you?'

'It's about my 'usband. He's been done for stealing an occasional table and I want to know if he'll go to jail.'

'Your husband, ma'am? Well, to start with, do you know if he's been charged with stealing anything else?'

'Yes, he 'as.'

'Can you tell me what?'

''E stole an occasional car . . . and an occasional video . . . and an occasional . . .'

Nigel slammed the phone down. 'Piss off!' I heard

through the glass. I replaced my receiver silently and buried my head in some paperwork. Maggie could be a heartless bitch when she wanted.

I left early, for once, and told Nigel not to hang about. I hadn't made a great contribution to the cause of law and order today, but I had other things on my mind. Five years of broken fingernails, caused by endless rubbing down and polishing, had finally come to an end. All the difficulties of finding obscure spare parts had been overcome and now the whole thing was assembled and sitting in the garage waiting for me. Patience isn't one of my foremost virtues, but I'd made great efforts not to spoil the restoration of the Jaguar by rushing it. Going slowly also helped to spread out the expenditure.

Jimmy had popped the keys through my letter box, as arranged. I just went into the house, picked up the keys, and went straight back out to open the garage door. It slid upwards like the shutter of a missile silo, to reveal its awesome contents. The evening sunlight slid slowly up the endless bonnet of the E-type and flicked over the windscreen. I took a few paces backwards and just stood there, staring at it. I've never been what might be called a car person – they're normally strictly workhorses to me – but I'd always regarded the E-type Jaguar as a work of art. The reverence I experienced as I gazed upon it was similar to that I had felt when I stood before Michelangelo's *Pieta,* or watched the sun set, one winter's afternoon, from the summit of Blencathra. Jimmy was right, except that I would have liked to have put the whole caboodle over the mantelpiece.

The phone was ringing in the house. I dashed in and grabbed it. 'Hello,' I said. It was as good an opening as any, and didn't give a lead to crank callers.

'Is that Mr Priest, please?'

It was a female voice. I thought I recognised it, but I wasn't sure.

'No, it's Charlie. Who's that, please?'

'Hello, boss, it's Kim, Kim Limbert

'Hi, Kim,' I replied with enthusiasm, 'sorry I missed your bun fight, did it go off all right?'

'Yes. Never mind that. Charlie, are you in trouble?

'No. I don't think so. Why?'

'I overheard a conversation today, well, more of a row than a conversation. It seemed to be about you.'

I was intrigued. 'Where was this?' I asked.

'Down at city HQ,' Kim replied. 'I don't start till Monday, but I thought I'd call in today to say hello. I was waiting to see my new boss when I was invited up to see the Assistant Chief Constable, Mr Partridge.'

I hadn't been invited to see the ACC when I made sergeant. 'Go on,' I told her.

'Well, when I got there I was informed that he'd just been summoned to the Big Chief's office. Hilditch's, that is. Would I forgive him, and he'd have a word with me some other time.'

'Mmm, sounds like I've a rival there. What happened next?'

'Next I got lost. I had a quick word with a girl I know in the outer office, then I must have turned the wrong way when I came out. I knew I'd made a mistake when the carpet came over my ankles. I found myself outside Hilditch's office. There was an unholy row going on inside, and your name was being mentioned. Well, shouted, actually.'

'Maybe they were making the short list for the next super's job,' I suggested.

'No way, Charlie. Hilditch was telling him that he wants you off the Force. Pronto and *sine die*. Mr Partridge tried to reason with him, but he wouldn't listen. He ordered him to have you suspended, as from tomorrow, or else. What have you been up to, Charlie?'

I thought about it for a few moments before I answered. Two possible courses of action occurred to me. The first one was very tempting, almost irresistible: invite Kim for a trip to a moorland pub in my new sports car to discuss the predicament. 'Kim, it's best if you don't know what it's about just yet. What you don't know can't make a pig's ear, or something. You just show 'em you're the best sergeant they've got, and forget what you heard. And I promise I'll tell you all about it as soon as I can. OK?'

'I suppose so, you're the boss.'

'And I'm grateful. Any time you want a transfer to CID, just let me know.'

'We've had this conversation before, Charlie. I'd be no good: my profile's too high. Good detectives are grey and anonymous, they merge with the woodwork.'

'Ah, but we have all the fun. Good luck with the job, Kim, and thanks.'

I was smiling as I put the phone down, but I had a feeling that I ought not to be. I gave myself a mental ticking off for having misplaced priorities, and trudged upstairs to pack a suitcase. Kim's call had helped me make a decision. I had a lot to do, and not much time to do it in.

Jimmy Hoyle told me, when I rang him, that the car was hunky-dory. He'd done a hundred and thirty, he claimed, on the M62 and she was as steady as a three-legged card table. But keep an eye on the oil level. I was about to ring Tony Willis, but I changed my mind and wrote him a note. Notes can't ask questions back. There were a few other things for him to attend to, but the main priority was the safety of Makinson and Rose. I instructed him to debrief them and act on whatever information they had gathered. I'd drop it through his letter box in the morning, on my way to Spain.

A good night's sleep seemed more important than an early start, so I rose at my normal time. It was a brilliant sunny morning, as if to give me a foretaste of what to expect. I put the Jag out on the road and left the other car standing in its normal place, up against the garage door. I pratted about for longer than I ought, checking this and that and wondering what I'd forgotten. I couldn't find any sunglasses, although I did have some, once, but I did find a baseball cap with NYPD on the front. Sparky's kids had brought it back from the States for me a few years ago. I pulled it on to my head and looked in the mirror. Not bad.

'OK, Frank,' I said to myself out of the corner of my mouth, 'let's go!'

The big engine rumbled into life immediately. I sat there for a few moments, feeling the car rocking gently beneath me, like the panting of a big cat – *panthera onca* – readying itself for the chase. It was inevitable that I thought of Dad, and wondered how much of his shadow I was still living under. I selected first gear and eased out the clutch. Going towards the high street an extremely glossy black Rover passed in the opposite direction. The two occupants were uniformed, and the one in the passenger seat had silver braid on the peak of his cap. I pulled the NYPD down over my eyes and shot past them.

After stuffing the note through the Willis letter box I filled up the fourteen-gallon tank. That should take me to the outskirts of Dover. There's a pay-phone at the garage, so I used it to ring the station. I told the desk sergeant that I wasn't very well and was having a day or two off sick, and to let Mr Wood know. He was very sympathetic because it was unheard-of for me to be off, and asked me what the problem was.

'Haemorrhoids,' I told him. Make it something unglamorous and they're bound to believe you.

'Ooh, nasty,' he confided. 'Have you tried Anusol? It's the only thing that works for me.'

Then I remembered what I'd forgotten. We'd defied the purists on two counts: Jimmy had fitted a pair of tasteful wing mirrors that the manufacturers had not deemed necessary, and I'd installed a radio/cassette player. Unfortunately I'd forgotten to throw in any cassettes. A quick detour took me to the record shop. I picked up a Dylan I hadn't heard, then made for the classical section. I was looking for S for Sibelius, but on the way saw Rimsky-Korsakov, and decided that perhaps *Capriccio Espanol* was more appropriate. Eventually, much later than I had wanted, I found myself heading cross-country to pick up the Ml southbound.

The E-type was a revelation. By modem standards it was heavy on the controls, and the performance was probably no better than lots of other cars, apart from the hundred and fifty miles per hour top speed. But what it did do, *par excellence,* was turn heads. Drivers pulled over to let me through, and then turned to wave a friendly hand. Kids in back seats gave me the thumbs up. When I stopped at a motorway cafe there was a constant procession of admirers gawping through the windows and standing well back to appreciate the graceful lines. I felt like a celebrity, and was surprised to discover that I enjoyed the feeling.

Dover was reached by late afternoon. After filling up and buying a European road atlas I investigated the queue for the hovercraft. It wasn't as bad as I had expected, and eventually they squeezed me on. I think they quickly regretted their consideration when they realised how long the car was, and how difficult it was to manoeuvre, but we did it. Forty-five minutes later we were in France. I followed another vehicle for a few hesitant miles, until I recovered from the shock of driving on the right. The Jag's poor rearward visibility, combined with the fact that the steering wheel was now on the wrong side, meant that I had difficulty watching what was happening behind me. The obvious solution was to drive faster, then I'd be going away from it all.

Immediate priorities were meal, bed, breakfast; preferably in that order. I drove steadily for about an hour, then, just as it was growing dark, pulled into the car park of one of the legendary Les Routiers. It was a disappointment, but bright and early next morning, stuffed full of croissants and twitchy on thick black coffee, I set about some serious motoring. Before going to bed I'd spent half an hour studying the maps and decided to travel south on the *routes nationales* rather than the autoroutes. My intended course would take me to the west of Paris, through Orleans and Limoges, and touch the edge of the Massif Central in Limousin country. It looked an interesting way to see some of France, and this was supposed to be a holiday.

France is a big place, I discovered, and my progress to the bottom of the map was tardy. But the E-type weaved its magic, and the sun was shining, and soon the familiar shadows of the avenues of poplar trees were flickering over the windscreen. I thought of all the impressionist paintings of these roads that I had admired, and wondered how many of them would be improved by the addition of a speeding Jaguar. The next time I visited a gallery I'd take a few fibre-tipped pens with me and see. Orleans was easily bypassed. It brought back memories of the only time I acted in a school play. We were doing Shaw's *Saint Joan,* and I landed the part of the Bastard of Orleans, purely on the grounds of being the only kid in the class who could pronounce it properly.

It was going to take me a lot longer to reach the Costa del Sol than I had anticipated. Impetuosity is not normally one of my traits, and now I was paying the price for my foray into that territory. Lack of planning; that was the cause of the problem. What the hell, who cares? Problem? What problem?'

I stopped in an unnamed village and dared to check out the local supermarket. Stocked up with bottled water, crusty bread, fresh grapes and other local goodies, I was soon on my way again. I also bought some aspirin, because the driving seat was giving me back-ache; and some sunglasses. Walking back to the car I put on the shades and gave the baseball cap to a little boy on a bike.

I reckoned on stopping for fuel at about two-hundred-mile intervals. I filled up four times that day.

There's a line in a song about the old men playing chequers 'neath the trees. The shadows were long and the light had turned a warm golden-yellow when I pulled triumphantly into the small town of Foix, at the foot of the Pyrenees. And there they were: old men in woollen cardigans and black berets, playing chess in the shade along the roadside, against a backdrop of a sunwashed hilltop chateau. I extricated myself from the Jag, gingerly straightening my back and stretching my protesting limbs. I was worn out and sweating. Beautiful cars, like beautiful people, have their deficiencies.

I'd parked outside a church, underneath a colossal cedar tree. I had a quick swig of bottled water and went for an exploratory walk. My schoolboy French was an embarrassment, but after a lot of gesticulation and even more laughter I found a small, deep-shadowed hotel that could feed and accommodate me for the night. When I took the Jaguar there, Monsieur le Chef-Patron was ecstatic, and insisted on my putting it round the back, away from the road. I felt welcome.

The evening blowout started with trout in a buttery sauce, followed by steak and whitebait, with olives. An unusual combination to me, but it went down well.

This was followed by a portion of cooked celery and then a salad. There was no menu; as I cleared one platter the next appeared. We finished off with a cherry flan that would have impressed my mother.

I wiped my chin on the big napkin. Madame was insistent with the cheeseboard, but I could only manage a couple of mousetrap-sized portions. As with the food, there was no choice of wine. And rightly so: they were the experts, and I submitted to their knowledge. My glass was filled with liquid that looked black until you held it to the brightest light. Then it glowed deep ruby, like St Anne's robe in the Leonardo painting. It was one of those wines that ambushes you. The first big mouthful left a slight prickly sensation on the tongue, and I decided that it was not really to my palate. By the end of the glass I was reconsidering this hurried appraisal, and by the third glass I was thinking that tomorrow was another day and could look after itself.

Monsieur asked me if I had enjoyed my meal. At least, I think that's what he said. I gave it Yorkshire's highest accolade: 'Not bad,' I told him, grinning like a euphonium, as he refilled my glass.

Next morning I felt as if I was coming round from unsuccessful brain surgery. Two aspirin for this hangover seemed as effectual as throwing ping-pong balls at a runaway train. Maybe the mountain air would do the trick.

'Never again,' I swore, not for the first time.

Normally, I like mountains. Human beings are supposed to have some primordial instinct that draws them, eternally, back to the sea. Not me, I go for the high ground. Today, though, the Pyrenees were just a barrier to my progress. The big engine ignored the gradients, but the mile after mile of hairpin bends took its toll on the driver. Perspiration was running down my arms when we were in the sunlight, then we would swing round a bend that seemed to go on for ever and plunge into shadow. The temperature would drop until the next hairpin brought us bursting out into the brightness again. I felt sick. A road signposted 'Andorra' passed by on the right. It would have been an interesting diversion, but I'd save that for the next time. I'd made myself a promise that one day I would return to Foix, but then it would be my destination and not just a stopover.

The first view down into Spain was not what I expected. The entire countryside below was covered by cloud, like a vast goose-down quilt stretching into infinity. Here and there pinnacles of vapour towered upwards from the undulating mass, as if trying to break free from it, and caught the morning sun. I pulled off the road and got out. It was one of those sights that makes you wish that everyone you had ever loved was there to share it with you. I had mixed feelings, though – soon I would drop down into it and it would slow my progress. I settled back into the driving seat and looked at the mileage on the speedo.

I was eleven hundred miles from home, but it felt like ten thousand.

It wasn't too bad. By concentrating hard, and with some fairly heavy braking now and then, I managed to keep up a good speed. After a while I caught a lorry. He was cracking on, and overtaking him would have been suicidal, so I just locked on to his taillights and settled down to follow him. It was a lot more relaxing.

I took stock of what I was doing there. It was difficult to come up with a good answer. Suddenly, looking for Cakebread's boat seemed a feeble reason for tear-arsing across Europe. There was the information in the note that Gloria had given me, but it didn't amount to much. We'd tried brainstorming possible meanings for PH and PM with the troops, but our combined grey matter had hardly raised a summer breeze.

I wished one of them was with me now. Tony Willis would be upped to inspector before too long, and I'd lose him from my team. He was young and ambitious, but he'd worked hard and deserved to move on. I'd let him run the show often enough, and known it was in good hands. The only thing that might hold him back was a sense of humour that he had difficulty containing.

Sparky was different. He was about as old as me but was still ranked as a constable. In spite of this he was one of the best officers I had ever known. He knew the theory, whether it be an obscure point of law or a piece of practical psychology, and he knew what on-the-street policing was all about. More than once he'd put his hand on my shoulder and told me: 'Let it go, boss, there's a better way of doing this.' And there usually was.

Only one thing scared Sparky, and it couldn't be hidden from: whenever he sat in an examination room he developed paralysis of the mind. He was OK talking to the top brass, and performed well in court, but stick an exam paper in front of him and he froze. We'd worked on it with him, and I'd spoken to various people about him, but in the last few years we'd accepted that DC David Sparkington was as high as he'd ever be. Police-wise, it didn't matter much – we could use him to the best of his considerable abilities without any problem. It was just unfortunate that he lost out on the pay. There was no reason for Sparky to contain his sense of humour, though, so we all benefited from that.

Then there was Gloria. Yep, I wouldn't have minded having Gloria with me, either. Distance changed my perspective on the brief meeting we'd had. I'd laughed at her enthusiasm for Cakebread's shabby world, and derided her eagerness to fall for his advances. The truth was that she was a young girl making the best of what she had. She'd found herself a job that she loved – a rare thing at the best of times – and I'd probably lost it for her. One day I'd like to make it up to her, but could I trust my motives? Probably not, I gladly admitted.

Most of all, I wished Annabelle was with me. I'd only met her twice, but readily confessed that I was smitten. It had taken her to make me realise that I'd drifted into an existence of compromise and second best. But not any more – from now on I was Going for Gold. She'd affected me on a more mundane level, too. I'd started polishing my shoes and wearing better shirts, just in case I bumped into her again. I'd even bought some decent aftershave; it must be love.

The cold, clammy mist suddenly began to glow yellow, as if each individual molecule was its own light source. Then, a few moments later, we burst out of it into the sun-drenched landscape of northern Spain. The sky was brilliant blue and the land all the shades of ochre. The lorry in front pulled over on to the shoulder of the road to let me through, and I gunned the Jag past him, waving a *gracias*. We were on our way again, and my hangover had nearly gone.

Outside Barcelona the road south became the Autopista Seven, for which I was thankful, but we were still about seven hundred miles from Marbella. I wanted to make it today, so there was no time for sightseeing. Do they have speed limits in Spain? No idea. I practised my Gallic shrug, in case I was pulled over. With a little effort I could bring my shoulders above my ears.

It was a long, hard day, but we did it. I grabbed packets and cans of whatever was available at the filling stations and dined on the move. The sun traversed the sky and the last couple of hours were driven in the dark. The Jag's headlights fell into the bimbo category – sexy to look at, but staggeringly dim. Just through Torremolinos a road sign read 'Marbella 45km'. Say thirty miles. That was near enough for me – I was at the end of my endurance. I pulled off the main road and found my way down towards the seafront, where the tourist hotels were. It was nearly midnight and I was well and truly japanned.

The first one I entered was called the Cala d'Or. It had a lounge with a piano and a small dance floor. The clientele still around were all over twenty-one, but it looked as if most customers had already gone to bed. I leant on the bar and had ordered a lager before I remembered my early-morning vow. The pianist was tinkling 'I Get Along Without You Very Well . . .' It felt in harmony with my mood, so I decided that this would do.

When I'd finished my drink and was feeling slightly less ragged round the edges, I made my way to the front desk. The receptionist was talking to somebody, but while I was waiting a girl came by wearing the characteristic blouse and skirt of one of the major British tour companies. I intercepted her.

'Excuse me, are you with Wilsons?' I asked. She was a big girl. I bet she was pushing at the leading edge of the company's unwritten rule about the preferred size of their representatives. Expanding the envelope, I believe it's called. The badge on her blouse said Stephanie Jones. I notice things like that: I'm a cop. The suntanned face split into a wide smile that didn't look too rehearsed.

'Yes, Stephanie Jones. What can I do for you?'

It was midnight, she'd been dealing with lost passports and punters with dicky pacemakers all day, and she was still smiling and touting for business. This lady had stamina.

'You're right, you are.' I pointed at the badge. 'Charlie Priest. I've just driven down and I'm looking for somewhere to stay. Can you recommend this place?'

'Nah! It's dreadful. How long are you staying?'

'Mmm, about a week.'

'This is probably what you're looking for,' she suggested. 'It's fairly quiet without being dead. The food's good.' Then, with a mischievous smile, she went on: 'At the Cala d'Or we cater for the more discerning holidaymaker.'

'Say it. You mean older, don't you?'

She laughed. 'It's nice here, you'll like it. Do you want me to book you in with us?'

'Will that save me money?' I asked.

Apparently it would. She attracted the receptionist's attention and the formalities were dealt with. I was glad to have met her; she might be a useful ally if any language difficulties came along. She was also looking more svelte with every moment. When we'd finished she turned to me and asked: 'Is that your swish sports car I saw outside?'

'Yes, it is,' I answered proudly. Maybe she was an enthusiast . . .

'Then I'd move it if I were you. You're in the chef's place and he's got a hell of a Latin temper.'

CHAPTER NINE

I took two aspirin and slid my aching body between the cool, crisp sheets. I'd done well; I told myself, but tomorrow we would start work properly. I wondered, briefly, if I still had a job at Heckley, then drifted into a deep sleep, interrupted only by a dream where I was dancing with a big, suntanned lady whose arms embraced me, and Hoagy Carmichael was playing the piano, very slowly.

Bright and early next morning found me still fast asleep. Eventually I awoke and just made it for the last ten minutes of breakfast. I went out blinking into the sunlight and took stock of my physical condition. I rotated one shoulder several times, then the other. Next I moved my head to the limits of its range, first side to side, then forwards and backwards. My fingers were still working and I was able to stand on my tip-toes. It looked as if I was alive, so I'd best get on with it.

I was at a place called Benalmadena. In one direction, within walking distance, lay Torremolinos, and to the other side, but further away, was Marbella. I didn't have to look far for boats to inspect: there was a marina right outside the hotel, and several others within sight. It made sense to eliminate the ones between here and Torremolinos first, and then go down to Marbella and work my way back.

How would I know which was Cakebread's boat? Well, I might see him on it. Then maybe the letters PH on the note were shorthand for its name. Another possibility was that he'd use the ABC theme or maybe his wife's name. Lastly was the western influence; he seemed to have a penchant for things cowboy. *Bonanza, Maverick,* or maybe even *Rednecked Asshole* were all contenders. There was plenty to go on, I was feeling confident, and it was a pleasant way of spending a couple of days.

It's difficult to be patient and vigilant at the same time. I read off the boat names but had to compare each with the checklist of possibilities, not just let them float through my mind. Hoping that a name will trigger something in the subconscious is not a reliable way of doing things. Fortunately relief was close at hand. All the way into Torremolinos, fronting on to the beach, is a succession of cafes, collectively known as the Carahuela. They all have imaginative names and prosaic menus, offering typical local dishes such as beefburgers and pizzas. After each small marina had been inspected I would relax with a coffee or a glass of Seven-Up. From now on I was a Seven-Up man.

Paella is one of my favourite meals. As I walked by the restaurants I studied the plates of the diners, and examined the menus, to see who did the biggest, saffroniest, prawniest paella. It was a disappointment: every place cooked it, but for two persons only. Yorkshire thriftiness wouldn't allow me to order a double portion just for myself. Ah well, to everything there is a purpose: I'd have to invite someone to share it with me. Wonder what night Stephanie is free?

I drew a blank on the first leg, but I was just practising. I'd learnt to walk past the 'Privado' signs on many of the jetties and walk up and down the duck-boards as if I owned them. It was hotter than I had expected, so I made my way back to the hotel and changed into shorts and a T-shirt. Driving to Marbella and then marina-hopping back to Benalmadena was the way I'd decided to manage the next leg, but I was delayed. The first thing I saw when I reached the car was that some Iberian imbecile had scraped a wing.

'It's only metal,' I told myself, without conviction, as I charged into the hotel foyer. The desk clerk was very apologetic and came out to look at the damage. He shook his head sadly as he surveyed it.

'How sad. What a lovely car,' he sighed. I began

to feel sorry for spoiling his day; a more considered inspection showed it to be only a little scratch. Eventually he composed himself and said: 'Come with me. I show you where you put car.' He took me back through the foyer, down a short corridor and through a couple of doors that weren't meant for the public. We were out the back, in a yard where the service vans did their deliveries and where the rubbish bins were kept. One or two hotel vehicles were parked here. 'Tonight you put car there,' he said, pointing. 'Will be safe from mad German drivers.'

The road into Marbella was busy. There are long stretches of dual carriageway, and on one of them I caught a brief movement over at the other side. It was another red E-type, but a convertible, travelling in the opposite direction. An arm was held up in a wave, but before I could take in any more the lorry in front braked hard and demanded my attention. It was loaded with fifty thousand live chickens, packed into minute wicker cages. I know where hell is – it's somewhere in the middle of a lorry-load like that.

The boats were in a different league to those I'd looked at in the morning. My eyes ached with the glare off white hulls and gleaming mahogany decks, with stainless steel and brass and probably even gold-plated fittings. Flags hung indolently and here and there a rope dared to tap gently against a mast. I learnt to say 'No stiletto heels' in five languages. I didn't see any silly cowboy names, though.

It was amazing how many of the British boats were flying the Union flag. You'd think that anyone who owned a few hundred grand's worth of yacht would be interested enough to find out that he was supposed to show the Red Duster. Some were even carrying small Union Jacks on the mast, instead of the Spanish flag, which should be displayed as a courtesy gesture to the host port. I wondered, briefly, how such morons made their money; then I remembered Cakebread and knew the answer. Unfortunately I didn't find a boat that looked as if it might belong to him.

Harbour by harbour I made my way back towards Benalmadena. I'd walk up and down the jetties, reading the names on the hulls. Some were clever, others were ordinary and a few made you think about the character of the owner. What sort of person would retire to the Costa del Sol to live on a boat named *Evasion*, *Palimoney* or *Lucky Flicker*? Then I'd retrace my steps back to the Jag and drive on to the next floating exhibition of wealth. If I'm ever rich I think I'll just Sellotape my bank statement in the rear window of the car. It'll save a lot of effort.

It was nearly dinner time when I arrived at the hotel. I put the Jag round the back, where it was out of the way. I was a lot happier with it there. The sun had sunk below the rim of the hills that lie inland, and they were etched, hard-edged, against the evening sky. I'd had a fruitless day, but I wasn't despondent. Maybe the task I'd set myself was hopeless, but I'd been on plenty of wild-goose chases before. Not this far from home though. At least nobody knew I was here, and there was no drain on the Force budget to be accounted for. And let's be honest, I was enjoying myself. I showered and changed into something more suitable and went to the dining room.

Those hills were inviting. If nothing turned up tomorrow I'd seriously think about abandoning the project and have a couple of days lost in the mountains. It was a long time since I'd walked a decent ridge. I sat down at an empty table, pushed all thoughts of crooks and boats out of my mind, and set about working my way through the menu, towards the inevitable creme caramel.

The food was better than I'd be having at home, when you took into consideration the service. In other words, no cooking or washing-up. Afterwards I ordered a pot of tea in the lounge and slouched in an armchair, assessing my fellow guests.

'Hello, how are you enjoying your stay?'

I turned and pushed myself more upright. It was Stephanie. 'Fine,' I answered, unsuccessfully trying not to look too pleased to see her. 'Dinner was good and I've caught the sun. What more could I ask for?'

'Good. I hear your car was bumped. Is it bad?'

'No, just a scratch. They've let me put it round the back, so it should be OK now.'

She apologised again, and was about to leave when I said: 'Can you recommend anywhere that does a decent paella? I've developed a craving while I've been here. Hope there's nothing wrong with me.'

She thought for a while. 'Anywhere on the Carahuela, I would have thought. I'm not all that keen on seafood myself, but I'll ask around.'

Ah well, make that paella for one, Manuel. 'Thanks. Maybe you can help me with one more thing.' She'd turned to go, but stopped and faced me again. I went on: 'I'm looking for a friend with a boat. A wealthy friend. Any suggestions where I might start looking?'

'If I knew I'd be looking there myself. Is this friend stinking rich?'

It occurred to me that she probably thought that I was quite well heeled. 'By Marbella standards, no; but by my standards, he stinks.'

'Try Puerto Banus. That's where they all hang out,' she said.

'All who?' I asked. Her reply had puzzled me.

She blushed and shrugged her shoulders. 'All . . . the rich people,' she answered, as she turned and left.

I was intrigued. People often ask me if I'm a policeman. If I went to a nudist colony, before long someone would say: 'Oh, hello, you must be the policeman.' Well, maybe that's an exaggeration. But Stephanie was different: she thought I was a crook. When she said 'All the rich people', what she was thinking was 'All the criminals'. It's an easy mistake to make. Tomorrow I'd have a long, hard look at Puerto Banus.

* * *

144

Puerto Banus is to money what the Vatican is to incense. It lies just outside Marbella, on the far side, beyond where yesterday's search had started. This was the big league. It was mid-morning when I arrived and parked the car between a Ferrari and a Cadillac, but there were elegant women walking about in cocktail dresses, accompanied by men in three-piece suits. Swarthy men, who kept their coats buttoned in the heat of the day. There was a definite pecking order for the boats. The biggest, with gold-plated names emblazoned across the front that would have looked reasonable above a cinema, were parked in the middle, immediately adjacent to the centre of the town. As you moved outwards they diminished in size, until, at the outermost berths, you had the half-a-million-quid wannabees. Egalitarian to a fault, I decided to start at one end and work my way through to the other.

In the afternoon I started at the other end and worked my way back to the beginning. All my instincts told me I was close, but my eyes couldn't find the evidence. I had a glass of wine and some tapas and resumed the search. This time I just followed my hunches, picking out the boats that I guessed might be the right size. Hunches are unscientific and usually unreliable; today was no exception.

'That's it, Mr Breadcake,' I said out loud. 'If you want me tomorrow you'll just have to come climbing mountains.' I found the car and drove much too fast back towards the hotel.

There is a *supermercado* in Benalmadena, so I decided to stock up with a few things that I might need the next day. As I swung into the car park I saw another red E-type, a convertible, obviously the one whose driver had waved to me the day before. I parked alongside it, but the owner was nowhere to be seen. I formed a picture of her in my mind and rehearsed a couple of opening gambits. In the supermarket I studied the weird concoctions available to tempt the different nationalities, and chose a jar with a German label that contained what looked like pickled testicles. They'd go down well in the office. I stayed with the basics for myself. I was low on T-shirts, so I grabbed a couple of those, too.

When I arrived back at the car a tall, elderly man was leaning on the boot of the other Jag. He beamed when he saw me. 'How do you do,' he said. 'I've been wondering who the old car belonged to.'

He had 'ex-pat' written all over him. He was wearing a checked shirt, with cravat, that would have looked more at home at Goodwood in winter, and had a respectable handlebar moustache. The freckles on his face had expanded with overexposure to the sun, and had started to join up with each other, so that he looked like a jigsaw puzzle of the Gobi Desert, before you'd put the pieces together.

'It's one of the fast ones,' I told him, adding, as I indicated towards his: 'Not one of those whippersnappers.' It was a fact that as the E-type evolved the engine was made bigger and bigger, but the car became slower and slower. They also ruined its looks – his later version lacked the wicked symmetry of the original.

He held out his arm for a handshake and said: 'George Palfreeman, with two e's in the middle.' He gestured towards the pavement tables and added: 'Fancy a snifter?'

'Charlie Priest,' I told him, 'as in Roman Catholic. Why not?'

I put the groceries in the boot and followed him to the cafe next door. We ordered a large whisky and soda for him and a pot of tea for me. An hour later he knew that I came from Yorkshire, but I had learnt his entire life story. It's a trick of the trade. The moustache looked RAF-ish, but in fact he was a Navy man, with two years commanding a motor torpedo boat to his credit, during World War Two. Settling down hadn't come easily afterwards, and he'd moved round the Empire before establishing himself in Spain. His wife had died a couple of years ago, and now he was another lonely old man, eager to cling to a new audience. He'd had an interesting life, though, so I didn't mind listening to his tales.

'You'll have to come to the club one night,' he suggested expansively. 'How about tomorrow? Have you anything on?'

Drinky-poos with the Brits didn't appeal to me. 'Sorry, George, I'm planning on going off for the day. We'll have to make it some other time.'

He looked thoughtful. 'What about the night after, then? It's a bridge night, but I've stopped playing. Everybody takes it too damn seriously. I could do with someone new to talk to.'

It was my turn to do the thinking. I didn't like disappointing him, so I said: 'That'll be fine, but on one condition. We're not going to your club, I'm treating you to a big paella on the Carahuela. They only make it for two people, so I need someone to share one with me.'

'Splendid!' he beamed. 'I'll really look forward to that.' He went away a happy man. It hadn't taken a lot. I went back to my room at the Cala d'Or and prepared for another journey towards la creme caramel.

At breakfast I loaded myself with enough carbohydrates to sustain me through a day's walking in the hills. Passing through the foyer I caught sight of my reflection in the big mirrors. I was wearing grey shorts, a grey T-shirt and grey trainers. For an ex-art student the overall effect could only be described as, well, greyish. I could desperately use a splash of colour. I poked out my tongue. It was vermilion, fading to lilac at the back, and covered all over with minute lemon spots. That should do it. I might have a dull exterior, but boy, I was colourful on the inside.

In fifteen minutes I'd crossed the coast road and cleared the edge of town. After a couple of deadends I finally found a track that petered out at the base of the hills, from where it was possible to gain access to them. Coming through the outskirts of the town, where the locals lived, I'd been amazed how many of the villas had big dogs – Dobermanns and Rottweilers – barking and slavering within their compounds. It appeared that this wasn't the peaceful, law-abiding community that I had believed it to be. The lower flanks of the hill were laid out with streets, complete with lay-bys and parking areas, waiting for the next speculator to come along and put up the money and the buildings. The biggest hill looked to be about two thousand feet high, with a smaller one to its right-hand side. The plan was to walk to the top of the small hill, then traverse the ridge to the summit of the big one. It was quite a modest walk by any standards, but I had the usual feelings of expectancy and well-being as the gradient steepened, and leg muscles that thought they had achieved redundancy began to protest at this unseemly disturbance.

I followed a path for a while, but it stayed too low, so eventually I struck off into the scrub. The ground was hard-baked clay, with sparse, evil-thorned scrub. In territory like this each bush or plant needs a certain catchment area to survive, and it never encroaches on to its neighbour's patch. This makes it possible to walk between them without difficulty, although my legs were soon covered in small white scratches. I puffed like an old tank engine for a while, but quickly struck up a rhythm in tune with the gradient. I was gaining height rapidly, and felt I could go on for ever. I'd have to do more walking, I'd forgotten how rewarding it could be.

The ground became rocky – outcrops of grey, porous boulders, probably volcanic in origin – and the air was heavy with the perfume of rosemary. It was hot. I took off my T-shirt and tied it round the strap of the knapsack I was carrying. It contained my camera and a small amount of food. And my Swiss army knife, of course; I never go anywhere without my Swiss army knife. I'm determined to use everything on it, one day. There was no wildlife of any sort to be seen, the probable explanation lying in the liberal scattering of shotgun cartridges I came across. Plenty of wild flowers were growing, though, including some spectacular lilies. I took photographs of them. One day, when I retired, I'd learn all their names.

The lower summit was reached quicker than I'd expected, but I wasn't complaining. I decided to have elevenses. I unpacked the bag in the middle of a big, flat rock, so that any marauding creepy-crawlies could be warded off. I was high above the coastal towns, with the Mediterranean stretching like a sheet of beaten gold into the distance. A crusty bread roll, with molten butter, was followed by rough pate and black grapes. I slit open the grapes with the small blade of the knife – the one I don't use for skinning crocodiles – flicked out the pips and stuffed them with pate. Heavenly! They exploded like sweet-and-sour flavour-bombs against my tastebuds. I wished I'd brought a ton of them. The kindest thing I can say about the luke-warm Seven-Up I washed the lot down with is that it hadn't travelled well.

Soon I was walking in the shadow of the main hill. The ridge was really a broad saddleback and the going was easy. At its steepest I could touch the rocks in front of me, but it wasn't necessary to use my hands to climb with. Then the slope flattened out and I emerged into the brilliance of the summit plateau.

I took in great gulps of the clear air and slowly rotated, my arms held out sideways. There were another three or four days of holiday left and I resolved to spend them out walking, not wasting my time looking for Cakebread. The view, all three hundred and sixty degrees of it, was breathtaking. Inland was a vast, arid plain, with mountains at the other side and specks of white indicating the presence of villages. I'd have to buy a decent local map.

I fitted the telephoto lens to the camera and began to pan around the horizon. The lens worked like a low-powered telescope, giving a view slightly better than the naked eye. I picked out the inland villages, then slowly turned in a clockwise direction. To the north were some mountain peaks with snow on them, glaring in the noonday sun. I lowered the camera, but I could barely see them unaided.

They must be the Sierra Nevada, I thought. I resumed panning, down the coast towards the hotel where I was staying. A few boats were tracking up and down, but most were stationary in the water, the occupants fishing or, more probably, just sunbathing. Down below, people were ordering their midday chips with chips, and embarking on the alcoholic trail that would lead to oblivion in about twelve hours' time. Up here the silence was exalting. I swung the camera down the coast, and Marbella swam into view. I focused beyond it, into the unknown. I couldn't remember what lay at the other side of Marbella.

It soon came back to me, though. There it was, like a full stop at the end of a sentence, or the buffers at the end of a railway track. The blue bulk of the familiar shape of the Rock of Gibraltar reared upwards, marking the southernmost tip of continental Europe. The Sierra Nevada to the north and Gibraltar to the south – so much reward for so little effort. I peered at the Rock again, and as I did so, adjusted the focus to see what was beyond. To the left of it, across the water, a range of blue hills was barely discernible against the glare of the sky, one peak slightly higher than the others. I lowered the camera and thought about it. They must be the Atlas Mountains, in North Africa; Morocco in fact. On the other side of those hills stretched five thousand miles of the Dark Continent. I'd never seen it before, but I was far from being immune to its allure.

I was gazing at the Pillars of Hercules, once thought to be the end of the world. I stood there, stupefied. 'PH,'

I said to myself. 'The Pillars of bloody Hercules.'

I was down the hill in well under half the time it had taken me to go up. I called into the hotel room to have a quick shower and collect my passport and wallet, and was on the road again in Olympic qualifying time.

CHAPTER TEN

The best suggestion we had managed during our brainstorming session had been 'public house'. Nigel narrowed the field somewhat with 'Poste House', while Sparky's contribution could be ignored, as it was unlikely that multi-million-pound art deals would be transacted in public toilets. I'd been thinking in terms of a public house of unknown name, but did I now know that name? Four hours after leaving the mountaintop I parked on a huge area of tarmac at the end of the isthmus that links the Rock with the mainland. An RAF Nimrod was standing at the other side of the road. As I was locking up, an eight-year-old mafioso sidled up to me and said something that included the words 'money' and 'car'.

I said: 'Go to hell, Miguel,' and climbed back in. I

drove towards the customs post with the intention of impressing the incumbent with my warrant card and asking him if I could leave the Jag outside his window, but he waved me straight past. I decided that it would save a walk and pressed on. I soon regretted it: the place was chock-a-block with tourists and looking for a parking place was like trying to find charity in Hull. Then I saw him. He was big, bonny and smiling: a wonderful British bobby, big hat and all. I pulled up alongside and flashed my card. I was deferential, though; he was the boss as far as I was concerned.

'I'm only on holiday,' I told him, 'but I'd be grateful if you could help me with a parking place for a couple of hours.'

'No problem, sir. Leave it in the visitor's spot at the station. That's what they usually do.'

'Fantastic. Where's the station?'

He started to point, then decided it was complicated and maybe he'd better come with me. The complication was one right turn, but he enjoyed the ride, and he let them know inside who I was. I deliberately didn't ask him if Pillars of Hercules meant anything. I preferred to explore; that way you discovered incidental things that otherwise you wouldn't have come across. There'd be plenty of time for asking if I became stuck.

I found it long before reaching the 'What am I doing here?' point. I wandered up and down a couple of streets – the couple of streets – and there it was. Tucked between a shop selling Hong Kong tablecloths and one with windows filled with expensive pottery figures was the only pub in the colony that didn't sound as if it belonged in the Cotswolds. Inside, though, it was pure Heart of England, from the glass riding boots in the inglenook fireplace, to the busts of William Shakespeare on the beer engines. It was moderately busy. The waiter on this side of the bar looked Spanish, but the man behind, presumably the landlord, was all Anglo-Saxon. He was big, with bare, pink arms that resembled pigs' carcasses. Round his neck was a gold chain that you could have used to drown a St Bernard, and on one wrist he wore a bracelet that had been carved straight out of the ingot with a blunt chisel.

'Good afternoon, sir. What would you like?'

Pleasant enough manner, though his voice was surprisingly light. He had blond hair and eyebrows that were paler than his skin. I ordered a half of lager and passed the minimum of pleasantries with him. The other clientele gave the appearance of being holiday-makers: young couple, three lads, a few older couples. Nobody with a violin case, drinking screwdrivers. I ordered a ham sandwich. York ham, of course.

When he brought it to me I said: 'I was supposed to meet a friend here on Tuesday, but I don't know if he meant last Tuesday or next Tuesday. You didn't notice a big, fat fellow hanging around, did you?'

He placed my change on the table. There was no visible reaction. 'No, there wasn't anybody in like that.' I asked for another lager, and when he came back with it he said: 'This friend of yours, does he have a name?'

'Yes.' I rocked back in my chair so that I could stare him in the face, and said: 'He's called Cakebread, Aubrey Cakebread.'

He held my gaze and replied: 'Sorry, never heard of him.'

But just off to my left the glasses rattled on the waiter's tray.

I finished my drink at a leisurely speed and made my way back to the police station. I hadn't caught a fish but I'd certainly stirred up the mud. Maybe the murk would attract a big one. I thanked the desk sergeant for his help and drove into the narrow gateway from the station yard. I stopped there, and looked both ways to see if the road was clear. It's a policy I've adopted over the years. It wasn't, and I had to wait for several seconds.

A man in a doorway opposite was having great difficulty lighting a cigarette. His body language was yelling: 'I know this looks suspicious, but I can't think of anything better to do.' It wasn't possible to be certain, but he looked like the waiter from the Pillars. I pulled on to the road and immediately stopped. In the mirror I saw him leave the doorway and hurry off. On the back of his T-shirt was a picture of a Greek bodybuilder carrying a club over his shoulder. What a prat. I chuckled at the ease of it all.

If I hurried I could make it to Puerto Banus with an hour or two of daylight left, so I did. It hadn't changed much, just put on its evening gown and dinner jacket. I had to admit it: the place had style. The loudest noise you could hear was that of wealth rubbing up to opulence. None of the boats had moved. I was reaching the point where I could name most before I saw them. I ordered a glass of house *tinto* in a pavement cafe and let darkness fall around me. There were worse places to be.

'Suki! Stop doing that. Be a good boy. Oh, Kimmy! You're all in a tangle. Come to Mummy.'

Northern vowels were breaching the peace. I turned towards their source. A peroxide blonde in a leopard-spot blouse and leather miniskirt had two dogs on leads. One of them was having a pee against a lamppost and the other had the lead wrapped round its legs. She untangled it and picked it up.

'Hurry up, Suki,' she said impatiently.

Personally, I'd have toe-ended the little bugger into the bay. When it had finished she waddled off, lucky Kimmy pressed to her bosom and Suki trotting alongside. She was wearing stiletto heels, and her skirt was so tight that her legs couldn't move in parallel – they had to oscillate around each other with each mincing step. If you'd placed a dry stick between her thighs the friction would have ignited it.

It was the dogs, though, that I was mainly interested in. They were a bit like Yorkshire terriers, but hairier and more softly coloured. I didn't know what a shih tzu looked like, but I'd have gambled Gilbert Wood's pension that I was looking at a pair. I left a three hundred per cent tip because I had nothing smaller and followed her.

The only description I had of Cakebread's wife was that she was an ex-beauty queen. The ex part was accurate, but I wasn't happy about the rest of it, unless you only had to enter to qualify. I followed her along the quay until we were down among the wannabees – the ones that it would only take me eight lifetimes to earn the equivalent of. She turned on to a jetty and then picked up the other dog to carry it up a short gang-plank. Ignoring the sign showing a lady's shoe with a line drawn through it she crossed the deck towards the cabin and let herself in. I watched from the shore. The boat was called *Pelican;* there was no need to look – I could remember it. Only because of its associations with Francis Drake, though: my powers of theoretical deduction had been a complete waste of time.

I sat on a bench on the dockside until nearly midnight, watching the lighted windows on the boat, sometimes turning to watch the beautiful women and their partners strolling by, resplendent in their evening finery. Lady Breadcake would either go to bed, in which case I'd go home, or she was right now changing into something stunning before hitting the town, in which case I would follow her. Plenty of people were promenading up and down, enjoying the warm night air. A couple of times I walked on to the jetty and strolled along it, hanging about as I passed the *Pelican,* but there was no sound to be heard.

I'm never sure if you can actually see a light go out. One moment it's there, a hundredth of a second later it's not. The windows at the front of the boat went dark, then those in the middle, sorry, amidships, and then the ones at the stern. It was as if she were working her way towards the door, before coming ashore. Some people were passing in front of me. I stood up and walked a few paces forward to lean on the railing.

Someone rattled off something in Spanish in my ear and a hand gripped my arm.

A pockmarked man was speaking to me, but it was the ugly black automatic he was poking into my side that demanded most of my attention.

He had the advantage of a gun, I had the advantage of unpredictability. Of the two, I'd have preferred the weapon, but you can only make the best of what God gives you. I swept his gun hand to one side and thumped him, hard, in the solar plexus. The air in his body burst out in a rasping gasp, bringing most of his stomach contents with it, and he went down like a tower of dominoes. His pal was more professional: he must have cracked me on the side of the head with his pistol. I saw a display that would have pleased Standard Fireworks and the next thing I remember is being on the ground, surrounded by legs and shiny shoes. It was impossible to tell if they were friendly or foe-ly.

I rolled on to my side. I was immediately grabbed

by strong hands and my arms were forced behind my back and manacled. They were definitely foe-ly. They dragged me to my feet and pushed me towards a car. I swayed about and kept my head down, trying to act a lot worse than I felt. The one I'd hit was sitting on the pavement, his back against a post. His face was the colour of a toad's belly, and the front of his shirt looked like a salad bar. We tore off with a squeal of tyres, and I did my best to take notice of where we were heading. I needn't have bothered: we arrived in about three minutes. They pulled me out of the back seat and bundled me towards the door of an imposing building. Several cars were neatly parked on either side of the entrance. They were black and white, and had POLICIA stencilled on the sides. These were the good guys.

Nobody read my rights to me. They just confiscated everything from my pockets, removed the laces from my trainers, took off the 'cuffs and threw me in a cell.

A sickly youth with a stupid grin was already in it. He put two fingers to his lips and said: 'Cigarrillo?'

'Yes, thank you,' I told him, in fluent Spanish.

There were two benches, for sleeping or sitting on, and a small sink in the corner with a single tap. It smelt as if someone had been pissing in it. I swilled round the basin with cold water, then washed my face. There was no mirror or towel, so I dried myself on the front of my T-shirt. The wound on the side of my head had bled a little, but it had stopped now. After a few minutes the guard's keys rattled in the lock.

Good, I thought, let's be getting out of here. He opened the door and threw me a blanket. There was an air of finality about his action. I rolled it into a pillow and stretched out on the vacant bunk. The youth was laid under his blanket. Trying to perform two functions with a single blanket was a form of torture. I resolved to write to Amnesty International, if I ever escaped from this dump. I looked across at my cellmate. He wasn't very big; if it became cold during the night I'd just have to steal his.

Morning came, although there were long periods when I doubted if it ever would. Like I'm told they do in hospitals, they woke me up just after I'd dropped off to sleep. A full English would have gone down well, but they didn't even offer coffee. The guard just told me to 'Come', grabbed me under the armpit and marched me upstairs. I didn't argue, I was in no position to, but I was amazed how compliant one night in jail had made me.

Capitano R. Diaz sat behind a big polished desk that could have graced a modest boardroom. He wore a blue suit with a dazzling white shirt. The silver stripes in his tie were echoed in his cuff links. The desk was clear, apart from the large brown envelope that had contained my meagre possessions, which were now coming under his scrutiny, and a nameplate that told me who he was. One of his lieutenants was also in the room. He studied the contents of my wallet for several minutes, the last few being devoted to my warrant card. Then he sat with his hands together as if in prayer, his fingertips touching his lips.

Finally he said: 'Sit down, Inspector Priest,' gesturing to a chair and passing my laces across the table. 'Would you be good enough to tell me what you were doing last night in Puerto Banus?' His English was about as good as mine, but his accent was sexier.

'Thank you.' It seemed impolite to put my foot on his desk while I replaced my laces, so I wrapped them around my fingers. 'I'm on holiday, Captain. Whilst I was here I heard that a known criminal one – I've had dealings with – was in the area, so I thought I'd watch out for him. I believe he may be staying on the boat called the *Pelican*.'

'And his name?'

'Cakebread.'

He turned to give an enquiring glance to the lieutenant, but he shook his head.

'Cakebread, did you say? Is that a common name in England?'

'No, sir, it's very unusual.'

He thought for a few seconds, then asked: 'This Cakebread; what did you intend to do if you saw him?'

I'd wondered about that myself. My brain did what passes for racing to think of a plausible course of action. The results impressed me. 'We think he may be involved in drug smuggling. I had information that

163

he was due back in England on Thursday, but I didn't know whether it was last Thursday or next. If he's still here, it must be next.'

'When you say: "*We* think he may be involved in drug smuggling," who do you mean?'

'Just myself, sir. My evidence is only hearsay, and I really am here on holiday. I'm acting completely without authority and apologise for the problems I've caused you.' I shrugged my shoulders and risked a smile. 'It's the only way I know to enjoy myself.'

He didn't return my smile, but he said: 'Yes, Inspector Priest, I know what you mean.'

I wondered if I'd be able to make myself a coffee if I killed them both, but decided against it – I was in enough trouble. I said: 'There is one other thing, Captain Diaz.'

He raised an eyebrow that invited me to enlighten him.

'Cakebread had a colleague called Truscott. Truscott supposedly died in a fire, but the body was unrecognisable. I think he may be alive, possibly living in Spain. I'd hoped I might see him.'

He stood up and walked over to the window. He looked out for a few seconds, then resumed his seat.

'Inspector Priest,' he began, 'it is a sad fact that there are many international gangsters living on the Costa del Sol. But not everyone who is wealthy is a thief. Well, not according to the law.' He gave a wry smile. 'We have many influential people visiting Puerto, very influential indeed. We are constantly alert for would-be terrorists and kidnappers. You were seen behaving suspiciously. That is why you were arrested. I apologise if my men were rough with you, but I am sure you understand that you were not in order. I am told you were quite rough with one of them.' He gave another hint of a smile.

'Yes, sir. Sorry about that. Is he all right?'

'He's not at work this morning. He was too close to you; I'm sure he will learn his lesson. When are you leaving Spain?'

I had a choice? I'd expected to be run out of town on a pole.

'In four days, if that's all right.'

'That's all right. Please leave word of where you are staying, and I would be grateful to receive a report and information on Mr . . .'

'Cakebread,' I offered.

'Yes, Mr Cakebread. You are free to go, Inspector, but I would appreciate it if you spent the rest of your holiday sightseeing. The Alhambra is very beautiful.'

'Thank you, I'll take your advice, and you'll have the reports as soon as possible. One small problem: I don't know where I am.'

'Don't worry, Ramon will take you back to your car.' He turned to the lieutenant and gave him some instructions, adding: 'Goodbye, Inspector.'

The surly Ramon dropped me off on the quay. He made no attempt to communicate in the car, so I busied myself rethreading my trainers. The Jag was where I'd left it. I fished my watch out of the envelope; there was time to make it back to the hotel, have a shower and catch the end of breakfast. I'd had a lucky escape. I left Puerto Banus without casting a glance in the direction of the *Pelican*.

I hung the 'Do not disturb' notice on the door handle and crashed out on the bed. Around lunchtime I had a walk round a few shops and bought an exercise book so that I could map out a report for Captain Diaz. I had coffee and a pastry and went back to the room to do the report. Then I dossed on the bed again until it was time to start getting ready for my appointment with George and the paella. I was ready for it.

Seven thirty sharp I walked on to the end of the Carahuela. George was already there, standing alongside his car. He looked pleased to see me.

'Charlie! How are you? Glad you could make it. I was a little early, so I had a look round for your car. Couldn't see it anywhere. Thought perhaps you'd gone off again for the day and not got back.'

'Hello, George,' I said. 'I'm fine, thanks. They let me put it round the back of the hotel, away from sticky fingers and lager louts. Where do you fancy eating?'

'Anywhere, I think most of these places are the same. How about this one?'

We'd walked past the first restaurant and were standing outside the next one. It had already attracted several evening diners, and a waiter was going round lighting the lanterns on the tables. It looked tempting and businesslike. He saw us hovering and came over.

'A table for two, gentlemen?' he asked in English.

I wondered if it was my Marks and Spencer, or George's *Country Life* look that gave us away. We sat down so that George had the view out to sea, while I could watch the four women at the next table. A perfect arrangement. No messing about with the menu: it was a carafe of the local red and the house speciality paella. I also ordered some water in deference to my recent brain operation.

Being with an attractive woman would have made it perfect. Sharing the evening with Annabelle Wilberforce would have been riches beyond my dreams. But in any company, quaffing soft red wine as the sun sinks behind you, eating passable food and sharing anecdotes makes a reasonable approximation of what heaven must be like. George was good company. Eventually, tongue loosened by the grape, I confessed that I was a policeman – off duty, of course – and we swapped service stories well into the night. We discovered that men in uniform have similar ways of relieving the tension or boredom of their chosen professions. Ways that were always funny, and usually vulgar.

Our laughter was echoed by the women at the next table. They were having a good time, too. I kept exchanging glances with the dark-haired one in the red dress. Every time George rocked his head back to give one of his guffaws, I gave her a smile. She smiled back. I had a feeling that I'd seen her in the Cala d'Or, but it could have been desire triumphing over reality.

George said he was OK to drive. He'd only had coffee over the last couple of hours, so he was probably right. He gave me his card and I promised to ring him before I went home. I meant it, too. We stood up and shook hands. It was an extended, jovial goodbye. George said something to the ladies at the table behind him, then noticed that we had a drop of wine left. He shared it amongst them with a flourish. As he walked to his car I caught the waiter's eye and gestured for another coffee. I sat down in the seat George had left, near the lady in red, and half facing her.

'Your friend enjoyed himself,' she said.

'Yes, I hope he did,' I replied, adding: 'I'm having quite a pleasant evening myself.'

I watched him reverse out of his parking place, then the long bonnet swung round and the Jaguar slid up the hill out of sight. There was a junction in about fifty yards where he would have to stop. As he pulled away a scooter engine burst into noisy life in the shadows just beyond him. Two youths were on it, and they followed George up the hill. The waiter arrived with my coffee. He put it down near me, but on the ladies' table; he was a professional.

'Would anyone . . .' I began.

There were two loud cracks, from what sounded like

a heavy-calibre pistol. I sat, frozen, for half a second that felt like an eternity, then I was up and running.

I jumped on to the low wall that separated us from the first restaurant, stepped in the middle of someone's table, scattering food and crockery, and cleared the wall at the other side. I was in the street. George's car was at the junction, the scooter alongside it. The scooter rider had messed up his getaway; he'd dropped the clutch too quickly and nearly stalled the engine. It was pop-popping and throwing up a cloud of blue smoke. I could catch him. I could catch the bastard and screw his fucking head off. Ten yards. The engine burst into full song. Four yards; he was screaming the engine, determined not to make the same mistake again. My outstretched fingers clutched for the collar of the passenger's jacket.

I grabbed a bunch of leather just below the collar, but I couldn't hold on to it. As they pulled away my fingernails raked down his back. There was a luggage carrier behind the seat. My hand curled around the metal and I was dragged off my feet. The rear wheel was spinning inches in front of my face and the exhaust pipe bellowing in my ears and eyes. Twenty yards along the road I let go and rolled over in the gutter.

George's car had run back a short way and come to rest against a lighting column. As I limped towards it a horrified couple embraced each other for comfort. George was slumped over sideways; most of his brains were on the passenger seat. I removed the wallet from my jacket pocket and put the coat over his head, to protect him from salacious eyes. Then I sat on the edge of his seat, one foot on the pavement and my arm around him, and waited for the police to arrive.

CHAPTER ELEVEN

Capitano Diaz was immaculate in brown suit and cream shirt, in spite of being called out in the middle of the night. We'd had language difficulties in the local station, so I'd suggested that he be sent for. He arrived within the hour, and now it looked as if he had taken over the investigation. I found his courtesy disturbing. If our roles had been reversed I hope I would have treated him similarly, but I doubted it. We were sitting in a bare interview room. My trousers were around my ankles and the police doctor was cleaning up my knees. He'd already trimmed the fingernails I'd nearly ripped off, carefully dropping the clippings into a specimen bag. I now sported two muslin finger-pokes on my right hand and my knees were stinging like hell. Diaz was asking the questions.

'You are saying, Inspector Priest, that Mr Palfreeman had a red Jagwar very similar to you own, and that the gunman mistook him for you? Am I correct?'

'Yes, Captain, I'm sure of it. The day before yesterday, before I was arrested by your men, I'd been to Gibraltar. I visited a pub – a bar – called the Pillars of Hercules, which I believe to be one of Cakebread's haunts. I let them know I was looking for him, and I was followed back to my car. Unfortunately I'd parked in the police station.'

'In retrospect, Inspector, that would appear to have been foolish of you.'

'Do you think I need reminding, Captain Diaz?' I snapped.

'Quite. I apologise. Even though you only met Mr Palfreeman two days ago you are obviously upset by his death. Please accept my sympathies.'

The doctor stood up and gabbled something to Diaz. Diaz translated: 'You are to keep the dressings on for as long as possible, then you should be OK without one. Why did you not tell me about Gibraltar when we met yesterday?'

I pulled up my trousers and shouted a thank you after the doctor as he left, then went on: 'It wasn't relevant at that time. However, I've written a rough report and it's all in there. It's in my hotel room.'

'Good. Yesterday we made some enquiries into your Mr Cakebread's movements. I'm afraid you missed him; he left Spain last Thursday.' He flicked through the pages of his notebook, then said: 'Here it is. He flies an aeroplane called a Piper Commanche, and according to his flight plan, he intended landing at . . . Teesside, after refuelling at Nantes, in France. He had one passenger, a man called Bradshaw. You know him?'

I shrugged, saying: 'Never heard of him. Teesside's interesting though. It's in the north of England, about a hundred miles further on than he need have flown.'

'Very strange. When you go home, maybe you should ask yourself why it is necessary for him to fly so much further. Do you not think so, Inspector?'

'Good point,' I admitted. 'We'll look into it.' I knew he usually kept his plane at Blackpool airport.

Diaz stood up: 'Come, Inspector, I will take you back to your hotel, then you can give me those reports. Can you walk OK?'

It was an effort. Both knees had scraped along the tarmac for several yards, and the doctor's ministrations, while no doubt of long-term benefit, had only aggravated the immediate pain. My fingers were singing a duet to each other, too. On the way to his car Diaz asked if this would change my leaving plans. I'd not given them any thought since the shooting.

After a while I said: 'I'll rest up for the remainder of today, then, if you've no objections, I'll leave first thing tomorrow morning.'

'None at all, but I'd appreciate it if you stayed near your hotel today, in case we need anything else. You realise, of course, that you may have to come back to give evidence.'

'If you catch them,' I said.

'We'll catch them,' he replied, as he opened the door for me. 'Of that, Inspector, you can be quite sure.'

I sat down, easing the material of my pants off my knees. When he was in beside me I said: 'Capitano Diaz, you are of a higher rank than me, and although we are in different forces I respect that. However, I'd like to point out that I am a plainclothes officer. If you call me Inspector all the time it destroys the point of it. My name is Priest, most people call me Charlie.' I wasn't sure what his reaction would be, but he'd been getting up my bodily orifices with his formality.

He turned to face me and held out a perfectly manicured hand: 'And my name is Rafael. Pleased to meet you, Charlie. I think you are my kind of police officer.'

We were driving along the coast road. Off to our right the sun was half out of the sea. It looked like a red tombstone, come to mark the first day for seventy-odd years of a world without George Palfreeman. I twisted in my seat and watched it slowly rise and detach itself from its reflection.

'You're lucky to live in such a beautiful place,' I said.

'Yes, I know. But there are beautiful places in the south of England, too. My wife and I have spent several happy holidays in Cornwall and Devon. You live in the north, I believe. Is it very industrialised there?'

I laughed a little. 'No, it's wild and rugged. I love it, but I wish we had some of your weather.'

'Ah yes, the famous English weather.'

'Your English is excellent, Rafael. Where did you learn it?' I asked.

'My wife was a lecturer in English at the University of Barcelona. We moved down here about ten years ago. Now she teaches English in a local school, we speak it at home and listen to the BBC.'

I pointed to the hotel and he swung into the gateway. We went round the back so he could see my 'Jagwar'. Then he accompanied me to my room and I handed over the rough drafts of the reports. We shook hands and he told me to take care. He tried to say something about George's death not being my fault. I already knew the speech, but it still sounded unconvincing.

I needed a shower, but didn't know how to have one without ruining my various bandages. I couldn't decide if I wanted breakfast or not, so I settled for two aspirin and stretched out on the bed. The housemaid woke me four hours later, but I excused her of her duties. I managed to have some sort of a bath, and changed into decent clothes. Diaz had told me that the British community would rally round and organise George's funeral – there was no need for me to become involved. Once or twice through the day I looked at the number he had given me and thought about ringing it, but I didn't. Tomorrow I would sneak away like a plague rat, leaving only death in my wake. I wasn't proud of it, but I didn't know what else to do.

I dined in the hotel, then settled my bill and told the desk clerk I would be leaving in the early hours. The woman in the red dress wasn't in the dining room. Then I lay on my bed, thinking, until it was time to get into it and try to sleep.

Dawn broke as I brought the car round to the front of the hotel and loaded the boot with my few belongings. I stopped a few miles up the coast, and looked out to sea. I'd been hoping to see the sunrise again, but there was a mist over the water, and the sun was obscured. It looked like being a hot day.

Driving is a good antidote for many things. You have to concentrate when you drive. If you drive fast enough you have to concentrate totally. I decided to take the autoroutes all the way. Not the best way to see a country, but you could pack a hundred miles into an hour. By early evening Barcelona was behind me. I refuelled and decided to have a rest.

Two hours later I was away again. The dim headlights were no obstruction to progress on the wide dual carriageways, and the E-type revelled in the type of cross-continent driving it had been designed for. I had a longer sleep, curled up in the back, near Lyons, and made it to the Paris *peripherique* in time for the rush hour. Afternoon tea on the hovercraft goes down well when your tongue has a relationship with your mouth like a sweep's brush has with a chimney.

You think you're there when you roll off the ferry, but it's not true. The longest mile might be the last mile home, but the other two hundred and eighty were just as gruesome. It was another six hours before I slammed the car door under my own neighbours' window and gratefully crashed out in my familiar bed. I'd been away just under nine days.

In the morning I looked at my mail. There were several never-to-be-repeated opportunities for me to win a total of three and a half million quid, and a note from Gilbert Wood. I sealed all the prepaid envelopes in the junk mail and put them on one side for posting. The post office needs the revenue. Then I opened Gilbert's note. It read:

> *Charlie,*
> *You've done the right thing being off. Hilditch has gone off his rocker. He sent ACC Partridge round with orders to suspend you for harassing Cakebread. Partridge was very embarrassed about it. Suggest you don't come back until after*

your holiday. Things may have cooled down by then.

Gilbert

PS Sorry about the piles. Have you tried Germaloids?

I swapped the cars round and went to the supermarket to restock the freezer. Officially I still had a couple of days' leave left, but I knew I'd be as restless as a foreskin in a synagogue if I didn't get back to work straight away. I wrote full accounts of my trip and ran off three copies. Then I rang Gilbert.

'Hello, Charlie,' he said. 'How're the haemorrhoids?' Funny how people always say 'haemorrhoids', but write 'piles'.

'I haven't got frigging haemorroids,' I told him. 'I just said the first thing I thought of. Sorry I had to tell you a fib. Do I still have a job or am I suspended?'

'God knows, it's a bloody shambles. Hilditch wants you sacked, but he's way out of order. Partridge is his own man, though, and would have done the right thing. He's got the measure of Hilditch, I reckon, but I didn't want to tell him what it's all about. As far as I'm concerned you're still with us. Where've you been?'

'Spain.'

'Christ, I knew it. Find anything?'

'Yep. Are you in tonight?'

'Sure. What time are you coming round?'

'Try this,' said Gilbert. 'Discovered it when I was up there at Easter. It's regarded by some as the finest single malt ever distilled.'

We were sitting in his little study, surrounded by his books and his small but growing collection of whiskies. He wasn't a great imbiber, but he enjoyed the good things in life, and considered the elixir of the glens to be one of the best.

'Make it a very small one; it's wasted on me,' I admitted.

'I'd no intention of making it a big one,' Gilbert countered.

I took a sip, and let it wash around under my tongue and down my throat. 'Mmm, quite pleasant,' I said, 'for whisky. What is it?'

'Linkwood,' he replied, with hushed reverence.

'Linkwood? Never heard of it. Japanese?'

'God, Priest, you're a peasant. Sit there while I fetch you a can of lager. What's that you've brought to show me?'

I passed him the sheaf of reports. 'Read those, Gilbert, while I savour the Linkwood. Then I'll answer questions.'

It took him nearly half an hour to get through them. Periodically he glanced up at me, then, towards the end, he said 'Jesus Christ' under his breath. Finally he lowered the sheets and sat looking at me for a couple of minutes. I gazed into my glass.

He said: 'You're lucky to be alive, Charlie.'

'Yeah. And George Palfreeman's unlucky to be dead.' I swirled the dregs of the straw-coloured liquid around the heavy tumbler. I didn't dare lift my head to look at him. 'Between those two statements and the Linkwood, we've got the makings of a nice philosophical evening.'

He went to ask Molly, his wife, to make some tea. I was grateful for the interlude.

Gilbert came back and sat down. We waited in silence until Molly brought the tea and left us. Then he said: 'First thing in the morning I'll call in the Serious Fraud Office. It's spread too far and wide for us to handle. Sorry, Chas, but you're off it from now on. It's a pity I didn't give you a bit more support earlier; we should have bowled Hilditch a googly – set him up, somehow.'

'Never mind. It was one of his predecessors who said hindsight was an exact science.'

'Doesn't make me feel any better. Are you coming in tomorrow?'

Tomorrow was Friday, the last day of my holiday. 'Yes, I'd like to.'

'Good. You'd better hang around the office – no doubt they'll want a word with you. Let Willis see the week out as acting inspector.'

'That's fine by me. What else has been happening?'

'I was just coming to it,' he said. 'We brought in young Rose and Makinson. They've come up with some good information. We're hitting four addresses early Monday morning, just when they're at their best. Only two of them's in Heckley, though. The city boys are looking after the others. Will you want to take over?'

I thought about it. 'No, if Tony's done all the planning, let him handle it. I wouldn't mind going in, though, if that's all right. A bit of aggression might do me good.'

'All right by me. I'll let Willis fill you in tomorrow.'

I went home and asked the word processor to run off copies of all the reports, for the Serious Fraud boys. According to the Data Protection Act I shouldn't store information like that on my computer, so I closed the curtains while I did it.

The first four people I met next morning asked me how my haemorrhoids were and suggested a variety of treatments. Then word must have passed round that it was a touchy subject, and concern began to diminish. I buried myself in the small hill of paperwork that Tony had decided I ought to know about, and fielded enquiries about my holiday. The first worthwhile phone call I received was from Diaz.

'Good morning, Charlie, or may I call you Inspector Priest? I thought you would be back at work today. How was the drive?'

'Hello, Rafael, it's good to hear from you. The drive was hard work, not to be recommended. Any developments?'

'Yes. One of my men was in a bar and he saw a youth wearing a leather jacket which had some interesting marks on the back. He brought him in. The stuff we took from under your fingernails was a perfect match. We now have the accomplice and the scooter, too.'

'Well done. No gun?'

'Unfortunately, no, but they are known to be associates of gangsters. Rest assured, they are the ones.'

'Good, thanks for telling me, Rafael. I've put copies of all the relevant reports in the post for you. They should keep you entertained for a day or two.'

He went on to tell me when the funeral was arranged for, and offered to send flowers on my behalf. After a shaky start, I decided that I had a lot of time for Capitano Diaz.

In the afternoon we had a briefing on Monday's raids. It was hard, but I had to drag myself down out of the clouds and start being a cop at Heckley again. There might be links stretching from our ram-raiders to Cakebread and Puerto Banus, but so far that was for the birds. Gilbert did the introductions and handed over to me. I split the troops into two teams and explained that Mr Wood was in overall command and Acting Inspector Willis was running the show in the street. I'd be going in with the marines. We then split up to study our separate targets. That's when I discovered the identity of the occupier of the house I'd volunteered to enter. He was called Willy O'Hagan. I'd never heard of him, but his record said he had one conviction – for armed robbery.

I put my finger on the relevant sentence and said: 'Looks like we'll need to be armed.'

'Sorry, boss,' said Tony. 'Didn't you know? Rose told us he keeps a gun in his car boot. I thought you were a bit eager to be up front.'

We were nearly finished when I was called to the phone. 'Priest here,' I said.

'Good afternoon, Inspector. I'm Chief Superintendent Fearnside, Serious Fraud Office. I'd like to see you, in about fifteen minutes, if that's all right.'

A real chief super, they meant business. 'No problem, sir. Are you coming here?'

'No. I'll be at the Little Chef near Cattleshaw. I'll see you there.'

I hesitated, remembering the last arrangement I'd made on the telephone. Fearnside must have read my mind; he went on: 'If you ask Superintendent Wood, he'll tell you that he recommended the place. I'll be in a black Granada.'

'Right, sir, I'm on my way, but fifteen minutes is pushing it a bit.'

'Then you'd better get moving.'

I rang Gilbert, more to tell him where I was going than to check on Fearnside. 'What's the coffee like in the Little Chef?' I asked him.

He laughed: 'OK, they do decaffeinated.'

'I'm going now.'

'Give 'em hell, Charlie.'

I parked a few spaces away from the Granada. There were two of them in it. We didn't go in for a coffee; as I approached the car the passenger got out. He let himself into the rear seat and gestured for me to join him. Fearnside was burly and prosperous-looking. He could have been a captain of industry. The one in the driving seat was tall and slim, and equally smooth. It was no good: if I wanted to get on I'd have to buy myself a suit. I took out my warrant card and offered it to Fearnside. He didn't look at it, but he got the message and they both showed me theirs. His aide-de-camp was an inspector called Longfellow.

The delights of production-line catering for hoi polloi apparently didn't appeal, for we went for a drive up on to the moors. I let Fearnside break the silence.

'Fascinating landscape,' he said. 'Absolutely fascinating. Am I right in believing the Bronte girls were from these parts?'

'That's right, sir, not too far away.' I wanted to add: 'And Robbie Burns, too,' but managed to stop myself. Eventually we pulled into a lay-by.

'Right, Inspector Priest, let's get down to business. Superintendent Wood has told us the main story, but we need a few details from you. First of all, tell us everything you can about Truscott.'

I didn't tell them everything I knew, just the relevant stuff. I also handed over the copies of the reports.

When I'd finished he asked: 'How do you believe the paintings were switched?'

'In the security van. The fakes were already in the van, laid flat under the carpet, or wherever. On the journey the genuines were removed from the frames and the fakes substituted. One of the guards riding in the back was about the same size as Truscott, so I'm assuming it was him. The tacks would go back into the same holes, so they still looked the same from the back, as well as from the front. The breakdown was to give them more time; the loud music covered the sound of hammering.'

'Breakdown? Loud music?'

Gilbert had obviously not gone into such detail.

'Sorry, it's all in the reports.' After a few moments' silence I said: 'I take it that the art world is making waves. Have the paintings been switched?'

He pondered on what to tell me. 'Unofficially, yes,' he confided.

I felt strangely pleased. I clean forgot to mention the Picasso, but later a chill ran through me as I realised that I'd gone away and left it hanging over the fireplace.

'And now, Inspector, let's hear about your Spanish trip.'

They dropped me off back at the restaurant. It was out of my hands now. They had the resources and the intelligence network to really crack who was behind the theft of the paintings. A little bit of me was sorry, though – George's death apart, I'd enjoyed

185

my foray into international crime. Nicked videos and pensioners' purses lacked the glamour of drug cartels and international smuggling. It was Friday evening. I dallied in my car until the Granada left the car park, then I went in and ordered an all-day, American-style breakfast.

CHAPTER TWELVE

I hadn't had enough time back to become snowed under with all the must-be-done-yesterday jobs that are usually threatening to engulf me. Usually I have a couple of hours in the office on a Saturday morning, and maybe spend some time coordinating any of the troops who might be working. But, apart from a brief phone call from ADI Willis, I had a weekend off. Tony asked me if I wanted to take over on Monday, instead of being on the pointed end, but I declined his offer. The exercise would do me good – I had two flights of stairs to run up.

The dead flies and streaks of yellow dirt that covered the Jaguar gave it a purposeful air, but they weren't good for the paint. I put it through a car wash and applied touch-up to the scrape. It was hardly noticeable. Then

I pushed it to the back of the garage and covered it with a dustsheet. In the afternoon I mowed the lawn and did some weeding. As soon as the garden looked only marginally worse than my neighbours', I stopped. Sunday, I hoovered. I love weekends like dentists love garlic.

We rendezvoused at the station at five a.m. Monday. People you've known for years always look different in situations like this. We were all wearing dark, casual clothes, with silent shoes, and one or two drew on cigarettes. There was tension behind the banter. Superintendent Wood liaised with the city teams and confirmed the plan. All four targets would be hit at six thirty-five. We had a final briefing, and then some of us went to the armoury to draw our guns. A Tactical Firearms Unit would be standing by, but those of us with the necessary training would carry personal weapons.

Hate is a word I rarely use, but it's in my vocabulary. I reserve it for describing my feelings towards guns. Holding a gun changes your personality as surely as does a mind-bending drug. I'd found it in everybody I'd ever seen with one, on both sides of the fence; including myself. In the Force, there are stringent tests of personality and ability before you can carry a firearm. In the streets, all you need is a hundred quid.

The standard issue is a thirty-eight, either automatic or revolver, according to the individual's preference, loaded with flat-nosed bullets. We are trained to shoot only if a life is in immediate jeopardy, so, if we have to shoot, we shoot to kill. The flat-nosed bullet has maximum stopping power, with the least chance of it going straight through the target and hitting somebody else. 'Maximum stopping power' means it makes a mess. 'The target' is the person you are trying to kill.

In the armoury, however, was a neat little Walther two-two automatic that had been found in a German tourist's handbag, and confiscated. I'd adopted this for my own use whenever I had to be armed. It fitted in my jacket pocket without the need for a holster. The macho types sniggered at it, but the way I saw things, if I had to use it, I'd already failed. I checked that it had a full clip of cartridges and that the safety catch was at '*zu*'. We'd carried firearms on hundreds of occasions, and practised for hours on the range, but, to the best of my knowledge, none of us had ever fired a shot in anger.

Our four cars came to a silent halt round the corner from O'Hagan's house. We were a measured hundred yards away. Uniformed officers positioned themselves where they could prevent the postman and the milkman stumbling into the action. The last couple of minutes ticked by, then the codeword came through on the radio. Ten of us got out and, leaving the car doors wide open, strode towards the three-storey terrace. The drivers would bring the cars after us. At our head was a big constable carrying a sledgehammer. We lined up in a prearranged order at the door and I nodded to the constable. The hammer hit the lock and the door bounced inwards about four inches and sprang back. It was held at the top. Two more blows and we were in.

We'd studied the layouts of similar houses, and knew that the rooms on the second floor were usually used as bedrooms. It was my job, with Nigel, to get to them as quickly as possible. That's where the action was most likely to be, but hopefully we'd catch them with their pants round their ankles. I took the stairs three at a time, but I was only halfway up the last flight when a character came round the top whirling a rice flail round his head. Unfortunately for him it was not much good in the narrowness of the staircase and it tangled round his arm. He had a game attempt at passing me, but I just doubled up and went for his legs with my shoulders. I felt his shins connect with me, then he sailed over my head and landed at the foot of the stairs with a crash that shook the beer cans in the kitchen. I turned to look down at the wreckage.

'I'll get him,' shouted Sparky, who'd found the first floor uninhabited.

'C'mon,' I said to Nigel, and cleared the last few steps.

I kicked open the first bedroom door. The bed bore signs of being recently vacated. I slid an unwilling hand between the off-grey sheets; they were still warm. Nobody was under the bed or in the wardrobe so I tried the next room. It was filled with junk, plus a stack of interesting, unopened cardboard boxes. The other bedroom was the biggest, and had a bed, wardrobe and chest of drawers. The sheets on the bed were colour coordinated with the others. Somebody had just got out from between them, too. Sparky and a couple more came round the landing to join us.

'Find anything?' I asked, putting my finger to my lips, then pointing upwards.

'No more bodies, plenty of loot, though,' Sparky answered, his eyes following my finger.

These houses originally had cellars and attics. When the attics were no longer required for the maid, or the kids, or the deranged mother-in-law to sleep in, most people blanked them off and demolished the stairs to make the bedroom bigger. This had been done here, leaving just a trapdoor to give access to the plumbing in the attic. The trap was above the chest of drawers, and it was open. Our second sleeping beauty was up there.

I pointed for the others to go downstairs.

'OK! Let's go,' I shouted. There was a gap at the side of the wardrobe to leave room for the curtains to go back. I slipped into it and gestured to Sparky to leave me.

'Right, we've done all we can here, let's go,' he said.

They banged and stamped down the staircases. I moved the curtain to one side and looked out. The front door slammed, but only Nigel emerged into the road. He spoke to one of the drivers for a few seconds, then the car tore off with much revving and squealing.

At, the end of the street he put on his siren and I listened to it fade into the distance.

I didn't have a long wait. There was a creaking of joists above my head, moving towards the trapdoor. After a few seconds, a pair of bare legs appeared. He sat on the edge of the opening, then dropped on to the chest of drawers. The upper half of his body was still above ceiling level. There was an easy way to do this. I put my hand in my pocket, and my fingers curled round the PPK. My thumb, without being told, eased the safety catch to 'auf'. He stood, half concealed, apparently reaching for something in the loft.

Then I saw the butt of a shotgun being lowered out of the opening. I stepped out of my hiding place. 'I'm an armed police officer. Put the . . .'

I didn't get any further. He ducked out of the trapdoor, swept the shotgun in my direction and pulled the trigger. I instinctively jumped back behind the wardrobe as the corner of it in front of my head exploded into sawdust and the window shattered. Stinging fragments peppered my face and eyes. I did a standing leap into the middle of the room, swung in his direction and pumped the trigger of the Walther three times. The figure swimming in front of me raised his hands in a futile gesture of protection, then toppled over, crashing to the floor, the shotgun clattering down alongside him. I lowered my head and blinked most of the debris out of my eyes, then put the pistol in my pocket and moved over to the body, just as Sparky, thirty-eight held in front of him, charged round the top of the stairs.

All three shots had hit him in the chest. I pressed

a finger into his neck, alongside the Adam's apple. 'Anything?' asked Sparky, quietly.

'Yes, there's a pulse,' I said. 'Let's take his vest off.'

We pulled the garment over his head and looked at the three wounds. They were small black holes, almost innocuous-looking, but the blood dribbling out of them was flecked with foam. Nigel and one or two others had joined us. I told him to go down and let ADI Willis know what had happened, and send for the ambulance. We had one standing by. He was back almost immediately.

'Go back and tell Mr Willis we need the SOCO and a photographer,' said Sparky.

I sealed the holes with my fingers, while Sparky checked the pulse. After a minute or so he said: 'We're losing him.'

We decided he was dead more or less as the paramedics arrived. Acting Detective Inspector Willis drew some marks on the floor with a fibre pen to indicate where he fell, just before they put him on their stretcher and rushed him away. I flexed my knees and wiped more bits from my eyes.

'Where were you when he fired, Charlie?' asked Tony.

I blew my nose and walked across the room. 'There,' I said, pointing to where a great chunk from the edge of the wardrobe had been blasted into infinity.

'And when you fired?'

'There.'

Tony and Sparky stood looking at me, each waiting

193

for the other to speak. I looked from one to the other. 'C'mon,' I demanded, 'what are you telling me?'

'Have you seen his gun, boss?' asked Sparky. 'Yeah, it fell near the bed.'

I walked over and looked down at it. 'Great,' I mumbled. 'That's just what we need.'

It was an ancient, single-barrelled job. He didn't have another shot left.

Chief Inspector Colin Brabiner was appointed investigating officer, and Sam Evans, the police surgeon, was asked to come and have a word with me. The Federation representative offered to appoint a solicitor to be at my side throughout, telling me what to say and what not to, and everybody I met gave what they believed to be support. Superintendent Wood made me coffee, the real stuff, and loaned me his office while I wrote my reports. Then he went with the 10 and Sparky to view the scene of the incident.

Sam Evans looks like a well-fed, but pale, Mahatma Gandhi. Premature baldness and a grey moustache make him look much older than he is. I'd first met him about ten years earlier, when I'd hurt my back falling down a fire escape. I did him a favour and we became good friends. He came over as soon as he heard the news.

'I'm supposed to make you an appointment to see Dr Foulkes, of the General,' he said. 'How do you feel about it?'

Foulkes was head of the psychiatry department. We used him for stress counselling. 'Unhappy, Sam. Can't you deal with it? I have mixed feelings about this psychotherapy stuff. No doubt some people need it, but I don't think I'm one of them. Leave well alone, I say.'

'If it ain't broke, don't fix it.'

'Exactly.' I put my ball-pen down. I'd become aware that I was clicking the cap on and off all the time we were talking.

'How do you feel about what happened this morning, Charlie?'

I had to think about this one. The truth was, I hadn't had time to feel much about it at all. After a while I said: 'Sad. I'm sad that a young man has had a wasted life and has died. The fact that I was the person who . . . who shot him seems . . . irrelevant. He was somebody's son, though. Maybe it just hasn't hit me, yet, but at the moment it's not bothering me. It's just more hassle stopping me getting on with the job.'

Sam nodded. 'I see,' he said. 'And, of course, you were in danger yourself.'

I shrugged my shoulders. 'That's what we get underpaid for.'

'Don't you think about the danger to yourself?'

'No. There shouldn't have been any.'

There shouldn't have been any. The words jangled in my brain. An innocent question, from someone who was trying to be helpful, had signalled a train of thought

195

that I would prefer not to follow. Was this why I was scared of seeing Dr Foulkes?'

I went on: 'The danger was there because I made a cock-up. An error of judgement. I was being clever, short-cutting normal procedures. It should never have reached the shooting stage. I brought that on.'

I remembered what I'd said to Gilbert about some aggro doing me good. I'd wanted to go in and prove that I was still as good as anyone. Bring-'em-back-alive Charlie had wanted to show that he could still do it; but this time he'd brought one back dead. Two, if you included George. The ball-pen slipped out of my fingers and fell to the floor. I hadn't realised I'd picked the bloody thing up again.

'Are you in trouble, Charlie? Do you think you'll be criticised?' Sam's tone was soft and concerned.

I took a long time to answer. 'I'll be all right. There'll be some searching questions, but we'll pull through. Deep down, I'm happy that I did the right thing; and that's what counts. I'll be able to sleep at nights.'

Sam made sympathetic noises, and waited for me to go on. I couldn't think of anything to add, so I told him what had happened in Spain. He looked shocked.

'Right, you've convinced me,' he stated. 'I'm grounding you, at least for the rest of the week.'

'That's no good, I've work to do,' I protested.

'Someone else'll do it. And I think you ought to see Foulkes. This is not really my field.'

'No, I don't want to see him.'

'Then you're grounded. Why don't you clear off to the coast for a few days, do some fishing or something? You need a rest and a complete change. There's life outside the police force, you know.'

'OK, it's a deal,' I reluctantly agreed.

'Good. Come and see me next Monday and we'll take it from there. Meanwhile, if you do need something to help you sleep for a night or two, you know where I am.'

'Cheers, Sam. How's Yvonne?'

'She's fine, thanks. A lot better. Sold a painting last week for sixty quid. Says she ought to be paying you commission. Why don't you call in to see her? While you're off work.'

'I might do that.'

Chief Inspector Brabiner didn't give me such an easy ride. I still had the Walther in my pocket when we met. I ejected the cartridge clip and placed it, with the gun, on the desk in front of him. He didn't look pleased. His main line of enquiry was why was I armed with a pea shooter and the others with pistols. We should have gone in brandishing Heckler and Koch rapid-fire assault weapons. This would probably have resulted in a siege, with laddo holed up in the loft, but, hopefully, he would have survived. It didn't matter that the street would have had to be evacuated, and all the neighbours found alternative accommodation. Thousands of hours of police time would have been consumed, while he hurled down roofing slates for the benefit of the newsreel cameras. A life would have been saved, and that was above valuation, even if it was a life dedicated to thieving, drug peddling, corruption of the young and the destruction of society. And he was right.

I felt depressed, and wished I'd accepted his offer to have a solicitor present. After nearly two hours he asked me if I had any questions.

'Only the obvious one,' I said. 'What's the outcome likely to be?'

He gathered his papers together. 'I'm happy with what I've seen and heard. It's a miracle you didn't have your head blown off. With any sort of luck, the inquest will come out in our favour. I'd say it was cut and dried. There's always the possibility, though, that some trendy lefty politician will jump on the bandwagon and try to make capital out of it.'

I smiled at the irony. 'I get called a trendy lefty,' I said. That's why we'd gone in how we did, instead of armed to the teeth like Captain Blackbeard's pirates.

'I know, but they'll still stab you in the back if it will help the cause.' He clicked his briefcase shut and smiled for the first time. 'You'll be all right. Our masters won't fall over themselves to give you a commendation, but plenty will think you deserve one.'

I shook my head: 'I don't need a commendation, just get them off my back.' But he'd made me feel happier.

* * *

I went home and made a corned beef and pickle sandwich, which I didn't finish, and a pot of tea, which I did. I tried watching some TV, without any enthusiasm, and dipped into a couple of books. They didn't grip me, either. In the smallest bedroom, the one I'd slept in as a child, were boxes of possessions that I'd brought back with me when I returned to live here again. I sat down in the middle of the untidiness and started opening boxes. Eventually I found the one containing a comprehensive collection of Ordnance Survey maps, relics of my days as a budding mountaineer. I thumbed through them, extracting the most interesting ones. My old rucksack still held my waterproof clothing, and the boots were sound if you ignored the mildew. I stuffed the treasure into the sack and took it downstairs.

The rucksack might have earned a place in a Museum of Scouting, but nobody would be seen dead carrying one like it these days, so I binned it. The boots were expensive leather ones and cleaned up beautifully. Then I settled down to pore over the maps. That evening the phone rang more often than a whore's doorbell when the party conferences are in town. All the calls were to wish me luck and offer support. One was from Mike Freer.

'Sheepshagger! How y'doing?' he greeted me.

'Gannet Breath! I'm OK, how are you?'

'Not bad. I was wondering if you could use a pinch of this stuff of yours in our safe. Might be just what you need.'

199

'Don't tempt me, Mike, I'm in deep enough already. I take it you've heard?'

'Yeah, you did well. The rest of the team send their regards. How are you feeling about it?'

'Fed up. Brabiner gave me a grilling this afternoon. Then there'll be the inquest. He thinks I'll be OK, but he made it clear that I broke the rules. Maybe you were right: it's not worth it.'

'Listen, Sheepdip,' he said. 'The only rule you broke was to move. If you'd stood still and let him kill you, everybody would be saying what a splendid fellow you were. Past tense. Right now the high and the mighty would be pressing their best uniforms and practising the purple prose. You weren't carrying a gun to scratch your arse with, you know.'

'Yeah, thanks. When are you taking me out for a swift half?'

'Sorry, Charlie, no can do for a while. It's the party season and we're busy. However . . .' he paused for maximum effect, 'I've some good news about your friend Parker.'

'The penpusher?' I asked.

'None other. We've tracked him down, plus one or two others he's involved with. Any day now we'll invite him to help us with investigations.'

'Invoke the law against him,' I suggested.

'Exactly. Stick him before the Great Invigilator. No doubt he'll produce some suitable invective.'

'Great. People like him have no backbone.'

'Invertebrate, true. Never mind, the information you gave us was . . . er . . . priceless.'

'Invaluable. Pity it can't be used.'

'Invalid. Wonder if he's got a maiden aunt in Scotland?'

'Inverness?'

We both started laughing.

CHAPTER THIRTEEN

I should have accepted Sam's offer of some sleeping tablets. A thousand thoughts were racing through my mind as I lay in bed, and, when I almost did drop off, the reports of the guns jolted me back to alertness. I listened to the World Service for an hour, then rose and dressed.

All my old oil paints were in the junk room, together with an easel. I found a board of about, but not quite, the right size, and set up the easel in the front room, before the Picasso. It was daylight outside when I finished. It would take three or four days to dry, then it could go over the mantelpiece in place of the so-called original. It might fool a hired burglar, working by torchlight. I washed my hands and fetched the duvet from the bedroom. I fell asleep on the settee, the smell of oil paints and natural turpentine bringing back memories of another life.

In the afternoon I rang Gilbert and arranged to see him later. Then I had a desultory meal, showered and went to the library. I spent a long time perusing books about walks in Yorkshire. The CID office is usually at its quietest in the late afternoon. When I entered only Martin Makinson and Nigel were there.

'Hello, Maz,' I said. 'Or is it back to Martin? How does it feel to have to come to work again?'

He gave a relieved smile. At first they both were uncertain how to deal with me. 'No problem, boss. All the sex and drugs was starting to get me down anyway.'

'Good, you did well. Which of you two is good at walking?'

Neither spoke. They both believed that the first to twitch a muscle would find himself pacing every pavement in Heckley.

'Hard luck, Nigel. You blinked first.' I had intended giving him the job all along. I put a bundle of OS maps and a library book on his desk. 'You are now the secretary of the CID Walking Club. We meet the first Sunday in every month, for a brisk expedition across the fells. Have a look at these and sort something out. It's about time you discovered more about God's Own Country, apart from the boozers and curry houses.'

Nigel surprised me with his eagerness. 'Great, boss,' he said, adding: 'Do you think many will want to come?'

'They will when they read the constitution. It's a pound a week to be a member, and membership is compulsory. All walks to finish near a pub, where we spend the club funds. That'll drag 'em in.'

Poor Gilbert had aged ten years overnight. He'd probably been taking non-stop flak since the shooting.

'Sit down, Charlie. Let's have a coffee.' He filled two mugs, then looked at his watch. 'Oh, it's not too early for a snifter, what do you say?'

I'd have preferred to have said 'No thanks', but I said: 'Good idea, get the bottle out.'

Gilbert poured two measures in our coffees and we settled down to put the world right. I told him about the new Walking Club.

'Hey, that could catch on,' he said. 'Might even come myself, if it's not too strenuous.'

'It won't be. We intend catering for all tastes, abilities, and the overweight.'

We discussed a few outstanding jobs, then he told me what Chief Inspector Brabiner had said he would put in his report. It sounded favourable. Gilbert delved into one of his drawers and slid a ten-by-eight black-and-white photograph across to me.

'If anything clinches it, Charlie, that will. Christ, you were lucky. I went cold when I saw the hole in that wardrobe.'

The print showed a uniformed constable standing in the alcove where I had been. Inches in front of his face was a jagged mess where the shotgun blast had blown away the edge of the wardrobe. A chill ran through my bones, too. 'Yes,' I remarked. 'I'm having a lot of luck lately.'

While we were sipping our coffee the phone rang. Gilbert answered it, making acquiescent noises into the mouthpiece as he listened for several minutes. He scribbled on his pad, then turned it so I could read it. He'd written 'Longfellow'. After a while he said: 'No, you won't catch him at home . . . He's here, that's why . . . Yes, in my office. I'll put him on.' He reached over with the handset and gave me a resigned look.

'Priest here,' I said.

'Hello, Inspector Priest. DI Longfellow, from the SFO. I'm afraid I've some not very good news for you.'

'Don't spare me, I'm feeling brave.'

'Pardon?'

'Nothing, go ahead.'

'I've rung to tell you that we've just searched various of Mr Cakebread's premises. They were all clean as a whistle. We also asked our Spanish opposites to turn over his villa and boat. They found nothing, too.'

Disappointment hit me like a ten-ton custard pie. 'Where, exactly, have you searched?' I asked.

'Everywhere he had registered; that's his premises in Welton, ABC House; his home—'

'The Ponderosa?'

'That's right; his aeroplane at Blackpool and a flat at Whitby. He spreads his largess between both coasts.'

'He certainly does. I didn't know about the flat in Whitby; do you have an address?' He read it to me. I went on: 'And you found nothing at all?'

'Nothing. Apparently the sniffer dog they put in the plane became quite excited, but nothing came of it. We've taken some sweepings up for analysis, but if we do find anything it will never stick. Looks like he's given us the slip, for the time being.'

'Oh. Well at least you sound as if you're happy that I haven't led you up a gum tree.'

'No, nothing of the sort,' he replied. 'He's up to his neck in something. We'll just have to keep watching him.'

'Will I step on any toes if I include myself in that?'

'Be our guest; you're on his doorstep.'

I was back on the job. 'OK, thanks for ringing.'

'There is one other thing,' he said before I could put the phone down. 'CS Fearnside had me dig out your file. You've been an inspector for a long time.'

I didn't like the sound of this. 'That's right, I'm going for the record.'

His reply caught me off-guard: 'Ever considered a sideways move?' he asked.

'Er, no, never,' I stuttered.

'Maybe you should. Fearnside was impressed. Could get you away from a tricky situation. Why don't you think about it?'

'I will. Thanks. Goodbye.'

I thought about it. Move down south – no way. End

of thought process. I handed the phone back to Gilbert, and when it was back in its cradle said: 'They've spun Breadcake and he's cleaner than a dog's balls. They can't manage without me, so will I spend some of my valuable time on the case? Then he offered me a proper job.'

Gilbert's eyebrows shot up. 'Offered you a job?'

'That's what it sounded like.'

'The cheeky bastard!'

Being off work gave me time to think, without the pressures of day-to-day policing. All we had on Cakebread was a collection of tenuously linked crimes, where some of the connections were thinner than boarding house Spam. What we didn't have was forensic evidence, something that would stand up against critical cross-examination by the best bent lawyers in the business. Money can buy you truth, but only, thank God, up to a point. Wednesday morning I rose ridiculously early, but I hung about at home to give ADI Willis plenty of time to deploy his troops. Then I went in to the office.

'Hi, boss,' Sparky greeted me. 'We were just having a discussion on the greatest labour-saving device ever invented. What would you say it was?'

'No idea. What's this in aid of?'

'It's the eldest lad's latest project from school. That's the sort of stuff they teach 'em, these days.'

'I thought you had only two sons,' stated Nigel.

'I have.'

'In that case he's your elder lad, not eldest.'

'But I've got three kids.'

'Well in that case he's your eldest child, but your elder son.'

'My daughter won't like that.'

'Why not?'

'She's elder than he is.'

'What's he thinking of so far?' interrupted Tony Willis.

'Sliced bread.'

'Sliced bread's not labour-saving. Cutting it with a knife's no effort, it's just that they're all different thicknesses. What do you think, Charlie?'

'Er, I agree.'

'The jumbo jet!' exclaimed Nigel, triumphantly.

'What about it?'

'Well,' he explained, 'four hundred people can fly from Manchester to New York in five hours in a jumbo. It would take them months to swim it. That's what I call labour-saving.'

'Hey, that's good,' said Sparky. 'He might use that.'

'Rubbish!' exclaimed Tony. 'What about the billion people who live in China? The jumbo hasn't saved them any labour.'

'In India they use them for moving logs,' I said.

Superintendent Wood walked through the door just in time to hear Sparky declare: '. . . but the main fault with the Criminal Justice Act is that it does nothing to address the problem of overcrowding in the jails.'

Gilbert said: 'Hello, Charlie, didn't know you were in.'

'I'm not, boss, it's just a quick social call.'

Gilbert placed some papers on my desk. 'Have a look at those when you have a chance,' he said. 'Not as riveting as the Criminal Justice Act, I'm afraid.'

I gazed at the dreaded annual budget forecast forms. 'I've just done them,' I protested.

'They were last year's. No hurry, tomorrow will do.'

He was halfway out of the door when I shouted to him: 'Mr Wood, what would you say was the greatest labour-saving invention ever made?'

Gilbert paused, one hand on the door handle. 'Brown underpants,' he stated, and walked out.

'Right, crimefighters,' I said, 'that is definitely the last word on the subject. I'll leave you to it.'

I stood up and walked over to my office. The main CID department is open plan, with a small room partitioned off in the corner which I grandly call my office. I do most of my work on a spare desk in the big office, leaving this room as open house for anyone who needs to work quietly, away from the rabble. I'd made a decision. The Cakebread Saga had gone far enough; it was time for drastic action.

I created a file. After the minimum of thought I called it 'Picasso Scam'. I gathered together all the reports and put them in the new file. Then I made a chart with all the disjointed events on it, and drew links between them, where possible. It was as obvious as a baritone in a convent choir that without the forensic we were going nowhere.

I rang Scotland Yard and asked for copies of the fingerprints of Cakebread and two associates of his, Bradshaw and Wheatley. Bradshaw was believed to be his co-pilot. Cakebread had not held a pilot's licence very long, and was not qualified for international flights. Bradshaw was. He was a one-time racing driver who had sought to sponsor his expensive tastes by avoiding paying the excise duty on a few thousand cigars, hence his record. Wheatley was involved in quite a few of Cakebread's business dealings. It was only hearsay, but he was a Rachman-like figure, involved in lots of dubious property deals. His only conviction was for petty theft, as a teenager. They promised to send me the copies as soon as possible.

Truscott and Eunice Cakebread had no convictions, so there was not much I could do about them. That left Ernest Hilditch. I was reasonably certain that our Chief Constable had lived a blameless past, free from the indignity of having his fingers pressed on to an ink pad and unceremoniously rolled on a sheet of paper. I'd have to use my ingenuity to obtain his dabs. I picked up the phone.

I was in luck; she was there. 'Hi, Kim, it's Charlie Priest.'

'Hello, Charlie, this is a surprise; how're you?'

'OK, thanks, but I need a favour.'

'If I can,' she said.

'Have you ever heard the saying "Friendship corrupts", Kim?'

'No.'

'Well it does, especially in our job. But forget it for now, I'd like to corrupt you.'

'You've been trying to corrupt me for years, Charlie, what's new?'

I smiled at the thought of it. 'Cut out the sex talk, Limbert, I've forgotten why I rang now.' After a moment I went on: 'Oh, yes, I remember – is the Chief's private secretary still Miss Yates?'

Kim said: 'The redoubtable Rita, it certainly is.'

'Good, I'd like a word with her, when nobody's there. Did you tell me you had a friend who worked in the outer office?

'That's right – Melanie. She's a cousin.'

'OK. What's the chances of finding out when I'll be able to catch Miss Yates with none of the top-brass around?'

'That should be no problem. Only one thing might stop me.'

'What's that?'

'Jealousy. Where are you? I'll ring you back.'

Nigel had left the office, so I wrote him a note. I explained where the file was and suggested he read it. Then I told him to contact Companies House and find out as much as he could about Cakebread's empire. If any of his contacts had records, obtain copies of their dabs. As an afterthought I suggested he clear it with ADI Willis.

Kim kept her word. 'There's an executive meeting at three thirty,' she told me. 'The CC is on leave and Partridge is in London. The desirable Miss Yates should be at maximum vulnerability any time after that. Let me know if you breach her defences.'

Rita Yates was a civilian. She had been private secretary to a long succession of Chief Constables and wielded power far greater than her status implied. Word had it that several CCs had had affairs with her. It was a recognised fact that most holders of the job died in harness, so to speak, but whether this was relative I had no way of knowing. At four o'clock I knocked tentatively on her office door and opened it.

Her perfume hit me with all the subtlety of a friendly Labrador. I'd seen her before, years ago, and knew her to be a stunner. Time had been kind to her. The blonde hair was now tastefully streaked, and a large pair of fashionable spectacles made the best of nature's perfidy. Her legs had been her most magnificent feature, but these were now concealed behind her desk.

'Miss Yates?' I asked.

'Yes, what can I do for you?'

The manner was abrupt; she rarely dealt with anyone below the rank of assistant chief constable. I went in and closed the door behind me.

'Priest, Inspector Priest, from Heckley,' I said. 'I've a . . . a little problem, and I'd like to ask your assistance to get over it.'

'If I can, Inspector, what is it?'

'Well . . .' I tried to sound uncomfortable, but it didn't require much effort, 'you see, Mr Hilditch had this book that was evidence in a case; and now we've found some fingerprints on it. Trouble is, we can't be certain that they're not his. Wouldn't do for us to release them and have everybody looking for the Chief Constable, would it?'

'I see,' she stated, 'so now you need something with Mr Hilditch's fingerprints on it so you can eliminate him from your enquiries.'

Phew! Couldn't have put it better myself. 'Quite,' I said. She thought for a while. 'I've washed his cup and the glass he uses. Let's see what we can find.'

She came from behind her desk and headed for the door into the adjoining office. The tight skirt emphasised the classy chassis. I followed her, tripping over the waste-paper bin on the way.

The Chief Constable's office was furnished in mahogany and leather. There were law books in a cabinet, drinks in another, and photographs from memorable moments in his career on the walls. Not a loose piece of paper to be seen anywhere. I had a look at the drinks cabinet and discovered that he was a Macallan man. That would gain him some of Gilbert's respect.

'What about his paperknife, Inspector?' Miss Yates was examining his desk. I turned to face her. Hell's goblins! She'd taken her spectacles off! The desk was totally bare except for a marble-based executive paper knife holder, essential for the job, complete with stainless steel knife. I held it between my fingertips and examined it as if I knew what I was doing.

'Smashing,' I said, 'do you mind if I borrow this for an hour or two?'

She perched herself on the corner of his desk. As I faced her she drew up one long leg and folded her hands around her knee. 'Not at all, Inspector. Did you say it was an interesting case?'

I dropped the knife into a plastic bag. 'Very interesting. I'd like to tell you all about it sometime. Meanwhile, I'd better have this examined. Then I can bring it back to you' – I gave her the smile – 'personally.'

Fingerprints were in the middle of a panic. Every white male in the city who could run a mile in under five minutes with his trousers round his ankles was in the process of being eliminated from enquiries. The constable laid aside what he was doing and gave the knife a brush-over with aluminium flake. It didn't show up too well against the bright metal, but he assured me there were some useful dabs present. He pressed strips of Sellotape over the smudges to lift them off. I could see them easily enough then. Chalk and soot are still used sometimes, but they have particles that squash flat when Sellotape is pressed on to them, distorting the image. This doesn't happen with the ally flake. The sticky strips are then placed on pieces of clear plastic sheet, to produce instant negatives, thereby eliminating half of the photographic process.

'Will they do?' he asked. 'Or do you want some contact prints making? They'll take a while, I'm afraid.'

'Make me some prints, please. There's no immediate hurry.' I wiped the powder from the paperknife, put it in an envelope with a note and posted it in the internal mail. The note read:

> Dear Rita,
> I've had to dash away. Thanks for the loan of the knife. (They were not Mr H's prints, thank goodness.) I haven't forgotten that I promised to tell you all about it.
> Charles
> PS I'd appreciate it if you didn't mention this to Mr H – it might not be good for my promotion prospects!!!

Or my breathing, I'd thought, as I folded it.

CHAPTER FOURTEEN

Hard physical exercise; that's what I needed. I retrieved the gardening tools from the back of the shed and spent the rest of the day digging the old vegetable patch. It looked better for it, but my hands were blistered and my back felt dodgy. That evening I hobbled to the nearest pub for a couple of pints. It's not my idea of a local, with its polystyrene beams and flickering electric candles. There were only four others in the place, all leaning on the one, short bar. They made little effort to move so I could be served. As I reached between them for my pint I accidentally let it drip on someone's portable phone. One of them was complaining that he'd had to drive the Rover all the way to Leeds to fill up, because that's where the company account was. I narrowly avoided puking down the back of his Pierre

Cardigan. It didn't work: next morning still found me drinking tea in the kitchen at four a.m.

I lunched in Whitby, after a three-hour drive, then went walkabout in the rain, looking for the address Longfellow had given me for Cakebread's flat. It was in an imposing Victorian terrace, on the north side, near Captain Cook's monument. I sat outside for over an hour, watching for comings and goings. Nobody came, nobody went. Whitby was as depressing as the weather, but without the possibility of changing in the near future. The front door of the building was not locked, so I entered and climbed the stairs. When I reached his door I took out the third key that had been in the envelope Gloria had given me. It wouldn't even go in the lock. If it had fitted I don't think I would have opened the door, but it would have been useful to know that I had the means to, at a more favourable time. Never mind, this wasn't the real purpose of my journey. I went back to the car and set off up the coast.

I'd scoured the Ordnance Survey maps and the only PM I found was a place called Port Mulgrave, near Staithes, to the north of Whitby, and only thirty miles from Teesside airport. Captain Diaz had suggested we ask ourselves why Cakebread flew to Teesside. I was working on the lines that the drugs were dropped to accomplices waiting in a boat. He'd be flying in unrestricted airspace, and could easily divert twenty miles out to sea. It'd been done before. Port Mulgrave looked the perfect spot to bring the booty ashore.

The east coast doesn't have the reputation of, say, Cornwall, as a hotbed of smuggling, but it happens. Not too long ago a major racket was exposed involving the importation of illegal immigrants, and recently a ton of cannabis was found on an oil rig service boat. The more I thought about it, the more I became convinced that I'd cracked the note's last riddle. 'Nineteenth-century port, used for exporting iron ore. Never commercially successful' was the only reference I'd been able to find in the library. It was time to investigate first-hand. In the car I had my old walking gear and a pair of binoculars; today I was an ornithologist.

It was mid-afternoon when I parked about a mile down the road from the turn-off to Port Mulgrave. The rain was coming down as if the second flood was already here. I changed into my waterproofs, stuffed the binocs down the front of my cagoule, and went for a walk. Half an hour later I arrived at the clifftop overlooking the port. There was a hotel that would have been a perfectly sensible place to park. The cliffs here are not like the ones at Bempton or Dover. Although the overall height might be just as great, they don't rise vertically from the sea. They slump against the land, at about forty-five degrees. Another noticeable difference is that they are not carved from chalk. Their chief component is mud.

A narrow path zigged and zagged down towards the broken little pier that jutted into the unwelcoming ocean. Skeins of rain flurried across the surface of the water. There were no buildings down there, just a couple of what looked like garden sheds, and a pair of boats dragged on to the shingle. I was hardly halfway down the path when two figures came out of one of the huts. I stopped and took out the binoculars. I had a good scan round, at nothing in particular, and proceeded downwards. I hadn't looked at the two men; I'd already noticed that they were carrying shotguns.

We met where the path levelled out. 'Afternoon! Not that it's a very good one,' I bellowed with enthusiasm.

They stood blocking my progress. 'Wouldn't go any further, if I was you,' one of them said. If Wales really does produce fine tenors, the East Riding should be famous for its baritones. This one sounded as if he gargled with bitumen.

'Oh, really. Why's that?' I asked.

'Shooting,' he stated. They were both wearing Barbour jackets that were pale with age, and the rain was running off their hats.

'Oh, thanks for the warning. What are you shooting?'

'Rabbits.'

'Hard luck on the rabbits,' I laughed. I stood looking around for a few moments, then pointed past them and said: 'Will it be safe if I just look for fossils for a minute or two, down near your boats?'

They exchanged glances, and the spokesman said: 'Aye, that should be all right.'

They followed me down. I told myself that this was

England, not Beirut, but I had to admit it was a good setting for a murder. They both went back into the shelter of the hut, but kept the door open, so they could watch me. I wandered up and down and kicked a few pebbles over. Once I took out my knife and squatted on my heels, closely examining nothing in particular. A squadron of guillemots came whirring over the wave-tops, as if on a suicidal torpedo run. I pulled out the binoculars and followed them until they vanished against the blackness of the rocks. It seemed a crazy place to build a port for the exporting of bulk cargo – they'd have to lug everything down the cliffs. But then I noticed the tunnel.

The cliffs were banked with scree comprised of shale, heaped up like mining spoil. Rusty rails ran back from the pier, and pointed up the scree towards the blanked-off entrance. The iron ore wasn't brought down the cliff; it was transported from inland by tunnel. I marvelled at the simple ingenuity of it: the tunnel would slope gently down, and the weight of the full wagons descending would pull the empty ones back to the top. Energy required, nil. I continued sweeping the binoculars, stopping here and there, but slowly drawing them towards the opening. I paused. The mouth was blocked off with a wall made of stone blocks. In the middle a stone had been left out, as if to allow some ventilation, but down at the bottom left-hand corner, partly concealed by scrub, was a bigger gap, large enough for a man to crawl through. Both openings were now sealed with breeze blocks. I continued the sweep, then put the binocs back down the front of my anorak.

The rain was even heavier than before. I stood gazing out to sea and took several long, deep breaths. Ah, wonderful! If nature had devised a better way to catch pneumonia, I'd yet to find it. I beat my fists twice against my chest, shouted 'Good afternoon' to the morons in the hut and set off briskly towards the cliff path. Out of the corner of my eye I could see that there was another, well-trodden path, leading up to the tunnel.

On the way down the mud had encroached up my legs until it reached my crotch. Going up, it made it to my armpits. Once I was back on the road the rain diluted it somewhat, but did little to improve my overall appearance. I couldn't have cared less, as I swung my arms jauntily on the way back to the car.

I had a lot of time to waste. I did some exploring in the car, heater at full blast to dry me out, and even managed a nap. It was well after opening time when I parked outside the Lobster Pot in Staithes. I'd chosen well, this was the pub that the old fishermen used. There weren't many of them, but it was a tiny place and their pipe smoke made the air so thick that the flies were hang-gliding. I leant on the corner of the bar with a half-pint and a packet of crisps. I was soon exchanging pleasantries with the landlord. Towards closing time, when most of the old-timers had stumbled away, he came to lean on my end of the bar. I bought us a Bell's each.

'Don't suppose you've a room vacant?' I asked. I'd seen the 'No vacancies' sign when I entered.

'Afraid not, sir. We've two small rooms, but an American family have taken them. Never guess what they're called.'

After a few seconds I said: 'Cook?'

'Correct. You could try the Cliff Hotel up the hill. Would you like me to ring them?'

'No, it's all right, thanks. I'll go home. I just had a fancy for getting quietly drunk on your whisky, then crawling upstairs to bed. It's a foul night outside.'

'I know what you mean. Have you far to go?'

'No, only to Malton. I've just had a day's birdwatching; probably have flu in the morning.'

He busied himself drying a few glasses. When he returned I said: 'How much fishing goes off, these days?'

'Virtually none,' he replied, 'just lobster-potting and some long-lining. It's a waste of time.'

'What about from Port Mulgrave? I had a strange experience there today.'

He looked interested, but not excessively so. 'What sort of experience?' he asked.

'Oh, nothing bad. I walked down the path and two blokes with shotguns warned me off. Said they were rabbiting, and I might get shot. It seemed funny weather to be rabbiting.'

He wandered round the room, collecting the ashtrays. Everybody else had left. I drained my glass.

'One for the road?' he enquired.

'No thanks; if I'm driving I'd better not.'

He came to stand next to me, and in a conspiratorial whisper said: 'The Lazenby brothers fished from Mulgrave. And their fathers. And their grandfathers. Last year they sold their boats, word has it, for ten times what they were worth. Bought a posh bungalow in Redcar and haven't been seen since. Some divers use the port now. You know what they're into, don't you?'

'Er, no.'

He lowered his voice even further, as if afraid that the walls might be listening. 'Wrecks.'

'Wrecks?' It wasn't quite what I was hoping for.

'Wrecks. War graves. There's dozens of 'em off this coast. And who knows what other things they're into?'

Other things; that sounded more like it. 'What other things?' I asked.

Just then the door burst open and Mr and Mrs Cook and their two offspring dashed in. They took off their raincoats and the landlord hung them somewhere to dry. The kids were packed off upstairs to brush their braces and go to bed, while Captain Cook and his mate settled down with a nightcap. I said my goodbyes and left. I had work to do.

I parked at the same place I had used earlier in the day, but this time I didn't don my waterproofs – they made too much noise when I walked in them. The steady rain had given way to the fine sort that just hangs suspended in the air, managing to soak your sheltered surfaces just as thoroughly as the top ones. Instead of walking up the road, past a string of houses, I cut directly across the fields. The night was blacker than a tomcat's soul. When I reached the clifftop I groped along the fence until I found the stile. I had my second pee, hoping that my bladder was responding to nervousness or overindulgence, and not incipient prostate trouble, and climbed over.

It was nearly impossible to keep to the path. Cattle grazed on the cliffside, and left numerous tracks that went off in different directions. I stared down at the ground, and placed my feet on the darkest patches I could see, sometimes with messy consequences. It took me a long time to reach the bottom. I did a left turn until I crossed the rails, then made another, up towards the tunnel entrance. The sheds were, thankfully, in darkness.

A hundred years of erosion had left the opening stranded several feet up. I did the last bit climbing on my hands and knees, pulling myself upwards with handfuls of grass. At last I made it on to a ledge at the entrance, and paused to regain my breath. Everything was as quiet as a tomb. The sea stretched out before me, still and lifeless, like southern beer. I took out a little torch and, cupping my hands round it, examined the opening. It was bigger than I had thought, but the breeze blocks weren't cemented in. I put the torch away and explored the joints with my fingertips. The topmost block had no weight on it. Quarter-inch by quarter-inch I worked it towards me until I was able to grip it and lift it out.

When I'd removed four I decided the gap was big enough. One by one I passed the loose blocks through the opening to the inside, then crawled through after them. Working by touch, I rebuilt the wall, slowly blocking off the pale patch of sky until the darkness was total. Then I switched on the torch.

It was a disappointment. The tunnel stretched away for about fifty yards, terminating in a fall of rubble that reached the roof. The first few yards were muddy, then it was firmer underfoot. The torchlight glinted on something in the mud, at the foot of the wall. It was a discarded condom, trodden into the ground after its brief moment of ecstacy. I couldn't imagine anybody going through what I had gone through to come in here for sex.

'Inconceivable,' I said to myself.

The dim light cast shadows at the far end. I walked towards them to investigate. A number of pallets were laid side by side, as if to form a dry base to stand something on. Alongside, roughly folded, was a large sheet of polythene, possibly used to protect the same something from drips from the roof. Whatever it had been, it wasn't here now. I closely examined everything, but failed to find anything incriminating. I felt certain that this was where they brought the stuff, but defence barristers usually had difficulty in accepting my word. I stood looking at the roof-fall for a minute or two, then turned and walked slowly towards the entrance.

As the torchlight swung up and down, the shiny white end of the condom winked at me. There was a machine in the pub near my house that sold flavoured ones. The banana had caught my imagination, and I'd wondered if the reason was because I liked bananas, or something more Freudian. When I reached the wall I bent down and examined the contraceptive with vicarious curiosity. I'd only ever seen the standard pink ones before. It was a different shape at the end, too . . .

It wasn't a condom; it was a glove. The thin, rubber type that surgeons wear. We keep a stock of similar ones, for if we have to handle certain items of evidence or search unsavoury prisoners, and the scene-of-crime officers carry them around with them. They're widely available, sold in DIY stores for yuppie decorators who don't want to get eau de nil on their cuffs. I took out my knife and carefully scraped the mud away. I pulled a plastic bag inside-out over my hand and gently picked the glove up, unfolding the bag around it. Maybe my journey had not been totally in vain, after all.

I dismantled the wall, crawled through and rebuilt it behind me. My boots had been slobbing about on my feet for a while, sucked down by the glutinous mud. What I didn't realise was that the weight of mud dragging on my bootlaces had pulled one of them undone. I dropped lightly off the ledge outside the tunnel, taking a quick step forward to regain my balance. Except that my foot didn't move because I was standing on the lace. I fell heavily, flat on my face, did a forward roll that would have earned a string of sixes for artistic interpretation, and slid fifteen feet on my back to the foot of the scree. A dog started barking.

CHAPTER FIFTEEN

I lay still for a few seconds, gathering my wits and my breath, then rolled sideways into the dense shadow of some bushes. The door of one of the sheds opened and a torch beam cleaved the darkness. The dog, a terrier, stood yapping at the night. I think it was as scared as I was. The beam scanned the cliffs, then went out. Thank God I'd rebuilt the wall. A voice said something to the dog and they both went back inside, closing the door behind them. I sat on the scree, my arms round my knees, staring at the shed for ten or fifteen minutes. When they'd had time to settle I silently made my way back to the cliff path.

Following the path upwards was easier, but by the time I reached the top I was wheezing like a leaky accordion. I had an old tracksuit in the car to change into, but I didn't bother. I carefully arranged it over the driving seat, to keep some of the mud off, and started for home. I was halfway across the North York Moors before my heart stopped trying to batter its way out of my rib cage.

The fingerprint people at city HQ work round the clock, so I went straight there. The sky was beginning to lighten as I pulled into the car park. I was dry by now, but caked in mud from head to foot, and had to show my ID to get past the front desk. The constable in Fingerprints viewed me and my evidence with scepticism.

'It's a bit of a mess,' he told me, unnecessarily, 'but we might find something. When you pull these gloves off they turn inside out, so the inside is now outside, andvcaked in mud. That's no good. If this was the first glove he pulled off, there'll be nothing on it. If, however, he pulled it off with his bare hand, we might be lucky.'

'You mean those prints would have been on the outside, which is now inside?'

'That's it.'

'So there's only a fifty-fifty chance of finding anything?'

He looked at the glove with disdain. 'Less than that, I'm afraid, Inspector. How urgent is it?'

'It's not desperately urgent, but it is important. I want your best efforts, we're talking about murder.'

He made notes on a pro forma pad, recording the

time, my name, et cetera. 'Right, sir.' He poked at the glove with the blunt end of his pencil and dislodged same of the mud. 'I think what we'll do is let it dry out, then give it the superglue treatment. That works best on rubber. Then we'll have a look at it under the ultraviolet. I'll have to wait until the fume cabinet's available, though. As you know, we're run off our feet – will Tuesday, possibly Wednesday, be OK?'

'Fine. I've some other work here too. Could that be ready at the same time please?'

He found the reference and made a note. 'Right, boss, will do. You look as if you've been run down by an avalanche, do you want a coffee?'

I smiled for what seemed the first time in ages, and said: 'It was only a small avalanche. No thanks, I'm going home.'

I showered and went to bed. I fell asleep in minutes. An hour and a half later the doorbell rang. I staggered across to the window and peeked out. Down below, the morning sun was reflecting off the shining pate of Dr Evans. I let him in.

When he saw the dressing gown he said: 'Sorry, Charlie, have I got you out of bed?'

'No,' I lied. 'I was just about to have a shower. Want a cup of tea?'

'No thanks. I was nearby, so I thought I'd call to see how you were.'

'Fine, Sam, I'm fine. Wasn't sleeping too well at first, but I dropped off OK – er – last night.'

'Good, good. How have you been spending your time?'

'Oh, this and that. I've done some painting, dug the garden. Yesterday I went to the coast, took your advice.'

The doctor stared at me, his eyelids blinking at regular, two-second intervals. After ten blinks he said, incredulously: 'You took my advice? You actually took my advice? You had a day at the coast?'

I gave him a grin. 'You were right, Sam,' I declared, 'there is life outside the police force.' I went back to bed with a smile on my face, but sleep had fled for the day.

I declared myself fit and well and resumed work Monday morning. The latest reports were placed in the file and I found Nigel's efforts in there. He'd discovered a comprehensive list of associated companies, and several names with records. He'd then looked up all the companies involved with these names. It was quite a tangled web. Fires and burglaries, usually just after a major delivery, were hazards that seemed to strike their warehouses with uncommon regularity. They had an awful lot of bad luck. Nigel had left a note saying he was off having a word with the insurance companies. Well done.

Mike Freer rang. Parker was now in the pen, but he wasn't writing home. They'd picked him up on the M62, the Porsche loaded to the gunwales with boxes of wraps, each one containing a twenty-five-pound fix.

Estimated street value, about fifteen thousand pounds; his profit, three and a half grand. Not bad for an evening's work. His house and several others had been raided, too. Findings included a crack factory and the first ice seen on the patch.

'We've done our bit,' said Mike. 'Now you boys can stand by for the backlash.'

Drug prices are controlled strictly by supply and demand. Ready availability creates a big market. A major supplier was now out of circulation, so the prices would soar. A user who paid for it by thieving, desperate for a fix, would have to step up his work-rate. That was the backlash.

Wednesday morning Fingerprints rang. 'It's Sergeant Miller, Fingerprints. Your photos are ready. Do you want us to post them to you?'

'Great, thanks. No, I'll collect them. Did you get anything at all from the glove.'

'Nothing spectacular, but better than it could have been. Several fragments, mainly from the thumb. All the fingers had turned inside out when the glove was removed, but the tip of the thumb hadn't. It'd got a bit smudged, though. It matches the other one, but it wouldn't stand up in court.'

'Eh? Which other one?'

'This other stuff you wanted. These contact prints. Says here they're off a paperknife. Weren't you expecting them to be the same?'

A sensation was welling up in my loins similar to the

time I accidentally wandered into the wrong dressing room at grammar school, after being clean bowled first ball, and realised that nobody had noticed me. The sixth-form netball team were just changing for a match. It was the most wonderful hundred and twenty seconds of my entire twelve years. I stared at the phone. Had I misheard him?'

'Sergeant Miller,' I said. 'Spell it out slowly. Are you saying that the prints in the glove match the ones on the knife?'

'Yessir. As far as we can tell they're from the same person.'

'You mean . . . you're convinced, but a jury wouldn't be?'

'That's it. There are several small, smudged impressions on the glove, which match with the ones on the knife, but nothing big enough to give us sixteen points of similarity in one dab.'

'Which the law requires.'

'To make it conclusive, yes.'

'How many points have we?'

'Three, maybe four, plus a couple elsewhere.'

'Mmm. You reckon it's him, though?'

'No doubt about it.'

'Great, I'm grateful for what you've told me. Any chance of a report for me by five o'clock, the full works?'

'No problem, Mr Priest. In fact, for you, four o'clock.'

I put the phone down, punched the air with my fists and gave a rebel yell. Nigel popped his head round the door, a big smile illuminating his tanned face.

'Won the pools, boss?'

I thumped the palm of my hand. 'We've got the bastard, Nigel, we've got the bastard.'

'Who, Cakebread?'

I calmed down, stared at him and shook my head. 'Sorry, Nigel, I can't tell you; not just yet. But I will do, soon. Do you know if Mr Wood's in?'

Gilbert was in an SDO's meeting at city HQ. I asked the secretary to get a message to him to ring me, pronto. He came out of the meeting straight away.

'I can't tell you anything on the phone,' I said, 'but there's been a development. I need to see you, soon as poss. What time will your meeting finish?'

'Are you talking about your friend in Lancashire?'

'Yes.'

'We try to finish about three thirty. Do you want me to come back to the office? I usually sneak off home.'

'No. Do you mind coming to my house? I'll get off a bit early.'

'OK, Charlie, I'll be there four thirtyish.'

'Thanks, boss.'

I made a pot of tea and struck out the biscuits. 'I'll be looking like tea and biscuits soon,' grumbled Gilbert, going straight for the chocolate. 'What's it all about?'

I told him about my trip to Port Mulgrave, and what I'd found in the tunnel. He listened with pained resignation. When I'd finished I slid the Fingerprints report over to him. After he'd had a chance to study it I told him: 'I know it's not conclusive – a good defence lawyer would tear it to shreds; but statistically, that glove was worn either by Chief Constable Hilditch or a Mongolian witch doctor in the tenth century. A court would give him the benefit of the doubt, but I know who my money's on.' I could feel my voice and my temper rising as I said the words.

We sat in silence for a while, then Gilbert said: 'So what are you going to do?'

'I don't know; it's out of my league. I suppose I should go to either the Home Secretary or HMI. I'd hoped you might have some ideas.'

'That prat in the striped shirt would sell the story to the tabloids.'

'Probably,' I sighed. 'So it's the inspectorate?'

'What if he just clammed up and denied everything?' asked Gilbert.

Suddenly I didn't feel so confident. 'He'd be retired on ill health, and I'd work out my time helping schoolkids across the street,' I answered.

'Correct. They'd say you were tired and emotional. What about seeing him?'

'It'd crossed my mind. He's not likely to break down and confess, though, is he? Or are you talking about a deal?'

'Possibly. How would you feel if he saved his own skin by grassing on the others?'

'Unhappy.'

'So would I; we could end up as incriminated as him.'

It was the first time Gilbert had used the plural; I'd been thinking I was in this on my own. I went into the kitchen to replenish the teapot.

After a few moments Gilbert shouted after me: 'How well do you know him?'

'Hilditch? Hardly at all,' I yelled back.

I poured us both another cup.

'I know him a bit better than that,' he said. After a while he went on: 'What if I went to see him?'

I felt relieved. Gilbert's responses so far were a disappointment to me. 'I'd feel better, but what's changed?'

'Nothing, but he knows you're conducting a vendetta against Cakebread. He'd be on the defensive. I'll just wave the file under his nose and say we've found his dabs in a cave used by drug smugglers. See what his reaction is.'

'It's a tunnel; they're not the Pirates of Penzance. Sounds good to me, though. What if he suggests a deal?'

'It's your case, Charlie. Who are you really after?'

'I don't know, but if he wants to talk turkey, the price is a shedful. I'll leave it to you.'

Gilbert finished his tea. 'I'll take this,' he said, holding up the file. 'I'll ring him from home, then let you know what's happening.'

'Cheers.'

I don't normally pass on the dirty work, but I was grateful to let this one go. It wasn't as cut and dried as I'd first thought. Gilbert rang me at seven.

'I'm just setting off. I'm seeing him at eight. He's moved to bloody Harrogate.'

'I've been thinking, Gilbert,' I said. 'Do you think you ought to have a driver with you?'

'No, you know the score. Wait up for me, I'll call in on my way back.'

An hour there, an hour back, an hour talking. That came to ten o'clock. Say eleven. I cooked a meal fit for a condemned man and hardly touched it. It passed the first hour, though. The next four weren't filled so easily. I tried luxuriating in the bath, with a couple of cans of beer, but the beer warmed almost as quickly as the water cooled. It had seemed a good idea. I watched some bad TV, then went into the garage to talk to the E-type. The dust sheets slid to the floor like a neglige off a beautiful woman. I ran my fingers along the curves, then unlocked the door and slid in. I sat there for a long time, thinking about people I'd known, messes I'd made. I wondered how much it would sell for.

It was after midnight when I went to bed, annoyed that Gilbert hadn't rung. Earlier, I almost called Molly, to see if he was home, but I realised that would only make her as worried as I was. I was still awake when I heard a car in the road, followed by the doorbell ringing. I knew straight away, from Gilbert's pallor, that something had gone wrong. I poured him a stiff Glenfiddich, with a very small one for myself. He downed his in one.

'Hey, this isn't Japanese muck, y'know,' I told him, pouring another.

'Cheers, Charlie, I needed that.'

When he'd composed himself I asked: 'How'd it go?'

He sat looking at his hands, as if wondering where to begin, then said: 'Bad, Charlie, really bad. I'd made it clear on the phone that he'd better see me. I think he had an idea what it was about. His wife was out, at a meeting, or something. I told him about the tunnel and the fingerprints. He said: "It's that Priest, isn't it, making wild accusations?" I said: "No, it's me, and there's nothing wild about that." I showed him one of the photos, one taken from the paperknife. I didn't bother explaining. He stared at it and started trembling.'

I had a sip of my drink and waited for him to continue.

'I asked him how well he knew Cakebread; thought I'd give him an opening. He didn't answer. After a while he said he needed a drink, did I mind if he fetched one? He stood up and went into the kitchen. While he was gone I had a look round the room, like you do. It's cluttered with all that stuff you see in the supplements; mass-produced special editions, as if he didn't know what to spend his money on. Then I saw the drinks cabinet in the corner. You'll never guess what he drinks.'

'What?' I asked, remembering the Macallan I'd seen in his office.

'Macallan,' Gilbert replied.

'Well at least he's got taste in whisky,' I said.

'I walked over and opened the door to the kitchen,' he continued. 'He was standing at the far end, with his back to me. It's a long room. I said: "Mr Hilditch," and he turned round. He was holding a shotgun, with the end of it in his mouth.'

'Oh, no!' I groaned.

'He just looked at me for a moment, then pulled the trigger.'

'Jesus Christ!' I said, putting my head in my hands.

'Do you mind if I have another?'

'Of course not.' I gestured towards the bottle. 'Help yourself, I'll run you home.'

'That wasn't the end of it. I was on the phone, trying to get some sense out of the local wallies, when I heard a car outside. It was Mrs Hilditch. I went out and locked the door behind me. She became hysterical. We had to drag her into a neighbour's. I think that was the worst part.'

I didn't have anything to offer, so I sat in silence. Gilbert took a sip and said: 'I'll say one thing, Charlie: it was bloody quick. He was dead before he hit the ceiling.'

CHAPTER SIXTEEN

Another aspect of the backlash caused by our successes with the heroin pushers was that raids on chemists' shops increased. The user who can't obtain a regular fix of his chosen pick-me-up has a pharmacopoeia of alternatives. The ingenuity of the desperate addict, or the greedy pusher, knows no limits. Drugs that were discovered or invented to induce sleep, kill pain or calm the raging mind were soon found to produce very different effects when taken in massive doses, or mixed into cocktails.

The barbiturates are the most favoured alternatives to heroin. They also cause more deaths than all of the others put together – except booze and fags, of course. The problem is that the fatal dose is not many times greater than the effective dose. As the taker builds up tolerance he has to pump in more and more to get the same buzz. Unfortunately the lethal level does not increase in the same way. One day the two lines cross and another dopehead takes a one-way trip. We find them hunched in squalid bedsits or sprawled in public urinals, choked on their own vomit. It's a long way from that first, laughing drag on a joint at someone's party.

As soon as we recognised an increase in raids on pharmacies we visited all those on our patch and advised them to improve their security. Some chemists were amazingly complacent, but we eventually reversed the trend. This led to an increase in domestic burglaries, and then armed robberies. We felt as if we were standing in the middle of the Serengeti Plain, waving our arms about, trying to stop the wildebeest migrating. Serious violence was hiding in the long grass. Fortunately, the figures soon settled down to something like the norm, but it wasn't due to our efforts: it was because supplies began to filter through again and the price dropped.

After long delays due to adjournments to allow for 'further investigations', the inquests into the deaths of O'Hagan and Hilditch were held. 'Expedient' is the kindest thing I can say about the first verdict. He'd been lawfully killed by a police officer who was not named, as it was not in the public's interest to do so. It wasn't in my interest, either, so I didn't argue. He'd fired the first shot, and suffered the consequences. Nobody mentioned that he didn't have a second.

If this was a whitewash, Hilditch got the full interior decorator treatment, complete with flock wallpaper. He was an overly conscientious officer, at the pinnacle of his profession, who had suffered a breakdown due to overwork. The rising crime figures, and his inability to stem them due to lack of resources, had caused him great distress. The Coroner said he'd borne an intolerable burden, and the Force would have difficulty replacing him. I wasn't there; I just cut the bits out of the paper and put them in the file.

Superintendent Wood had given evidence to Her Majesty's Inspectorate, and they interviewed me. They took copies of everything in the Picasso file. Nothing spectacular happened, but over the next few months and years jobs would be shuffled around, strangers from afar appointed in key positions, and traps set to snare the renegades. All most of us would ever know about it would be the odd, unexpected resignation.

We held our own inquests, of course. After hearing the shots, Sparky had come running into the bedroom, not knowing what to expect. Nigel, who wasn't armed, had followed close behind. We'd been lucky this time, but under different circumstances it could have turned into a three-nil defeat. Gilbert gave me carte blanche to nail Cakebread.

* * *

All Monday mornings should be wet and foggy, particularly in November. This one set the standard for the others to be designed around. I'd just fired a rubber band at the window to see if I could make the raindrops run down faster when Nigel poked his head round the door.

'Can I have a word, boss?' he asked.

I swivelled my chair back to the desk. 'No, I haven't heard anything.'

'It's not about promotion,' he said, coming in. 'I was wondering if you watched *Northern News* on Saturday?'

'No, I didn't. My cup of tea was going cold, so I watched that instead.' The onset of winter brings out the jollity in me.

'Pity. You won't have heard, then, that Percy the cat has turned up.'

I was worried about Nigel: he'd adopted a role model, and I wasn't sure that I approved. 'Close the door,' I told him, resignedly. 'Sit down and tell me all about Percy the cat.'

'Well,' he began, hardly able to contain his enthusiasm, 'apparently, last Thursday, there was a fire in a small warehouse, near the middle of Oldfield. Nothing special, didn't make the local news. The only casualty was Percy the cat, who was thought to have perished in the blaze. In fact, they blamed him for knocking over a heater and starting it.'

'Fascinating,' I said. It was marginally more riveting than racing raindrops on the window.

Nigel went on: 'Well, on Saturday, to everybody's relief, Percy turned up without a singe. That's a story. Made *Northern News* and an interview with Linda Lovett.'

'So he's not a ginger cat,' I suggested. 'No, white. Why?'

'Never mind. Tell me more. I presume there is more, or are this feline's exploits the sum total of your reason for disturbing my morning?'

Nigel was enjoying himself. He said: 'When I saw it on the news, I couldn't help wondering who Percy's master was, so this morning I've made a few enquiries.'

'And . . .'

'And he was Chief Mouser for Brian Wheatley Developments.'

I leant forward in the chair. 'You mean they owned the warehouse?'

'Yes.'

Well done, Nigel. I almost smiled, until I remembered that I'd smiled once already that morning. No point in becoming hysterical.

'Is this the same Wheatley who's Breadcake's sidekick?' I asked.

'Yes, boss. I've checked our list of his companies, and it's there.'

I nodded my approval. 'Good work, Nigel. Now let's have a think about our next move.' Then I added: 'On second thoughts, you've probably worked it all out. What do you suggest?'

'Nothing much, really. The building was in an old area of town, probably not worth much. The site may be valuable. Then there's the contents. It would be interesting to see what he's claiming for.'

'How do we find that?'

'From the insurance company.'

'And who tells us who they are?' I asked. Nigel knew as well as I did that if at all possible we wanted to avoid involving the Oldfield police.

'The fire brigade? Presumably they'd have to confirm that the place had burnt down.'

'It's worth a try. See what you can find out.'

Nigel left and I turned back to the raindrops. The window was covered with new ones, nowhere near as interesting as the ones I'd watched earlier. Here we go again, I thought. Where would this avenue lead us? Was I really conducting a vendetta against Cakebread, as some people believed? I was convinced that I wasn't, but I was biased. 'Keep shuffling the pieces,' I told myself, 'then, one day, they'll all fall into place.'

It was lunch time when Nigel came back. He had a look on his face like Percy must have done when Linda Lovett embraced him.

'Any success?' I asked.

'Mmm . . . The local fire station is in Rochdale Road, Oldfield. I spoke to the station officer and they have confirmed details of the fire to RDW Insurance. Their claims manager, in Manchester, is a Mr Rollison.

He's already had a claim from Wheatley and he smells a rat.'

'He's not letting the grass grow under his feet, is he? What's the claim for?'

Nigel paused for maximum effect, then told me: 'A cool three hundred thousand pounds. Two hundred and twenty-five of which are for the contents. Wheatley claims that the place was stuffed to the rafters with antique furniture.'

I shook my head with disbelief. 'How many times do the prats think they can get away with it?' I wondered aloud. 'So what's happening next?'

'Mr Rollison has asked Wheatley to see him this afternoon. Wheatley claims to have an itemised list of everything that was in the place, and Rollison has asked him for it.'

I allowed myself that second smile. 'We need that list,' I said.

'In the morning,' replied Nigel. 'I've an appointment with Rollison at nine o'clock.'

'Get your coat,' I told him, rising to my feet. 'It's dinner time. I'll buy you a Tomlinson's pork pie in the Golden Scrotum.'

I went to Manchester with Nigel. I didn't want to steal his glory, but I'd contacted the fire brigade and arranged to visit the burnt-out ruin afterwards, with Sub Officer Des Brown, of Green Watch. Or was it the other way round? To say Mr Rollison met us with enthusiasm is a bit like saying that Dante was quite pleased to see Beatrice. He pumped our hands and ordered coffee.

'Do you think it was arson?' he eagerly asked.

'No idea,' I replied, before Nigel could open his mouth. We were both studying copies of the list that Mr Rollison had ready for us. 'We think some of these items may have – er – originated in our area.'

'You mean they were stolen!' he declared.

'Now, now, Mr Rollison, that's not what I said. Let's just say we're . . . interested.'

The lists contained brief descriptions of items of furniture, date of purchase, name of dealer or auction house and price paid. Appended to it were photocopies of all the receipts.

'It's a very comprehensive list,' observed Nigel. 'He obviously didn't keep the receipts in the warehouse.'

'Did you see the originals of the receipts?' I asked.

'Oh, yes,' replied Rollison. 'He brought the originals, but wouldn't let me keep them, which is reasonable enough. I had them copied here. They looked genuine to me.'

We finished our coffees and thanked Mr Rollison for his cooperation, recommending that he didn't rush to pay out until he'd heard from us.

'What do you suggest I tell the investigation department, Inspector?' he asked.

'The truth, Mr Rollison,' I replied loftily. 'It's always the best policy.'

On the way to the fire station I asked Nigel if he knew anything about antiques.

'No, not much,' he said, with characteristic understatement, adding: 'My mother has a couple of nice pieces.'

'Really?' I replied, stifling a smirk. 'In that case, from now on you're the station's expert.'

We'd had the foresight to take our own wellington boots. Des Brown supplied us with yellow plastic safety helmets and took us in a station van to the warehouse. It was a narrow building, four storeys high, in a long terrace that had been purpose-built for another industry in another age. The ground floor windows and door were boarded up, and black streaks of soot reached upwards from them. First impressions were that it had been an inferno.

'You were lucky to contain it to the one building,' I observed.

'Yeah,' Des replied. 'Fortunately the ones on either side are empty, so we were able to get into them and cool the walls. These places are well built structurally, but there's a lot of timber inside. They're a headache to us, but the whole area's scheduled for redevelopment. The sooner the better.'

He'd taken a jemmy from the car boot and was levering off the boards from the door. When they were removed he went through and we followed. The first floor had vanished completely. Above that were just blackened ribs to indicate where the others had been.

The roof was intact apart from one small patch where the sky was visible. The air was still hung with smoke, and when you looked up the light from the empty windows created a cathedral effect.

'Where did it start, Des?' I asked.

'We don't know. The story is that there was a small office over there, where you can see the stairs were. It was stuffed with cardboard boxes and other combustibles . . .'

'Like cans of paraffin?' I interrupted.

'Possibly,' he replied, with a smile, 'but plastic bottles leave less evidence. Anyway, they think they may have gone home that evening and left the electric fire on. The cat was roaming around . . . et cetera, et cetera. It's a good story; we can't fault it.'

'Did your forensic people find anything?'

''Fraid not. Too much water damage.'

I gazed at the floor with dismay. It was a tangle of charred joists, partly submerged in black slurry. I gestured towards Nigel with my hand. 'Nigel's our antiques expert,' I explained. 'OK, Nigel, tell us what we're looking for.'

Nigel took a moment to gather his breath and his thoughts, then began: 'Well, most antique furniture, and this was furniture, is held together by glue and well made joints. The non-combustible parts are the fittings, such as hinges, handles and escutcheons. These were usually made of brass, and should have survived the blaze. Other decorative features might be made from marble, glass or . . .'

'Right,' I interrupted, 'let's see what we can find.' I kicked my feet in the mess, feeling for anything small and solid. It was a hopeless task and a difficult situation. We were trespassing on another force's territory, which made it impossible for me to call in a search party, and we were looking for something that we didn't really want to find. The temptation was to make a desultory search, find nothing and regard it as success.

Des saved the day. He was grinning broadly when he announced: 'I've an idea; how does this sound? We've some job-experience kids with us this week, all said they want to be firemen. It's a pain in the backside finding things for them to do – non-stop questions all day long. I could send them down here this afternoon, with a supervisor, and tell them to sift everything metallic out of that lot. Would that be a help?'

We accepted the offer like a banana republic dictator accepts a medal. In return we offered Des his lunch, but were pleased when he declined. We cleaned up in the fire station, and after a quick mug of tea and a laugh with Green Watch stormed back over the Tops to our own side of the lines.

An auction house in Leeds had supplied one of the expensive pieces on the claim. I sent Nigel on a preliminary recce to see them. If the search of the ashes showed that there had been some valuable stuff in the building then we were barking up the wrong tallboy. But if our instincts were right, we had no time to waste.

I wrote a brief report and spent the afternoon shifting paperwork. Much of it was the usual comical stuff: vernacular accounts of the exploits of our clients, complete with expletives. Some of it wasn't funny at all, just part of the endless procession of the sad, the mad and, occasionally, the bad that passes through our hands. Sparky came in, looking weary. He'd been interviewing witnesses at an unsuccessful bank robbery.

'Any luck, Dave?' I ventured.

'Fantastic,' he declared. 'He was black, or maybe white; between five feet four and six feet, and possibly walks with a limp. He's wearing a very distinctive coat: one side of it is leather and the other is an anorak.'

'That narrows it down. Tell me, do you know what an escutcheon is?'

'No, Charlie, but I'd have it looked at if I were you.'

Nigel arrived just before five. 'I saw Mr Somerby himself,' he told me. 'He's a lot younger than I expected; must be the son. He was amazingly helpful and open. He remembered the escritoire – it's a writing desk – because they'd had it in for a quite a while. They were trying to sell it for an old lady. It was a beautiful item but her reserve was too high. They'd put it through auction a couple of times before without it moving.'

'Did he say what the reserve was?' I asked. 'Yes, seven and a half thousand. When Wheatley started bidding Mr Somerby recognised him. Apparently he'd been going round the sales for over a year, buying the best items, often at top prices. Mr Somerby said that when he started bidding for the escritoire he couldn't believe his luck. The last genuine bid was at three grand, then Wheatley joined in. Somerby took him up to the reserve, then knocked it down to him. I was staggered when he admitted that.'

'So Mr Somerby did the auctioneering himself?'

'Yes. Sorry, boss, didn't I say?'

'Never mind. Anything else?'

'Well, yes.' He hesitated, then went on: 'Because he'd been so frank with me I showed him the list. He remembered several of the pieces; said they were all fine items. But they didn't . . . coalesce was the word he used.'

'Coalesce? What did he mean by that?'

'He meant that there was no rhyme or reason behind his buying, no pattern to it. Wheatley wasn't going to make a quick profit, because he paid top prices; he wasn't furnishing a house, because who needs four commodes; he wasn't forming a collection, because they were all from different periods . . . and so forth.'

'I get the message. Mr Somerby sounds useful to know. Hope you pointed out that we're only acting on suspicions, so far.'

'Never fear, boss. Then he showed me some of the things in their next sale. Told me the reserves on one or two that caught my eye. I might make a small investment with him after next payday.'

'Sounds like he's a good salesman. Fireman Des hasn't rung. I'll call him in the morning. C'mon, let's have an early night for a change.' I had a feeling that it might be our last for a while.

Des's call dragged me out of the morning briefing, before I'd had a chance to say my piece. 'You've a good job,' he declared. 'Rang you last night but you'd already gone.'

'Home for a snatched bite, Des. We don't have the luxury of three-shift cover like you. How did the kids go on?'

'Great!' I could hear him chuckling at the memory. 'We gave them oilskins, and they came back looking like black slugs. Had to hose them down in the yard.'

I smiled at the picture. 'What did they find?' I asked. 'Any escutcheons?'

'Not a one. I've two buckets here, filled with all sorts of bits and pieces, but nothing that looks antique.'

'Can you tell what they are?'

'Yes,' he replied. 'Hundreds of nails, out of the floorboards; quite a lot of hinges – the type used on modem kitchen units; a few handles made from aluminium or monkey metal; steel drawer sliders, that sort of stuff.'

'All MFI rather than Chippendale.'

'Exactly. What do you want me to do with it?'

'Any chance of a brief report, saying what you've just told me?' I ventured, pushing my luck.

'No problem,' he replied.

'Great,' I declared. 'In that case, if you don't hear otherwise from me in a day or two, you can chuck 'em in the skip.'

I thanked him for his help and promised to let him know the outcome. So far, over the months, I'd promised several people that I'd keep them informed. It was a tool I used to good effect: they gave me information, I satisfied their natural curiosity. It was a fair exchange. When the time came I'd run through the list and pay my debts. One of the unmentioned penalties suffered by the law-breaker is that he loses his right to privacy. His misdemeanours become public currency. Tough turds.

'So what we need to know,' I told Nigel, when I found him, 'is where are the antiques now?'

'Abroad,' he said.

I'd decided that was the best bet myself. 'Expand,' I ordered.

'Some of the pieces are quite well known, at least locally. The further away they are off-loaded, the safer it is.'

'Australia?'

'Maybe not that far. America's a better market. If he sells them over there at a small profit, and gets paid out by the insurers, he won't have done too bad, will he?'

'Then we'd better frustrate his efforts, hadn't we?' I pulled the Yellow Pages directory out of my drawer and slid it across to Nigel. 'There are fifty-two entries under Shipping Agents in there, I've just counted them. One for every week of the year, except you haven't got that long. Give them all a ring and see who's done business with Brian Wheatley Developments lately.'

Nigel's face fell. 'It'll take all week, boss,' he stated.

'Nonsense. Just pray that they're all computerised. You could always give your friend the auctioneer . . . I've forgotten his name . . .'

'Mr Somerby.'

'That's right, Somerby. Why not give him a ring, see if he thinks we're on the right lines. He might have a suggestion about who has experience in transporting antiques. What was it you were thinking of buying from him?'

'A couple of paperweights, by a French maker called Baccarat. It's my parents' thirtieth anniversary soon; I thought they'd make a decent present.'

'Mmm, they sound nice. Give him a ring, see what he says. All in the third person, of course: no names. Then offer him twenty percent less than he's asking for the paperweights.'

'Right, boss. Can I use your office?'

'Sure. Tell you what, I'll take Jeff Caton off what he's doing and let him help you. Fill him in with the details. I'll be upstairs, somewhere.'

Young Caton was on a futile mission knocking on doors at the Sylvan Fields housing estate, asking deaf and blind people if they'd seen or heard anything. He was glad to come in from the rain. I caught up with Gilbert and told him what we were doing.

As soon as I was able to off-load most of the other pressing cases, by a combination of delegation or simply placing them back at the bottom of the heap, I went out to do some investigating of my own. One of the auction houses on the list of suppliers had been burgled about ten years previously, and I'd handled the enquiry. I decided to renew my acquaintance with them.

The old gentleman who ran the place, Mr Oliphant, was still there, looking appropriately older and frailer than before.

'They'll have to shoot me to get rid of me,' he said, after I'd reintroduced myself. 'I don't do any auctioneering now, but I like to be surrounded by all these beautiful objects. The trouble with being in the business is that you don't make anything your own. Everything has a price, everything is for sale. My house is filled with bric-a-brac, but the good stuff goes under the hammer, I'm afraid.'

'That's business, Mr Oliphant,' I replied. 'Sentimentality is a luxury neither of us can afford.'

'Quite, quite. Now, how can I help you?'

I produced the list that Wheatley had supplied, and read from it: 'Do you remember selling this item? It's an early Victorian mahogany drum table, inlaid with marquetry in a geometric design.' I told him the price paid and the date of the sale.

'Oh, yes,' he replied immediately, 'I remember it well. It was a superb piece of workmanship. It was perfect, except that someone had started writing a letter on it and pressed too hard, leaving an imprint. All the dealers said this ruined it, and fifteen thousand was way over the top, but I disagreed. I thought it added to the charm of the piece, but not many share my sensibilities. Anyway, this chap Wheatley obviously agreed with me, so he bought it.'

'I don't suppose you've a catalogue with a photograph or a fuller description, have you?'

'Why, of course. Why didn't I think of that?' He rose unsteadily to his feet and made his way over to a bookcase. 'What did you say the date of the sale was?' he asked.

I told him, and in a few moments he produced the appropriate catalogue and found the page for me. I was studying it in a noncommittal way, wondering how else I would have used fifteen grand, when Mr Oliphant enquired: 'Is there a problem with it, Inspector? Has it been stolen?'

'Yes,' I answered, 'it's been stolen.' Technically, I suppose it had. 'This writing,' I continued, 'was it possible to read what it said?'

'Yes, but it wasn't anything enlightening or salacious, I'm afraid. It just said Dear . . . I think it was William.

That was impressed into the marquetry, then it ran on to the mahogany and became too faint to read. I like to think it was written by a young lady, too distraught to realise what she was doing.'

'You're a romantic, Mr Oliphant. Tell me one other thing. Which shipping companies would you recommend to export a collection of antiques?'

CHAPTER SEVENTEEN

Nigel and Jeff beat me to it. When I arrived back they were beaming like they'd been invited to be guest speakers at a nymphomaniacs' convention. Nigel gave me a thumbs-up.

'You were right, boss,' he told me. 'From now on, I'm going to listen to everything you say.'

'Go on,' I prompted.

'Well, I offered him twenty percent less than the reserve, and we settled for fifteen, all thanks to you.'

'Great. Did you say they were Baccarats?'

'That's right. Why?'

'They've got them in Pricefighter, at four quid for a box of six. They look very nice. Anything else?'

'Er, yes, one other thing. A shipping agent called Big Ocean Transport picked up six crates of furniture from

Brian Wheatley Developments five weeks ago. They were sent down to Southampton and packed into a container. From there they set sail last week on a boat called *Alpha Carrymaster,* bound for the Big Apple.'

'You mean New York?'

'Yes, boss. We now know all about cargo manifests, customs papers and carnets. Apparently the agents handle everything.'

Cocky sod. I drummed my fingers on the desk and gathered my thoughts. Big Ocean were on the list Mr Oliphant had suggested.

'When do they arrive in New York?' I asked.

'Saturday morning, all being well.'

I drummed and thunk some more. 'Where's the *Alpha* whatsitsname registered?'

Nigel's smile slipped. Got him. 'Never asked, boss. Does it matter?'

'Yes, it could be important. Have you got a passport?'

'A passport?'

'Yes, a passport. A thin book with your photo inside. Red now, but the proper ones were dark blue.'

'Yes, boss. Why?'

'What about you, Jeff?'

'You bet!' he replied with enthusiasm.

Jeff Caton was every bit as competent as Nigel, but under his shadow in the personality stakes. In many ways he was more reliable, but lacked Nigel's occasional flair. They were a good combination.

'Someone ought to go identify the loot,' I explained, 'but first, we need to know what we are looking for.' I produced the photo of the Victorian table that Mr Oliphant had given me.

'This is item six on Wheatley's list. We can further pin it down by some writing that's been imprinted either here or here, near the middle of a short side. We need more information like that, relating to three or four other pieces. See what you can find. Go together, but don't mess about: we've no time to waste. Meanwhile I'll see if I can raise permission for you to go over to the States.'

They were out of the office and down the stairs quicker than a Big Freddie's Steakburger gives you indigestion.

Superintendent Wood wasn't in, so I bypassed him. As the cost of two fares to America wouldn't come out of his budget, it seemed reasonable to assume he wouldn't mind. I needed permission to go ahead from an Assistant Chief Constable, so I rang Trevor Partridge.

Not long ago he'd been after my scalp, but Hilditch's suicide had put a more favourable complexion on our relationship. Now he was feeling aggrieved because he didn't land a promotion in the ensuing shuffle, but that was hardly my fault. He asked me how I was, listened to what I said, appreciated the hurry and gave me the OK. Thanks, Trev.

The North American Tourist office in Leeds wasn't

quite as accommodating, but I laid it on good and thick, and convinced them that there really was a conspiracy to assassinate Mickey Mouse that only we could foil. They eventually found places for Nigel and Jeff on the Friday morning flight from Manchester. I think the deal was that they had to help serve the meals, but I didn't mind. Today was Wednesday. I remembered that the pubs are open on a Wednesday round here, so I turned out the light and went to one.

Interpol have an office in London. I rang them early next morning. I rang them again a little later, after they'd arrived. They were interested and helpful.

'What authority do my men need,' I asked, 'and can you find me a contact for them?'

'All they need is authority from the local chief. We'll arrange that. We'll have to come back to you with a contact. Do you know where the boat is registered?'

'Yes, Monrovia.' I'd done my homework.

'OK. In that case it's important not to touch the stuff until it's on the dock. While it's on the ship it's out of our, or the American, jurisdiction. Stay there, we won't be long.'

They weren't. 'Right, Inspector Priest, here's what's happening. Your boys contact Lieutenant Tony diPalma, at 120th Precinct HQ. That's Staten Island.

They look after the docks. We'll have somebody there, too. They want to hit the receiver at their end, so the suggestion is, if the identifications are positive, you liaise directly with diPalma and coordinate the raids. Is that acceptable to you?'

I had a choice? 'Sure, that's fine,' I told him. 'Can you give me a number for diPalma?'

Suddenly the feeling hit me that I'd put Nigel and Jeff into something really heavy. They'd made one decent identification yesterday afternoon, and had gone straight on to the job this morning. I'd spoken to them both on the phone last night, and told them to pack a suitcase. I walked wearily up the stairs to Gilbert's office and informed him of what I'd done on his behalf.

'What was Partridge's attitude?' he asked, when I'd finished. He was making small talk while he juggled the situation in his mind.

'Helpful,' I replied. 'He didn't raise any objections at all.'

'Mmm, that's how I find him. Pity he didn't land the Chief's job. We really ought to make young Newley acting sergeant, don't you think? His promotion should be through any time.'

'Yes, I was about to mention it. One of them ought to be upped, and Nigel's been in on it from the very beginning.'

'Right, I'll see what I can do.' He fiddled with his pen, then said: 'So what's the programme from now on?'

'Tomorrow,' I stated, 'is Friday. They fly to New York, introduce themselves to Loot . . . Lieutenant diPalma. Saturday the boat docks. Sunday, hopefully, the container will be on United States territory and they'll have access to the contents. If we've done good we could be knocking on Wheatley's door sometime Monday.'

'Well it sounds straightforward enough. Charlie, how would you feel if we called in the Fraud Squad?'

So that's why the old bugger was being so edgy. He was afraid I'd be annoyed at having my show taken away from me.

'Come off it, Gilbert,' I replied. 'You know me better than that. Call in the Yorkshire Light Infantry if it helps. Why? What are you thinking?'

He shrugged his shoulders. 'I'm sorry, it's just that you've a lot invested in this one. I was thinking he's probably up to his neck in all sorts of things. Why limit our enquiries to this little scam? They might be able to find something in his files.'

'Right, good idea,' I replied. I was delighted with the suggestion. 'Then we'll need a Special Procedures Warrant.'

'Signed by a judge,' sighed Gilbert. 'Shouldn't be too difficult to find a sympathetic one; they all live in houses stuffed to the rafters with quietly mouldering antiques.'

'Ah, yes,' I told him, 'but they were new when they bought them.'

I drew a column of numbers on a sheet of paper, representing the twenty-four-hour clock, then I wrote another column alongside showing the corresponding time in New York and pinned the sheet on the wall. It looked as if diPalma should be at work so I dialled his number. He was around, somewhere. They transferred me. I was transferred several more times. Eventually a voice out of Damon Runyon came on and said: 'Yes, Father?'

'Pardon?' was the best I could do.

'DiPalma here. How can I help you, Father?'

'Hello, Lieutenant. This is Inspector Priest, from the British police force; Charlie Priest. A couple of my men are coming over to see you, so I thought I'd make contact and introduce myself.'

'Ha ha! They just said some priest was after me. How are you, Charlie?'

'Fine. I never actually signed a vow of chastity – it's just worked out that way.'

'Hey, man, you must have married my wife's sister. Call me Tony. When do your boys arrive?'

Acting Detective Sergeant Newley and Detective Constable Caton were taken to the airport by Mad Maggie and seen safely on their way. I'd given them strict instructions about contacting me after every stage of the enquiry. They were armed with photographs of several items from Wheatley's list and had spoken to three of the previous owners. From them they had received extremely detailed descriptions, so they were now able to positively identify at least four pieces. I'd have preferred it to be more, but it should be enough. I stayed in the office and wore out the carpet.

When Maggie arrived back she reported that they were safely airborne and on time. 'Oh, and Nigel said not to forget it's the walk on Sunday,' she added.

It had slipped my mind that it was the weekend for the Walking Club to go out. We'd had five or six expeditions and it had been a huge success, although a few were dropping out now the bad weather was here.

'Dammit!' I said. 'I had forgotten. Where are we supposed to be going?'

'Edale,' she told me.

'Derbyshire. Ah, well, that's not too bad. We could be in the pub by lunchtime.'

Nigel rang me late Saturday night to say the *Alpha Carrymaster* had docked dead on schedule. Everybody was friendly and later that evening they were hitting the town with some of the boys from 120th Precinct. I looked at my mug of cocoa and dressing gown and felt old, but decided I had no desire to trade places with him.

The walk went well, even though it was misty on the high ground. We went over Kinder Scout to have a look at the Downfall. This is the only waterfall in the world where the water travels upwards. The breeze was obligingly from the right direction, so we had a good display, to the disbelief of those who hadn't seen it before. Then I showed Sparky's kids how to plot a compass course over the cloughs, back to Edale and the pub.

I was home well before Nigel was due to ring. 'Bad news, boss,' he said when he did come on. 'The container's off the ship, but we haven't been able to get to it. Should be OK for tomorrow.'

I wasn't perturbed; things never run as smoothly as planned. If this was the only hitch we'd done well. 'Don't worry about it,' I told him. 'Ring me same time tomorrow.'

It would have been nice, though, to know we weren't on a wild-goose chase. I went upstairs to have a shower, then remembered I'd already had one, so, after making a couple of phone calls, I went to the local instead.

I was grateful for the delay – I awoke on Monday morning feeling dreadful. Must have been something I'd eaten. Fraud Squad were itching to get their hands on Wheatley's files. We were planning a cross-border raid to arrest him soon after we received positive news from Nigel, timed to coincide with similar action in New York. We reluctantly agreed to allow the Americans the pleasure of delivering a seven a.m. knock at the door; we'd have to be patient and wait until lunchtime.

Nigel rang earlier than expected. He didn't mess about: 'Success, boss,' he told me. 'We've identified the ink stain in the drawer of the Queen Anne bureau, that's item eleven on the list; the wrong hinge on item thirteen, George III writing cabinet; the bit knocked off the leg of item two, Chippendale dressing table . . .'

'The chipped Chippendale,' I said.

'Pardon?'

'Never mind, go on.'

'Er, and item six, the Victorian table with the writing, that you found.'

'Well done. What about the rest of it?'

'Everything here could be on the list, as far as I can tell, but there are a couple of items on the list that aren't here, if you follow.'

'Yeah. He probably siphoned off one or two choice pieces for his private collection. So you're confident that we can put Operation Bang Brian Behind Bars into action?'

'You bet, boss.'

'OK, tell Loot . . . Lieutenant diPalma – my pal Tony – that we are *go* for tomorrow. I'll be in my office from six a.m., *your* time. Is Jeff with you?'

'Sure, boss, do you want him?'

'Yes, please.'

'Hi, boss, it's Jeff.'

'Hello, Jeff, how's it going so far?'

'Great, a bit different from back home though. We've been out on patrol a few times. It's a crazy place, not my cup of tea.'

'Have you been invited on the raid tomorrow?'

'No, not so far.'

'Good, keep out of it if you can, but it's up to you. If

you do go, keep an eye on Goldenballs, you know what he's like.'

'OK, boss.'

'Ring me in the morning; 'bye.'

Sparky went over first, to locate Wheatley and keep tabs on him. His office was built on to the side of his rather desirable converted farmhouse, and he was at home. Nearer the time, a team from Fraud Squad joined Sparky. All I was waiting for was a call from diPalma, then I'd send them in. The phone rang, but it was DC Sparkington.

'It's Dave, boss. Wheatley's just received a visitor.'

'In a car? Could you see his number?'

'No, not all of it, only the letters – ABC. It's a Rolls Royce. Just thought you'd be interested.' I rang diPalma. Fortunately he was in.

'Hi, Charlie, we're just moving into position. What time is it with you?'

'Happy hour. Can we make a slight change of plan, Tony? How about if I say we go in, say . . . forty-five minutes from now?'

'No problem. That makes it . . . seven-o-five local time.'

'Got it; five past the hour. Good luck.'

I passed the change of plan on to the team outside Wheatley's house, then dashed downstairs and into the car, determined to be there, with them.

For once there were no roadworks, so I made it

with nearly ten minutes to spare. Billy Morrison, an inspector with the Fraud Squad, was in overall command. I walked up to his car and he wound down the window.

'Hello, Charlie, you're keen. Thought you were staying out of the cold,' he said.

'Hello, Billy. I want to take a dekko at Cakebread. I've a score to settle with him, sometime.'

'Do you want to take over? It's your show.'

'No, be my guest. I'll try to keep out of your way.' He looked at his watch, saying: 'Twelve o'clock. Are we to wait five minutes?'

'No,' I replied. 'Let's go.'

Billy, Sparky and myself went up to the house. The others stayed handy outside the gate. Three right hands dipped into inside pockets and removed warrant cards. A woman answered the door; ash-blonde, glamorous, made-up and bejewelled. Billy did the talking.

'Police, madam, we'd like to see Mr Wheatley.'

She looked flustered for a second, but quickly recovered. 'I'll, er, I'll see if he's in,' she said, and attempted to shut the door in our faces. Billy was too quick for her though, and we all followed him into the hallway. It oozed expense. Not taste, not class, just expense. Bit like the woman.

'Who is it, darling?' said a voice, and a man came out of a doorway in front of us. He had bleached hair, long at the back, and a suntan. He looked like an ageing pop singer who'd fallen into a time warp. He was half into an overcoat, and Cakebread was immediately behind him.

'Are you Brian Wheatley, sir?' asked Billy.

'Yes. Who the hell are you?'

'DI Morrison, and this is DI Priest and DC Sparkington. Do you mind going back in there, please, we'd like to ask you a few questions.'

I watched Cakebread's face as my name was mentioned. His eyebrows shot up so far they nearly dislodged his toupee. Wheatley huffed and puffed and made mysterious threats, but we all ended up back in the room he had left a moment earlier. The desk and chair could have come from the oval office.

'Who are you, sir?' Billy asked Cakebread, but it didn't sound polite.

'My name's Cakebread, and this is outrageous! We're just on our way to an important lunch appointment. You can't come barging in . . .'

'Shut up and sit down,' I ordered.

To my disappointment he did both. My next line was going to be to threaten to stuff his ferret down his throat, but I never got to deliver it; you never do.

Billy offered Wheatley a picture of one of the antiques, saying: 'Do you recognise the piece of furniture shown here? It's a Queen Anne bureau.'

'No,' he replied, without looking.

'Do you recognise this list?'

'No.'

'It's a list relating to a claim you made recently on RDW Insurance.'

'No comment.'

'Fuck me!' said Cakebread, looking exasperated. 'You're not still trying to pin one of them on us, are you? Why don't you stop wasting your time and ours?'

I said: 'Six weeks ago you forwarded six crates to the United States, via Big Ocean Transport. Could you tell us what was in them?'

No reply.

'Brian Wheatley,' began DI Morrison, 'I'm arresting you on a charge of attempting to defraud the RDW insurance Company. That'll do for starters. You are not obliged to say anything, but anything you do say will be taken down and may be used in evidence against you. We also have a warrant to search these premises, so can we have your keys? It'll save us damaging the locks.' He patted a filing cabinet and held up the warrant.

Wheatley looked shocked, but the defiance soon returned. 'These files are confidential; you've no right to look at them,' he claimed triumphantly.

'Unfortunately for you, sir, that's not true. This is a Special Procedures Warrant, which gives us access to everything. Your keys, please.'

He stared at the sheet of paper in disbelief, then tossed the keys on to the table.

'Dave . . .' said Billy, gesturing with a nod towards the prisoner.

Sparky moved round the desk and handcuffed him. 'Just one hand, sir,' he said. 'It's a long ride, and we don't want you to get cramp, do we?'

'Where are you taking him?' demanded Cakebread.

'Heckley.'

'Heckley! Don't worry, Brian, I'll ring Simon, he'll be there before you are.'

You know you've got trouble when they're on first names with their briefs. Sparky, myself and another DC took Wheatley back to Heckley, leaving the Fraud boys loose on the files. Rather them than me. Simon was Simon Mingeles. He didn't beat us back, but his reputation had already preceded him. Word had it that he would have mitigated in favour of Vlad the Impaler, on the grounds of him not being allowed sharp toys as a small boy. We weren't worried; it was a good nick, as long as we played it straight.

Next morning Wheatley appeared before the local magistrates, for committal to the crown court. We'd attempted a taped interview with him, but, at Mingeles's prompting, he'd just delivered a succession of 'No comments'. It was his right to do so. We didn't push it, and the interview was terminated in a couple of minutes. He'd have a bigger problem in front of a judge, when confronted with the evidence. Mingeles had a long, whispered conversation with him, no doubt about their tactics to ensure that he was given bail. Our chances of keeping him in were slim, so we didn't try.

'No opposition to bail,' said the prosecutor from the CPS, before Mingeles could practise his oratory. Wheatley didn't get value for money from him that morning.

The Fraud Squad found plenty to interest them in Wheatley's office, and it looked as if the Inland Revenue and the VAT inspector would also be having words with him. In New York, diPalma's men had made several arrests. They'd found a cache of stolen property and a small quantity of drugs. None in the shipment, though. They were pleased, and so was I.

Maggie popped her head round the door and announced that she was leaving for Manchester, to pick up Newley and Caton; their flight was due in at one p.m. I rewarded myself with a cooked meal in a cafe on the high street. It had the added attraction of not being licensed: I'd decided to make a more determined effort to go teetotal.

By late afternoon I'd put our case against Wheatley down on paper, with the rider that other charges would follow. Transcribing the taped interview didn't take long.

'How many lower-case is in gullible?' asked Tony Willis.

'Four,' I told him.

'Thanks.'

'Pleasure.'

Then the phone rang.

'DI Priest, Heckley Police,' I said.

'Boss, it's Maggie,' she said, without her normal self-assurance. 'I'm still at Manchester airport.'

'What's the problem, Maggie?'

'The plane. It was delayed, but it landed nearly an hour ago. I'm in security now. We've checked the passenger list and Jeff and Nigel weren't on it.'

CHAPTER EIGHTEEN

I must have been mad to send them to New York. This was my war, my private vendetta, I should have handled it myself. An image of George, slumped over the passenger seat of his E-type, flashed through my brain, as it had done, on and off, during the sporadic disturbed nights I'd had since. Training and instinct soon took over, fortunately.

'When's the next plane, Maggie?' I asked.

'Not till this evening, boss.'

I thought for a few seconds. 'Any chance of the airline checking with New York to see if they're booked on a later flight?'

'We've tried. They're supposed to be ringing back, but they're taking their time.'

'OK. Give them this number, then get yourself home.'

Outside, darkness had fallen an hour early. Black clouds were piling up on each other, gathering themselves for the onslaught and blotting out the twilight. I picked up the phone, considered dialling Gilbert, then rang diPalma instead.

'It's Charlie Priest in England, Tony. They weren't on the plane. Any ideas?'

'Hell, no. What do the airline say?'

'They're not answering our calls. Can you check if they caught a different flight?'

'Sure. I'll check with Immigration. Stay where you are.'

At least he had no bad news for me. Half an hour later he rang me back. 'They've handed in their immigration cards OK. I haven't confirmed which flight they were on, but all flights are overbooked, so it's likely they were bumped on to a later plane. Don't worry, Charlie, they'll turn up.'

'No doubt, thanks for checking.'

I looked out of the window and watched the cars leaving. Tony Willis, with his raincoat on, shouted from the outside office to see if I was going home. I shouted back to him and shook my head.

It wasn't a long wait. Command and Control, on the ground floor, had a message for me. ADS Newley and DC Caton were in a South Yorkshire Traffic car being blue-lighted up the Ml. They'd landed at East Midlands airport and our Traffic boys would be picking them up at the border. Should be home in about an hour. They'd ring me from there.

'Get a message back to them,' I growled. 'I'll see them in my office in an hour.'

I made a mug of tea, swung the electric fire in my direction and put my feet up on another chair. I sipped the tea and thought about alternative ways of earning a living. When Vanessa left me I lost my head for a while, made a spectacular fool of myself. Then, one day, I sat down and reviewed the situation. The conclusion I reached was that Truscott had possibly done me a favour. Our relationship was always on a knife-edge, and would probably have collapsed some other time in the future. She was beautiful, and I was glad I'd been married to her. Now she was gone, and I was glad of that, too. But someone, a talentless little rat ten years older than me, had stolen her with his big ideas and even bigger ego. That's what had hurt. Once I recognised it, I came back to life.

Now I was on the roller-coaster again: lows and highs following each other in rapid succession. I went through the past year in my mind. Someone in my position should always be able to compartmentalise the job; not let the grubbiness rub off on to his private life. That was the theory, and usually I managed it without any problem. I'd turned over corpses and tried to comfort shattered lives, then had a couple of pints in the pub and slept like a hibernating squirrel. Not always, but usually.

But now I was getting obsessive, and it worried me. Aubrey Bastard Cakebread was the root of the problem. Putting him behind bars was like a vast chasm that stood between me and a shining land at the other side. Was there anything I wanted more than that simple goal? Yes, there was: Annabelle Wilberforce's affection. The realisation jolted me awake. Would I trade Breadcake's freedom for Annabelle's love? Any time, it was no contest. But not just yet; maybe I could have them both.

Nigel and Jeff looked like last week's lettuce sandwiches when they walked in. Nigel was carrying his briefcase, Jeff a paper bag. I took my feet off the chair and kicked it towards them.

'Sit down,' I said.

Neither of them spoke. I couldn't tell if they were contrite or annoyed.

'Do you realise that they're dragging the East River for your bodies?' I told them.

'Sorry, boss,' they mumbled.

'Well, what happened then?'

'Er, at the airport, do you mean?' asked Nigel.

'Yes, at the bloody airport.'

'We . . . well, we missed the plane. No, we didn't miss it; it was full, so they wouldn't let us on. They were overbooked.'

'You were late for it?'

Jeff decided to help Nigel out: 'Yes, boss. We'd been out with some of the lads from the precinct. They got us to the airport a bit late, and the plane was full. We're sorry if we've caused a fuss.'

I breathed a big sigh. 'Never mind,' I said. 'Apart from that cock-up you did a good job. I suppose we should have let you stay over another day. You look dreadful, how do you feel?'

'Tired.'

'Rough.'

'Serves you right. How much sleep have you had in the last few days?'

'Hardly any.'

'None.'

I shook my head and managed a smile. 'Then you'll find it a struggle to have a report on my desk by nine in the morning,' I said.

Nigel lifted his briefcase off the floor. 'We did it on the plane,' he replied, producing the document, adding: 'It needs typing, though.'

I reached across and took it from him. 'OK,' I said. 'In that case you'd both better have tomorrow off, to catch up on your sleep. But stay by the phone.' That cheered them up.

'We brought you a present, boss,' said Nigel, gesturing towards Jeff. Jeff passed the paper bag to me. Inside I found a baseball cap. I held it in both hands, peak towards me, and read the logo on the front. It said: 'NYPD'.

'Thank you,' I told them, 'I'll always treasure it.'

I went home after ringing Maggie with the good news.

'The brainless pillocks!' she yelled. 'Wait till I see them.'

I had a feeling they hadn't escaped as lightly as they thought. I cooked a decent meal and ate it all. After I'd washed up I took out my diary and sat by the telephone. I picked the phone up a couple of times, then put it down again. The third time, I dialled Annabelle's number. There was no reply. Ah, well, at least I'd tried. I suppose that was progress of a sort.

Maggie had calmed down by the time the Terrible Twins reported for duty on Friday morning. Gilbert Wood suggested we join him later in the day for a celebratory snifter. I had to dash out to a bookmaker's office in town that had been held up at gunpoint. All that was taken was the cashier's wallet, containing ten pounds and two credit cards. He was so shaken he didn't have the wit to say he'd just been to the bank and there was three hundred quid in the wallet, like they usually do. The gunman had given him a hard ride because there was nothing in the till: nine o'clock in the morning is not a sensible time to rob a bookie's office.

The worrying part was the gun; from the description it could be real. He was almost certainly the character who'd tried to rob a bank last week. He was armed and he was stupid: a dangerous combination. I sent Martin Makinson and John Rose to interview the witnesses, suggesting that they invite along someone from Victim Support. Jeff Caton went to talk with the local intelligence officer and find out who was out and about in town. An ounce of inside information is worth a swagbag full of questions and answers. I hadn't been back in the station long when Maggie walked into my office. She wasn't her usual ebullient self.

'What's the matter, Maggie?' I asked, 'You've lost your sparkle lately. Am I working you too hard?'

She sat down and sighed. 'I don't know, Charlie. Things are just getting on top of me at the moment. It'll pass.'

'What things? Anything I should know about?'

'Oh, this and that. Like Nigel the other day. I was stupidly upset when they weren't on that plane. It was obvious they'd only missed it, but all sorts went through my mind.'

'I know what you mean, Maggie,' I told her. 'I felt the same way. Maybe we both need a holiday. If you want any time off, take it. You've plenty in the bank.'

'It's all right, but thanks. Now I've just taken a call about Julie Simpson; remember her?'

'Mmm . . . remind me.'

'Those girls we arrested in the New Mall. She's the one you caught.'

'Oh, I remember. She was the last woman I put my arms around. Not bad-looking; she'll be a stunner in a year or two. What's she done now?'

'Not now, she won't be,' said Maggie. 'Her solicitor's just been on the phone. She's in the General Hospital. Day before yesterday they amputated one of her legs. Gangrene.'

Maggie was usually as hard as old horseshoes,

but now she just sat there, talking in matter-of-fact monotones. I could see Sparky through the window. When he caught my eye I made a 'two teas' gesture to him. He nodded and went over to the kettle.

'Poor kid, what happened?' I asked.

Maggie sat back in her chair and looked at me. 'Have a guess,' she invited.

'You don't mean . . . injecting?'

She nodded.

After a while I said: 'Jesus Christ, we're living in a cesspit.'

Tea and work are my recipe for survival. We drank our tea and I off-loaded the armed robbery on to Tony Willis. Then I took Maggie to have a word with Julie Simpson's parents.

They lived in a respectable house just off one of the big estates. It was probably a council house which they had purchased. The garden was tidy and several alterations had been made to the outside. They were both at home. Julie had complained of pains in her leg for several days, and had stayed off school. She wouldn't see the doctor, though. When her foot turned black Mrs Simpson sent for him and he had her ambulanced straight to the General.

'Have you been told what caused the gangrene, Mrs Simpson?' asked Maggie.

She nodded and sniffed. Her husband replied for her.

'They said she'd been injecting drugs. Heroin.'

We asked about her friends, where she went at night, who might have influence over her. They knew nothing, apart from the two girls Julie was arrested with. Julie was just a typical teenager, with a typical secret life.

'Does Julie have her own room?' I asked.

'Yes,' replied her mother. 'Her older sister is married. There's just the two of them.'

'Do you mind if we look through it? You never know, we might find something.'

Mrs Simpson led us upstairs. She said: 'I've tidied it up. It's usually a dreadful tip; you know what teenage girls are like.'

I didn't, so I stayed silent. Maggie said: 'Yes.'

The room was neat, and more childish than I expected. A row of teddy bears sat across the pillow and the wallpaper was more suitable for a nursery than the room of a girl burgeoning into womanhood. Several posters of stripped-to-the-waist pop stars doing strange things with microphones added a note of conflict.

'Mrs Simpson, could you possibly leave us alone?' asked Maggie. 'Julie might not be very pleased if she knew you had looked through her things.'

I looked quizzical, but Mrs Simpson saw the sense of what Maggie said, and left us to it. I went straight to the drawers at the side of the bed, but they were locked. Maggie cast an expert eye round the room. Near the window was a brass rubbing, in a heavy frame, presumably done by Julie in happier times. It was half concealed by the curtain, and easily overlooked.

Maggie lifted it away from the wall and a key fell into her hand.

'Feminine intuition,' she said with a wink.

'I'm impressed,' I replied.

The top drawer contained mainly cheap jewellery. Underneath was some surprisingly sexy underwear for a sixteen-year-old, and a couple of hard-porn magazines. Now I knew why Maggie had wanted the parents out of the way; or I thought I did.

I was mistaken. In the bottom drawer we found a three-month supply of the Pill and two packets of condoms. Maggie held one of them up.

'She's sensible about some things,' she said, 'but I don't think her mum and dad would agree.'

'Put them back, Maggie,' I told her. 'I need some fresh air. And a drink.'

I picked up one of the teddy bears and took it downstairs with me. 'When do you visit Julie?' I asked her parents.

'Just in the afternoons,' said Mr Simpson. 'We don't like travelling on the buses at night. You don't feel safe.'

'How's she bearing up?'

'Not very well, but she was still a bit groggy yesterday.'

'Do you mind if I call in to see her? Not to question her, just to see if I can cheer her up.' I held up the teddy bear. 'I'll take him along, maybe tomorrow night.'

They didn't mind. They wouldn't have minded if I'd

offered to sell her to the King of Tonga. Not because they didn't care, but because they'd taken just about as much as they could. Maggie came down the stairs and joined us.

'I don't know where we've gone wrong,' sobbed Mrs Simpson. 'She was such a good girl. It all started about eighteen months ago . . .'

I looked at my watch. 'We could give you a lift to the hospital,' I said, 'If you'd like to go now.'

They thought about it for a second or two, then declined. They wanted to do some shopping first. Maggie took Julie's mother by the arm and told her not to be too hard on either herself or Julie. They went through into the kitchen.

'Do you work?' I asked Mr Simpson.

'No, I was made redundant fifteen months ago.'

'Where did you work?'

'Anderson's Engineering. There twenty-two years.'

'And now it's gone.'

'Yes.'

When Maggie was ready we left and went to the pub for lunch. Neither of us felt very talkative, so we ate our sandwiches quickly and quietly, then set off for the second girl's home. Sharon Turner was a year younger than the other two, but we believed her to be the major influence in the gang. We could have been wrong, though. She had escaped when we confronted them, but the others gave us her name when we showed them the video. Walking up their path we were aware of the

Turners being a rung or two lower on the ladder of luck than the Simpsons. The front garden made mine look like Sissinghurst, and a big Alsatian was going berserk in a compound at the back.

Sharon answered the door. 'Mam, it's the police,' she yelled over her shoulder, before we could speak.

Mrs Turner appeared with her indignant head on. She fell into the category known to anthropologists as Big Fat Slags. 'What do you want now?' she demanded.

Maggie introduced us and asked if we could come in and have a word with her. The room we entered illustrated the triumph of hopelessness over poverty. The floor covering stuck to your feet as you walked across it. Two toddlers with angelic faces, wearing only tattered vests, smiled up at us. We didn't sit down. Sharon was hovering near her mum, so Maggie said: 'Alone?'

When Sharon left us, Maggie asked Mrs Turner: 'Do you know Julie Simpson?'

'Yeah, she's the one who grassed on our Sharon,' she replied.

'Did you know she'd had a leg amputated?'

'I heard. What's that got to do with us?'

'She had gangrene, through injecting drugs. They were stealing to pay for drugs. We believe Sharon might be at risk, too.'

'Nonsense. My Sharon don't do no drugs; she's a good girl. It's them other two what got her into trouble. She didn't know what they were doing. I asked her if she knew and she swore she didn't. That's good enough for me. She wouldn't lie to me.'

We were wasting our time. 'Has Sharon left school?' I asked.

'Er, no. She's a sore throat, so I kept 'er off today.'

'Is there a Mr Turner?'

'Yes, he's out, though.'

'Out where?'

'I don't know. Just walking round. Sometimes he helps a pal down at the allotments.'

'What's your husband's first name, Mrs Turner?'

'Eric. Why? He hasn't done owt.'

'Just for the forms we have to fill in, love. You know how it is.'

'Mrs Turner,' said Maggie, 'we'd like to have a look in Sharon's room. Do you mind? We could easily get a warrant, but I'm sure that's unnecessary.'

It was a brave try, Maggie, but futile. The Turners wouldn't let the rat-catcher in without a warrant.

The third girl, Claire Clegg, lived in a different part of town. I threw the keys to Maggie and told her to drive while I used the radio. Five minutes later I knew that Eric Turner had served time for burglary and handling, and his wife, Vera, was a convicted prostitute. They'd both been clean for the last ten years.

'Could be they're making an effort,' suggested Maggie.

'True,' I replied, 'let's give them credit for that. There's sod-all else we can give them credit for.'

'Did you see the two little ones?' she asked.

'Yes, they were bonny, weren't they.'

'They were beautiful. It makes you sad when you think of the life they'll have.'

'Well,' I declared, 'on the whole, I think I'm glad that I haven't any kids. I should hate to think I'd brought anyone into this world.'

'Oh, I don't know,' Maggie sighed, with a hint of sadness.

I felt I was close to rattling forgotten skeletons, so I changed the subject. 'C'mon,' I told her, 'let's see what Claire's mum has to say.'

Claire's mum was a single mum, but I didn't know what the circumstances were. She was attractive, but her face was becoming lined before its time, and there was a touch of neglect in her hairstyle. She needed someone to smooth the lines. Under different circumstances I might have volunteered to try, and not in a furtive way. She invited us in and offered tea. Maggie was surprised when I accepted. The news about Julie caused the furrows to deepen.

'You say she was injecting heroin?' Mrs Clegg said.

'Mmm.'

'And you think Claire may be?'

'It's a likely possibility.'

'But . . . but wouldn't I know? Surely I'd be able to tell?'

'Not necessarily,' replied Maggie. 'The highs and lows would probably pass off as normal teenage swings of mood. People on heroin look just like the rest of us, most of the time.'

'Heaven knows, we've been getting plenty of moods, the last eighteen months.'

'Tell us about it, Mrs Clegg,' encouraged Maggie.

'Oh, I don't know,' she sighed. 'It's easy to blame someone else, but they were all as bad. The trouble all started when the Turner girl started going to their school, but that's no excuse; she should know right from wrong.'

'It's not so clear-cut,' Maggie told her. 'Taking a few pills seems harmless enough at the start, and it doesn't hurt anyone else. Then things get out of control. Someone starts pushing them heavier stuff. Your daughter's not bad, she's just come into contact with unscrupulous people, and she may be at risk.'

Mrs Clegg's cup of tea remained untouched. 'It's such a disappointment,' she said. 'It's tough bringing up a child on your own, but we'd come through the bad years. Claire's father died in a road accident when she was five. We were just starting to enjoy ourselves. Claire was borrowing my clothes, and I even tried some of her outfits. I'd taken her out for meals, that sort of thing. One day, I knew, she'd bring a boyfriend home, and that would be me out in the cold, but before then I'd hoped we could be friends for a year or two. Like big sister and kid sister. Then, all of a sudden, she hated me; couldn't stand the sight of me; everything I said was rubbish. I don't know where I went wrong . . .'

She started to cry. I finished my tea and let Maggie do the Marje Proops bit. Each to his own. When the tissues were put away I said: 'Mrs Clegg, would you mind if we took a look in Claire's room?'

'No, of course not,' she replied with a sniffle. She led the way upstairs and opened the door for us.

'It might be better if you left us to it,' I suggested. 'Claire will be annoyed with you if she knows you've been through her things. You can always say we had a warrant.'

Maggie gave me a sideways look. 'You're a fast learner, Charlie,' she said, when Mrs Clegg had gone.

The room was more in the style I had expected. The ceiling was black, with luminous stars and zodiac symbols on it. Large posters, with swirling, circular patterns or images from the occult adorned the walls. Hieronymus Bosch would have liked it. Only the teddy bears gave a clue to the former life of the room's occupant. The drawers in the small bedside cabinet were locked. We searched around, without finding the key.

'What does the feminine intuition say?' I asked. 'It says the key is hanging round her neck,' Maggie replied.

I leant over the cabinet and put my hand between it and the wall; it was open at the back. I placed the table lamp and the few other pieces on the bed, then wrapped my arms around the cabinet and lifted it bodily.

'Then let's try some male aggression,' I grunted,

walking backwards away from the wall. I placed the drawers where Maggie could get behind them. She removed her jacket and squeezed her bare wrist through the narrow gap into the top one. It wasn't necessary to remove much, because she could tell by feel what most of the stuff was.

'Clothing, mainly,' she told me. 'Underwear . . . something silky . . . bra . . . suspender belt. Hey, Charlie, you ought to be doing this.'

I'd been thinking the same thing. After a few seconds' silence a puzzled expression flicked across her face. 'This feels more like it,' she mumbled to herself, and a moment later she extricated a small tin box with a hinged lid. It said *Zubes* on it. I remembered keeping a spider in a similar one when I was a kid. They don't make useful boxes like that any more.

Maggie prised the lid open and studied the contents. Then she turned the box so I could see. A wicked-looking syringe lay on a folded tissue, cornerways across. 'Fancy a pick-me-up, boss?' she said, without smiling.

CHAPTER NINETEEN

'Jesus, Maggie, mind your fingers,' I said. She slid the box across to me and delved back into the drawers. Wrapped in a pair of tights she found a twist of cooking foil, as if wrapping a home-made sweet.

'That's what we're looking for,' I told her. After more groping she produced a cardboard packet. It was pale blue, and I noticed the Boots logo. 'What is it?' I asked.

Maggie held it so I could read the label. It said: 'Clear Blue', and underneath: 'Home pregnancy testing kit'.

'I've seen enough,' I said, adding: 'You'd better give me a lift back with the drawers; I think I did my back getting them out.'

We decided to take the wrap straight round to Drug Squad at city HQ. On the way there I asked: 'Do you think the girls were on the game. Maggie?'

'Dunno,' she replied. 'Probably not. Just having it away with the boyfriend, most likely; or the bloke who supplied. Maybe it's the same person. Let's give them the benefit of the doubt.'

We'd forgotten about the Friday afternoon traffic. It's one of life's little mysteries why there are so many more vehicles on the road on a Friday afternoon. Waiting for the lights to change, Maggie asked: 'Charlie, why didn't you tell Mrs Clegg about the wrap and the syringe?'

'No idea,' I replied. 'Just a spur of the moment thing. She's enough on her plate.'

'Would you have given the Turners the same break?'

'No,' I replied, after some consideration, 'probably not.'

Maggie gunned us across the junction as soon as the amber flashed on.

'I thought amber meant "Prepare to start",' I said, as the G-force relaxed its grip.

'What did you think of Mrs Clegg?' she asked. 'She was attractive, in a careworn sort of way, don't you think?'

'Er, yes. It was a nice home, too.'

Maggie turned to me and smiled. 'I think you fancied her, Charlie.'

I smiled back at her. 'These days, Maggie, I fancy anything. It's a phase I'm going through.'

An old lady was walking on the pavement, with a poodle on a lead. 'Look at that!' I exclaimed, turning in my seat and wolf whistling at the dog.

We pulled into the HQ car park. 'You could always try Vera Turner, Charlie. She'd probably accommodate you.'

'No thanks. If I'm ever that desperate, I'll jump in the Calder,' I said.

Maggie gave her lewdest laugh. 'You and Vera – it'd be like throwing a chipolata up a ginnel,' she giggled. She was still chuckling as we went into the building.

We gave the Drug Squad the evidence and asked for a report as soon as possible. I left word for DI Freer to ring me. He caught me at home later that night and invited me out for a pint.

'Oh, go on, then,' I said, in the pub, when he pointed towards the beer pumps. 'But I'm limiting it to one.'

'Good idea,' he replied. 'True temperance is moderation.'

'Is it? Who said that?'

'Peter Yates.'

I was puzzled. 'The solicitor with Jack Berenson's?' I asked.

'That's Peter Gates. Peter Yates founded Yates's Wine Lodges.'

'Oh. Well he would do, wouldn't he.'

'Would do what?'

'Would say that true temperance was moderation. He could have added that the only genuine way to appreciate abstinence was to get totally rat-arsed now and again.'

'Mmm, you might have a point. Cheers.'

'Cheers.'

We found an empty table and sat down. I looked around the pub; the average age of the clientele was about nineteen.

'So where did the works come from, Charlie?' Mike asked.

I reminded him about the girls, and told him about Julie.

He licked froth off his lip and shook his head. 'They never believe it can happen to them. What'd she been doing?'

'I don't know the details, just that she'd been injecting. I was hoping you'd be able to tell me.'

'It depends on where she's been sticking the needle in,' he replied 'or what the dope was cut with. Milk powder's the favourite over here. In America some sadistic bastards sell it with powdered glass in. She probably injects it between her toes. Not very hygenic, but the marks don't show. Sometimes they go for the femoral vein, in the groin. If they hit the artery they're in big trouble.'

I squirmed at the thought of it. After a few minutes I asked him if there was anything big in the pipeline. No pun was intended.

He shook his head. 'No, 'fraid not. At the moment we're reduced to spying on the needle-exchange schemes. We're picking up plenty of small fry, but nothing significant. Our policy is "hit the users", but only because we don't know who else to hit. Your Mr Cakebread is the favourite. He's a lot to answer for. We've been trying to watch him, but it's too intermittent. Lack of resources, as usual.'

We discussed various ways of smoking him out, ranging from the possible but ineffective right through to the absurd. I went on to orange juice and surveyed the talent. I decided that vitamin C was all the stimulus I needed.

'Would you like to be young again, Mike?' I asked.

He pursed his lips and looked round the room. It had become packed with the Friday night crowd of revellers, heading for a night on the town. The delights were the same as in our youth, but the temptations and the dangers were much greater. Pot and Purple Hearts had been replaced by dirty drugs that could kill in a dozen sordid ways, with the spectre of AIDS overshadowing everything. His gaze settled on the gyrating bum of a tall, mini-skirted girl who was standing, glass in hand, about a foot from his face. Blonde hair hung down her back and her thighs were a navigation hazard.

'Yes,' he announced, gravely.

'Me too,' I added, unnecessarily.

* * *

297

Billy Morrison of the Fraud Squad rang me at the office with an update on Wheatley's affairs. I was impressed – the main attraction of working for the Fraud Squad is they don't usually work weekends. He sounded hurt when I pointed this out to him.

'We'll be doing him for false accounting, among other things. Just thought I'd let you know his books don't balance,' he said.

'In what way?'

'Well, let's say he's living way above his apparent means. His companies are losing money, or, at best, breaking even. But he has a lavish lifestyle and it's not done on credit – he's no major debts. Most of his properties are paid for, as are the Range Rover and the Porsche.'

'So what we need to know is where does he get the money?'

'That's about the size of it.'

'What does he say about it?' I asked.

'Oh, there's a few deals in the books, associated with large injections of cash, but they don't stand up to scrutiny. We can't get anything out of him, thanks to that creep of a lawyer. The real reason I'm ringing is to ask you about this drugs thing; are you any closer with that?'

'No, it's come to a standstill.'

'Pity. If we could find a smell of drugs on him we could screw him with the 1987 Drug Trafficking Act. Confiscate the lot, with a bit of luck.'

'I get it: we say he gained the money through trafficking, then the onus is on him to prove otherwise.'

'That's the theory.'

'OK,' I replied. 'I'll bear it in mind.'

I didn't get the chance to. A message came up from Control and Command that a silent alarm had been activated at the York and Durham Bank in the high street. I went downstairs to listen to the action.

The intensity of purpose in the control room was almost tangible as I walked in. The sergeant looked up from his desk and lifted one finger towards his lips to silence me. He was listening on his headset.

'OK . . . OK . . .' he said. 'Good, good. So you stay there and round up the witnesses, then tell the other two to get off towards the motorway.' He turned to the WPC who was also listening and making notes. 'Did you get all that?'

She nodded as she wrote.

'Right, then divert all cars to the ring road, except Lima Sierra. They're too far away. Put them on the motorway, watching the westbound lane. Tell them what to look for; and we want no heroics – he may be armed.'

He removed his headset and turned to me. 'Sorry about that, Mr Priest,' he said.

'That's OK. What's happening?'

'That was young Henderson.' He gestured towards the microphone. 'Him and Wilson were first there, but the culprit had already left. Believe it or not, someone took his number, or at least, most of it. He's in a red Ford Escort that sounds like one that was stolen earlier this morning. Jenny's circulating it.'

'Was he armed?'

'Yes. A handgun – "like cowboys use".'

'How many cars is "all cars"?'

'Two of ours, one from City and a Traffic.'

'Mmm. Where's the nearest Armed Response Vehicle?'

'Halfway to Lancashire, unfortunately, but we've turned them round and they're heading this way.'

'Good. Any idea which way the crook was heading?'

'He started up the hill, but he may have gone round the one-way system and left it in any direction.' I wondered if I'd obey the one-way signs after sticking up a bank. Probably.

'OK. Jenny – repeat to all units that under no circumstances are they to approach the target. Strictly locate, follow and observe.'

'Yes sir.'

'Tom – have someone contact City and raise a firearms unit. Then let West Pennine know there may be some fast traffic coming their way. I'll try and organise the helicopter, before I ruin Mr Wood's lunch.'

Molly was just about to put the Yorkshire puddings in. I took pity on him and told him we could manage, strictly on condition that the next time Molly made Yorkshires, I was invited.

We alerted adjoining forces and listened to the banter on the radios. The sergeant knew the area better than a Buddhist monk knows his navel. He instinctively read the mind of the fleeing man and directed the cars under his command accordingly. I tried to follow the action on the big map. The net was slowly tightening, but there were some frighteningly large holes in it. Gilbert walked in. I gave him an update on the action.

'Where's the nearest ARV?' he asked.

Jenny overheard the question. 'They're just coming off the M62, sir,' she replied.

'Sorry, Charlie, didn't mean to take over.'

'No problem. Have them stand by, Jenny, until we know where laddo's heading. Do you want me to get out there, boss?'

'No, you handle it from here.'

Things went dead for a while. It looked as if he'd sneaked through the cordon. If he was heading for the motorway we might latch on to him in a few minutes, otherwise he'd be out of our patch and we'd have to rely on our neighbours. Then there was a sudden burst of static from the speaker.

'We've got him!' shouted an excited voice.

'Call sign and location? Let's have proper radio procedure, lads,' demanded the sergeant.

'It's Lima Tango,' someone yelled back. 'We're on

Parkside. He's gone the other way. We nearly hit him on the bend. Doing a . . . bloody 'ell! . . . done a U-turn and pursuing.'

'Lima Tango . . . whereabouts on Parkside?'

'Near the park, skipper, heading south. The park's on our left. He's turning left on to the Parkway; we've lost sight of him.'

The sergeant pointed towards the map. 'He's either heading for the Meadowlands or he's making a break for the Bradford Road,' he suggested.

'Lima Tango to control. We've regained contact. On Parkway, heading out of town. Just passing B & Q. He's about two hundred yards ahead and we're gaining.'

'How fast's he going?' I asked.

'Control to Lima Tango. What is your speed?

'About sixty.'

'Back off. Don't get any closer.'

'Zulu 99 airborne, Mr Priest,' interrupted Jenny. 'Requesting directions.'

I spoke directly with the chopper pilot, giving him some very unaeronautic bearings. We got him there, though. Then we contacted City to see what units they had available and to tell them to switch to our channel.

'Zulu 99 to Heckley Control. We've made contact with target.'

'Control to Chopper; can you make a low pass in front of him; make sure he knows you're there?'

'Will do.'

I turned to Jenny. 'Then blast him with your missiles,' I whispered.

'He's turning right,' someone yelled over the radio.

'Meadowlands,' stated the sergeant. He relayed the information to the other units in the vicinity.

'They're getting excited,' I said to the sergeant. 'Tell them not to chase him, leave it to the chopper.'

He passed the message on. Some of the villains who lived on the Meadowlands estate liked to think it was a no-go area, and the newspapers eagerly promoted this view. It wasn't, though. The area was rife with crime, but it was the pain-in-the-arse variety, committed by fourteen-to-eighteen-year-olds. Boys in men's bodies, but not old enough to draw the dole. They burgled each other's houses, then probably went for a drink together. Everybody knew who the culprits were. Even the respectable people – who were in the vast majority – could name a string of villains, but a brick through a window, or the threat of a firebomb, discouraged any contact with us. Who could blame them? The protection we could offer was negligible.

'Lima Sierra here. Approaching Meadowlands, where do you want us?'

'Don't know yet,' came back Lima Tango. 'Heading towards the big roundabout. Speed, nearly seventy.'

'Lima Sierra, this is Control. Get to the flats if you can, and wait. Lima Tango, back off and leave it to the chopper. Understood?'

'Yes, skip,' said a relieved voice, 'backing off. He's turning right at the roundabout, heading towards the flats.'

I was standing at the end of the console, alongside the sergeant. Gilbert was standing at the back, leaning on it and drumming his fingers. There was a burst of noise as everybody spoke at once.

'Repeat message,' ordered the sergeant.

'Lima Tango here. He's knocked a kid off a bike. Stopping to give assistance.'

'Zulu 99 here. I caught it on the video. Looks serious. Suggest you send for an ambulance, Control.'

'Will do. You stay with that, please, Lima Tango.'

'Understood.'

Gilbert thumped his fist into the palm of his other hand and walked over to the window.

'I'll do it,' I said. I had a quick look at the map to verify the street names, then rang the hospital.

'Zulu 99 to Control, he's heading for the right-hand block. Make that the southernmost block.'

'Did you read that, Lima Sierra?'

'Yes, understood. Heading that way now.'

I got straight through to Casualty, thank God.

'We can see him. He's seen us, doing a U-turn.'

'Follow him but don't give chase. Repeat, don't give chase.'

'Understood.'

A new voice came over the air: 'ARV Zulu Bravo to Control. On Heckley bypass. Any instructions?'

'Yes, Zulu Bravo. Turn on to Parkway, heading north. He may be heading back your way.'

'Firearms unit leaving city HQ,' said Jenny.

Another couple of cars from adjacent forces radioed in to say they were in the area. It looked as if he were panicking. If he'd managed to run into the flats we'd have lost him. They were a twenty-storey warren, named in memory of Hugh Gaitskell, one-time leader and unifier of the Labour Party. Now they stood as a monument to a social plan that had gone badly astray. They had more windows made of plywood than glass, and glue-sniffers and graffiti artists followed their pastimes unhindered.

'Hello, Heckley Control, this is India Romeo, we're coming out of Westland Road on to Dobgate. He's just gone by the end, heading towards Dudley.'

'OK, India Romeo. Follow, but don't chase. Understood?'

'Understood.'

'Zulu 99 to Control. He's turning on to the Heckley bypass. He must be doing about seventy.'

The bypass wasn't a purpose-built road. It was just a string of existing streets that had been linked together and given priority, to ease the rush-hour traffic flow. He wasn't going to get far at seventy miles per hour. The big question was would he kill anybody when the inevitable happened?'

'He's crashed! This is the helicopter. He's just bounced off the side of a bus.'

'What's his status?'

'Stationary. The car's in someone's garden. It wasn't too bad, though. Standing by.'

'India Romeo, where are you?'

'Approaching; we can see the chopper.'

'Zulu Bravo, where are you?'

'About half a mile away. We can see the chopper. Should be with them in a few seconds.'

'India Romeo; don't approach the suspect; he's believed to be armed. Wait for the ARV.'

'Right, skip.'

I needed a cup of tea. I walked over to the little boiler on the wall, filled it to the MAX mark and pressed the ON button. It was a struggle stopping myself giving advice to the men in the cars, telling them to stay well out of trouble. They were big boys; they'd had the training. Let them get on with it. Gilbert didn't look any happier than I felt.

'Wonder how the kid on the bike is?' he said, when I arrived back at the console. I just shook my head. Making enquiries about his health might make us feel better but wouldn't help him; sadly, we had other priorities.

'India Romeo to Control; we're there. He's standing outside the car. He looks shell-shocked.'

'Control to Romeo, keep your distance and wait for the ARV.'

'The passengers are getting off the bus. A woman's giving him a bollocking.'

'Does he look armed?'

'No. Now he's walking towards us.'

'Tell him to lie on the ground,' I said to the sergeant.

'Control to Romeo; order him to lie on the ground.'

Silence.

'Control to Romeo; what's happening?'

'He's lying on the ground.' More silence, then: 'India Romeo to Heckley Control, have arrested and handcuffed suspect.' We could hear the ARV's siren in the background. He went on: 'Here comes the cavalry, too late as usual.'

The boiler on the wall started to whistle. Jenny and I made everybody tea while they tied up the loose ends.

We were passing the cups round when Lima Tango came back on the air.

'Victim despatched in ambulance. Two other children were the only witnesses. Have them in the car and taking their details. We'll, er, need the FatAcc Investigation boys over here. Will you arrange it, please.'

They were referring to the standard procedure that swings into action after a fatal accident.

'Understood, will do,' replied the sergeant, gravely. 'Do you know his identity?'

'Yes, from these other two.'

'How old was he?'

'Thirteen

'Do his parents live nearby?'

'Yes, in the maisonettes.'

'Sorry to ask you this, lads; but how do you feel about . . .'

'No!' Gilbert held his hand out and interrupted the sergeant. 'Tell them to stand by. I'll be there in a few minutes. It's about time I made myself useful.'

None of us said anything. We were all afraid he'd ask us to go with him.

The heroes of the chase began filtering back to the station. The India Romeo crew were from City, so they were doubly pleased at making a good arrest on our territory. Their euphoria soon subsided when news of the young boy was given to them. We handed out tea and thank yous and wondered what Gilbert was finding to say. A constable brought me a big handgun in a plastic bag, found in the offender's car. It was at least a foot long. I held it up to feel the weight; its lightness told me it was obviously a replica. The others gathered round to gawp at it – it was a fearsome-looking brute. You could almost hear 'The Call of the Faraway Hills' welling up in the background. I looked at a constable who I knew to be an authority on such things.

'What do you reckon, Buntline Special?' I asked him.

He examined it through the plastic bag. 'Navy Colt,' he declared. 'Worth a fortune if it'd been real.'

'I bet the poor girl in the bank wet her pants when he stuck it under her nose,' someone said. 'It scares me just lying there.'

The villain was called Shawn Crabb, with a couple of other, fancy names in the middle. I stood in the doorway of the charge room as he was being processed. The custody sergeant read him his rights, emptied his pockets and made him sign for the contents, then charged him with armed robbery. He complained that he was ill; said he had 'flu and needed a doctor.

'Were you injured in the crash?' asked the sergeant. He shook his head.

'I'll ring for the doc,' I said, and phoned Sam Evans. He could buy me a drink out of his call-out fee.

The press were soon on the phone and I found myself fending them off with the standard platitudes. 'Further charges may follow' usually satisfies their readers. When Sam arrived I went down to the cells with him. Crabb, wearing one of our neat paper one-piece overalls, was sitting on the bunk, wrapped in a blanket. He said he was cold. Sam gave him a comprehensive examination, mainly to ensure he hadn't been hurt when he rammed the bus. The true cause of his sickness was plain to see: both arms were covered in needle scars and new sores.

'You've got to give me something, Doc,' he moaned.

Sam pointed to the scars. 'What are you injecting?' he demanded.

'Smack,' Crabb replied, his head lolling forward.

'Heroin?'

He nodded.

'How much? Do you know?'

He shook his head. 'No, all I can get. It's all shit nowadays.'

'I'll leave some pills with the sergeant,' Sam told him. 'They'll make you feel better.' Upstairs he rummaged in his bag and put a few white tablets in a container. 'Give him two of these every four hours,' he instructed.

I picked them up. 'What are they?' I asked.

'Aspirin,' he answered, with a bleak smile.

Cold turkey is not regarded as the ogre that it once was. It's not pleasant, but it's no worse than many everyday illnesses. At one time methadone was prescribed to ease devotees away from heroin, but the latest thinking is that this is a more addictive drug, with even more evil side-effects. Crabb was expecting methadone but he was in for a disappointment. I volunteered to take him his first dose.

'These are the pills the doctor left for you,' I told him, after I'd been let into his cell again. He reached out for them, but I clenched my fist around the bottle and pulled back from him.

'First of all, I want same information from you. Who do you get your drugs from? A name for a tablet; that's a fair exchange.'

He begged, pleaded and cried, but he wouldn't give me a name. He bought them from a bloke in a pub. He wasn't sure which pub. I thought about wiring his testicles to the pelican crossing outside, but I doubt if it would have helped.

'Does the name Cakebread mean anything to you?' He swore he'd never heard of him. 'OK,' I said, pocketing the tablets, 'have it your way,' and shouted for the jailer to let me out. Upstairs I placed the unopened bottle on the custody sergeant's desk. 'Give him another couple in four hours,' I told him.

CHAPTER TWENTY

It was after dark when I arrived home. It had been a long day. I had a tin of soup, then showered and shaved and drove to the General Hospital. She was propped up on her pillows. Apart from the dark shadows beneath her eyes, her face was as white as the bed linen. The ward was buzzing with visitors, but none were by her bed. She watched me approach.

'Hello,' I said. 'Remember me?'

She gave a little nod, but seemed unsure.

'I'm the policeman you duffed up in the New Mall a few months ago,' I explained. She stared blankly at me. There was a cage over her legs, holding the blankets off them.

'I, er, brought you a couple of magazines.' I put *Just Seventeen* and *Elle* on her cabinet. 'The man in the newsagent's said they were suitable. I got some funny looks, reading them on the bus. Do you mind if I sit down?'

I pulled the chair alongside the bed. 'I haven't come to ask you any questions, Julie. I know your mam and dad can't make it at night, and I don't do much on a Saturday, so I thought I'd come to see you. It was either you or the telly, so here I am.'

She didn't say anything.

'Is it hurting?' I asked. She nodded. 'Do you want me to ask the nurse to give you something?'

She shook her head. 'No thank you,' said a little voice.

'Do any of your school chums come to see you?' Another headshake. I wasn't wording these questions very well.

'They don't!' I exclaimed. 'Why do you think that is?'

She shrugged her shoulders. 'I don't know,' she whispered. 'I think they don't know what to say to me.'

'Well, you've got a point. I'm not sure what to say to you myself. Mind you, I've no kids of my own. The only time I speak to teenagers is to say "Don't do that" or "Put that back" or "Bugger off or I'll nick you".'

She gave a hint of a smile. I delved my hand into my jacket pocket and pulled out the little teddy bear. 'Oh,' I said, 'I nearly forgot. He said he was missing you, so I brought him along.'

She reached out and took him from me. This time the smile reached a little further. He was the scruffiest of all her teddies, so I guessed she'd had him the longest, loved him the most.

'I wondered about bringing you some chocolates,' I told her, 'but they didn't have any for under fifty pence, so I decided you were probably on a diet and wouldn't have appreciated them anyway; so I didn't buy you any.' I took a deep breath. 'That's my excuse.'

She looked downcast. 'There's no point, is there?' she mumbled.

'No point in what?' I asked.

'Being on a diet.'

'No, not for someone as skinny as you, but I thought you girls were always on diets.'

Her eyes flickered towards the cage over her legs. 'Nobody will want me now,' she said, her eyes filling with tears.

'Of course they will. There's someone waiting for all of us, somewhere. It's taking me a long time to find mine, but that's another story.'

'Not when you've only one leg.'

'Rubbish,' I told her. 'Did you ever hear of Douglas Bader?'

She sniffed and shook her head.

'Well, when I was a kid Douglas Bader was a big hero. He lost both his legs in a plane crash. Below the knee, like you. Both of them. He learnt to fly again and shot down umpteen German aeroplanes in the Second World War. He played golf, learnt to ballroom dance and married Muriel Pavlow. I was upset about that – I was in love with her myself. And he refused to walk with a stick. If he could do it, anyone can.'

She didn't look very impressed.

'Mind you,' I added, 'nobody liked him – he was a complete arsehole of a bloke.'

She tried to laugh between the sobs. I think I cheered her up. I asked her if I could call again, and she said I could. Better still, I offered to send along some of the handsome young bobbies I worked with. She blushed at that prospect.

I should have eaten, but I had no appetite. I rang Gilbert to give him moral support. A chief superintendent from Huddersfield was investigating the death of the youngster on the bike. There was plenty of evidence that our car was well back, not involved in a Hollywood-style chase, and the chopper had videoed the whole incident, but no doubt we would be criticised from the usual quarters. I felt I needed a drink, so I poured myself a generous Glenfiddich. I don't like whisky, so it couldn't really be called succumbing to temptation. Then I fell asleep in front of the television. TV does that to me – I don't even have to switch it on.

Next morning my mouth felt like the inside of a dead marsupial's pouch. I ate my favourite breakfast of double cornflakes, with six sugars and the top off the milk, with tinned grapefruit for pudding, and drove to the newsagent's for a couple of the Sunday heavies. Two hours later, as I was trying to decide which set of patio furniture to send for, Mike Freer rang.

'Hi, Sheepdip. Didn't think you'd be up yet,' he said.

'Then why did you ring?' I replied.

'Too much bed is bad for you. Did you know that Fangio said he was scared to go to bed, because most people died there?'

'He must have had a big bed. Did you ring for a reason, or are you just determined to keep me from pruning my herbaceous shrubs?'

'No, or to put it another way, yes. Talking about herbaceous shrubs, has it been a good year for your Gloxinias?'

'I don't know. You'd better ask our Gloxinia.'

'Ah, yes; wonderful girl. I tried to ring you yesterday, but you were up to the goolies in it, from what I gathered. What happened?'

It sounded as if we were talking business now, so I related the story of the chase and its consequences to him. When I'd finished he said: 'It sounds as if Crabb has been growing desperate over the last few days. I'm not surprised. We got the analysis of that wrap you brought in, and it's not a pretty picture. That's what I rang to tell you about.'

'Go on.'

'Well, for a start, it was about ten percent heroin.'

'That doesn't sound much.'

'It's not. Thirty or forty percent is the norm. Which means that your average everyday addict has to inject three times as much for a decent high.'

'Which is bad news for them.'

'It is. For a start, if they ever buy some of the good stuff they could accidentally overdose. Meanwhile, they're pumping vast doses of the contaminants into their bloodstream, which is even more worrying.'

'I see. Tell me what was in it.'

'Well, the main constituent is milk powder. Not too dangerous in itself. Dilute milk won't carry a lot of oxygen around your body, but it won't poison you. Then there was flour – the stuff you make bread with; and, lastly, plaster of Paris.'

'Plaster of Paris!' I exclaimed.

'Yep, or something similar, such as Polyfilla.'

'But that could harden, couldn't it?'

'It tends to settle out. Actually the flour is just as bad. They both cause blockages.'

'Jesus. What's happening? Are the pushers growing too greedy?' I asked.

'Not sure. Maybe not. It could be that demand is so high that a few occasional users have decided it's a good way to make a quick buck, by cutting their own supplies with any white powder they can find under the kitchen sink and selling it on. Kids flogging it in the playground to finance their own habit, that sort of thing. It's called enterprise.'

'Market forces.'

'Exactly.'

I thought about what he'd told me and remembered the conversation I'd had with Billy Morrison of the Fraud Squad. I asked: 'Mike, what's the chances of hitting Cakebread with the Drug Trafficking Act?'

'You mean the Drug Trafficking Offences Act, 1987?'

'That one.'

'Slim. There've been one or two prosecutions, but the drug end of it was well proven. You'd have to do that first, before you could strip his assets. When Cakebread was turned over he was clean, wasn't he?'

'Like Mother Teresa. What happened to the parcel that was planted in my car?'

'Your half-kilogram of Bogota's best; it's been incinerated, along with a load of other stuff. Listen, Charlie; I hope you're not thinking what I think you're thinking. If you are, forget it. Hear me?'

'It was just an idea.'

'Well don't have any more like it. They're not worth it, Charlie. Keep repeating "Pension, retirement, pension, retirement". OK?'

'I hear you. Thanks for ringing.'

It was definitely too cold to prune the shrubs, so I put a CD on the player and stretched out on the sofa to listen to it and relax. In deference to the sabbath I'd selected my Thomas Tallis. I played it loud, to impress God and the neighbours. I like the English composers, even if some of them have names that wouldn't make the Jockey Club members' enclosure. It's good music to think to; sort out your mind and make decisions. Inspirational, even.

Too many people were being hurt. We were catching the little fish, victimising the victims, while the hammerhead swam free. I lay staring at the ceiling as the choir's final, triumphant chord faded into the ether; then I slipped into my trainers and leather jacket and went out to the car. I'd decided to go shark fishing.

Sunday afternoon is probably as quiet as it ever gets down at the station. Most of the squad cars were in the yard, one bearing a dented wing, evidence of a memorable Saturday night for someone. The front door of the building was locked; I spoke into the microphone to gain admittance.

Sergeant Jenks was in the charge room, with a PC and a miserable wretch who was being fed into one end of the sausage machine that would cough him out into the magistrates' court on Monday morning. Jenks looked up when I poked my head round the door.

'Hello, Mr Priest,' he said. 'We weren't expecting you. Anything special?'

'No, Sergeant. I've just called to collect something from my office.' I nodded towards the frightened little man. 'What's he in for?'

Jenks shook his head and tut-tutted. 'Trumping in church, sir,' he said.

I glared at him, long and mean. 'Hang the bastard,' I pronounced.

Upstairs, I pulled open my bottom drawer. The brown envelope addressed to our late Chief Constable was still there. I reread the note it contained. The mysteries of PH and PM were solved; now was the time to exorcise the rest of it. I wrote the number for the alarm, 4297, on the back of my hand with a ball-pen, and pocketed the three keys.

Ten minutes later Heckley was falling behind and below, as I gunned the car up the moorland road that led into Lancashire. The radio tuned itself in to the local station and I sang along with the music, slapping time on the wheel with my fingers. All the songs were new to me, but you feel you'd heard them in the cradle after the first two lines. I felt good; activity is the best antidote for depression.

Even on a bad day the moors look all right. Today was still and clear, for a change, and they were at their benign best. It was only temporary, though: moody malevolence was never more than a breeze away. A million years of rain and wind has smoothed off every sharp edge, every jutting crag or soaring pinnacle. The hills roll and curve sensuously, with the valleys cutting deep cleavages between them, The shapes they make are animal, rather than geological.

Man's tentative grip is seen only in the valleys. Bold

mills stand foursquare to the elements, their chimneys long grown cold. Rows of solid workers' terraces are now the homes of painters and the makers of thick wooden jigsaws and other primitive toys; guaranteed to make your children believe that Santa Claus hates them. Cotton and worsted that once clothed and carpeted the world have been replaced by politically correct dolls and pottery that grinds the enamel off your teeth. I love it all.

Going down the other side the patchwork of the Lancashire plain was visible almost to the coast. Soon I was driving through the middle of Oldfield, rattling across the market square with its ancient cross, and heading out towards Welton and ABC House.

I drove past the gatehouse at the front entrance. Apart from the rows of mute lorries and security vans, the only vehicles parked there were a small motorbike belonging to the gateman and Breadcake's Rolls Royce. Dammit, I hadn't expected him to be in today. I settled down to watch, from as far away as possible. After an hour I rang his home, The Ponderosa, on the mobile phone.

'Hello,' said a female voice.

'Hello, is Mr Cakebread there?' I asked.

'No.' She didn't give much away.

'Oh. It's Mr Curtis here, of Curtis's. I'd like a quick word with him, soon as poss. Are you expecting him?' Curtis's were the local Rolls Royce dealers.

'Yes, he shouldn't be long.'

'Good, I'll try a little later. If I miss him could you ask him to give me a bell sometime tomorrow?'

'Yes.'

'Thank you. 'Bye.' Click.

At least it sounded as if he was due to go home soon. He did, just before the end of the Radio 4 play.

The cobbled lane that runs down the side of ABC House was deserted, apart from a couple of vehicles parked outside the factory next door. I left my car behind them and walked back to the side entrance of the building. I knew that two of my keys fitted the small door that was inset into the big sliding one. Without looking round I unlocked the deadlock, then the Yale, and stepped inside. A small red light was blinking on the burglar alarm unit on the wall at the side of the door. I typed in the number and the light turned to a steady green one. He hadn't changed the code, I was in. I closed the door, leaving the latch off.

It had possibly been a weaving shed, or something similar, in days gone by. Now it was just a big empty space, devoid of any machinery. Across the other side were a couple of disabled lorries, cabs tipped forward and entrails laid neatly on the concrete floor, waiting for their mechanics to resume work on Monday morning. A security van stood on blocks, minus its wheels. It was gloomy without the lights on, the only illumination coming from a row of windows up near the roof. Away to the right was the main entrance – a big concertina door that led out into the yard – and the office block where I had met the desirable Gloria. The offices were a two-storey affair, easily accommodated within the height of the main building. A flight of metal stairs led up to the next floor. I wondered if the door at the top of them gave access to Breadcake's private suite, with its deep carpets and wonderful matching colour scheme. There was a good way to find out.

I padded across to the stairs and climbed them two at a time, hauling on the handrail and extracting the third key from my pocket as I moved. I paused at the door and looked around. The place was as silent as a turkey farm on Boxing Day. I tried the key. It turned. I let the door swing open and surveyed the room. It was windowless and dark. I didn't want to put the lights on, so I left the door wide open. It still took a few moments for my eyes to accustom themselves to the gloom. It was a big room, with an odd assortment of furniture. There were two or three easy chairs and a huge table that might have come from a drawing office or a school laboratory. But what really caught my attention was the familiar face, staring unwaveringly at me through the gloaming.

CHAPTER TWENTY-ONE

I gazed back at it with a deal more fascination than when I'd seen the original in the Louvre, many years ago. It was the *Mona Lisa,* but the picture wasn't hanging on the wall: it was on an easel, as if waiting for the artist to add the finishing touches.

I turned it a few degrees, so that it received more of the light from the door. It was good. Oil paints are slow to dry; the different colours drying at different speeds. The earth colours, as used in this painting, might take a couple of days, whereas a red might need a week or more to be touch-dry. Total dryness can take up to a year. I tested the surface with my fingers, to feel what it could tell me. Not much. He could, of course, have been working on it for months, developing minute areas with infinite patience.

That hint of a smile on her face doesn't fool me. I reckon someone in the room has just broken wind, and, being a lady, she's desperately trying to pretend she didn't hear them. I think she'd look better with a big, lecherous grin. If the paint wasn't completely dry I should be able to do it with my fingertips. I tried to draw the corners of the mouth upwards, pressing hard on the surface. It was too late. She looked a little more as if she was about to lose control, but not as manic as I'd hoped for. I glanced around for materials, then pulled open the drawer in the table.

All his paints were neatly laid out, as per the rainbow. I went straight to the short end of the spectrum and selected a colour. Cadmium scarlet, perfect. Squeezing the paint directly from the tube on to the canvas, I gave her a luscious, Monroesque pout – although it did look as if she'd applied her lipstick while riding a horse.

I placed the squashed tube back in the drawer without putting the top back on and moved up the frequency range. Something had to be done about those eyebrows and the receding hairline. Chrome yellow; a bit cool, but it'd do. I gave her two arching brows, then, working outwards from the parting, masses of looping, blonde curls. Bet she'd always wanted to be a blonde. Half a tube of lamp black provided eyelashes that looked like lawn rakes. I closed the drawer and examined my handiwork. Well, at least it was original.

At that point I should have left. I'd penetrated their empire and guaranteed them a bad case of dysentery when they found out. I should have organised twenty-four-hour surveillance. Over the years, there've been a lot of things I should have done, but didn't. Besides, I've always had an interest in interior decoration. I just had to have a look at Mr Cakebread's private suite. I presumed that was where the door at the far end of the room led.

The handle turned silently and the door swung inwards when gently pushed. It was almost pitch black inside, except for a flickering blue glow reflecting off the shiny surfaces. As the door swung wider I saw the source of it. High in a corner was a small black-and-white closed-circuit TV monitor, showing the big door at the side, where I had entered the building.

'Come in, Charlie,' said a familiar voice, and the lights flashed on.

Rudi Truscott was standing at the far side of the room. He had a smug expression on his face and a Smith and Wesson in his hand. It was a Lady Smith, one of a neat little series of weapons designed for American women to carry in their purses. It was a thirty-eight, though, and would fell a moose at this range.

'Pizza Express,' I said. 'Did anybody here order a *quattro stagioni*?'

'Sit down,' he commanded, gesturing towards an armchair, 'and keep your tiresome humour to yourself.'

Ouch! That hurt. He placed himself on an upright chair at the other side of the room. I glanced round at the furnishings. There was a lot of lilac. The style was

Puffs Boudoir, with heavy Cocktail Bar influences.

'Nice room,' I said. 'Did you choose the colours?' No answer, just a contemptuous stare.

'I, er, I saw your painting.' I gestured towards the outer room. 'It's good, one of your best. But surely you're not going to try to heist the *Mona Lisa,* are you?'

He sniggered. 'No. While I am confident I can reproduce Leonardo's masterpiece, he unfortunately used inferior materials. I am unable to do justice to the surface cracks that it is covered with. The picture is just a little present for the wife of a friend. She says it's her favourite painting.'

'Good,' I replied, nodding my approval. 'Good. I'm sure she'll appreciate it. Tell me, what's her second favourite: the white horses galloping through the waves, or the Burmese lady with the green face?'

'You're a sarcastic bastard,' he hissed. 'You always were. But we won't have to put up with you for much longer.'

'Why? What are you going to do?' I asked. It seemed a reasonable question. I was genuinely interested.

'You'll find out.'

'I'd never have thought of you as a killer, Rudi,' I told him. 'I'm not.'

'Aren't you? What about old Jamie?'

'Who's old Jamie?'

'You remember. The tramp whose body we found in your cottage. We've been looking for you for his murder.'

Fear flickered across his face for a moment. The gun wavered alarmingly. 'I didn't kill him,' he hissed. 'He . . . died.'

'Did he? And what did you do to help the process? Give him a litre of Bell's and tell him to get it down? It amounts to the same thing in my book.'

His eyes flashed up towards the TV monitor and he smiled. 'Fortunately, Priest, your book is not the one we're working from.'

I followed his gaze. The big door was open and the Rolls was coming through. As it slid shut again Truscott said: 'Get up, it's time to go.' He pointed towards the exit. 'Walk slowly, and don't try anything.'

I walked slowly. Very slowly. I was hoping he'd come up close behind me, but he was wary. 'Faster!' he snapped.

We were approaching the painting, which was angled away from us, towards the outer door. I glanced back at him and said: 'Yes, it's a really nice picture.' We'd reached it now. I went on: 'It needed a few small alterations, though, so I made them for you. I hope you don't mind.'

I grabbed the top of the easel and turned it so he could appreciate my handiwork. With the lights on it wasn't *La Gioconda* any more; it was Barbara Cartland, after being ravished by the Chipping Sodbury chapter of Hell's Angels.

His face contorted in horror: 'You bastard!' he screamed.

328

One second later the picture, with easel still attached, hit him in the mouth and I was out through the door.

Cakebread was opening the boot of the Rolls. He looked up when he heard the commotion and his natural look of self-satisfaction turned to panic when he saw me. I was down the stairs in three leaps and already running when my feet hit the ground. Truscott fired. The bullet ricocheted off the concrete in front of me, nearly hitting Cakebread.

'Three seconds, dear God,' I prayed. 'Three seconds, that's all I ask, with my hands round his throat.'

I nearly made it. With five yards to go Cakebread delved into the boot and spun in my direction. I found myself charging towards the pitiless black orifices of a sawn-off shotgun.

Plan B. It wasn't much, but it was all I had. I executed a body-swerve and change of direction that would have graced any football field in the world, and headed for the door. But you can't outrun a twelve-bore.

The noise, the pain and the impact all hit me at once. The blast caught me in the right side, spinning me round. My legs tangled and I went down. The only thought in my head was 'keep moving'. I rolled over and over. Then I was scrabbling forward on my hands and knees and finally on my feet again. I thumbed the door catch with my free hand – the one that wasn't holding my guts in – yanked it open and spilt out on to the welcoming pavement.

* * *

329

Penny Throstle owns a craft shop in the new riverside development at Oldfield. She sells rugs and blankets that she weaves herself on a Victorian floor loom, purchased when the company that had hitherto owned it fell victim to advancing technology and cheap imports. She was given the option to buy the three similar ones in the mill at the same knockdown price, so she took those, too. The intention was to use them for spares, or restore them for sale to another small operator. Fortunately she did neither, and all four are now in use.

The rugs are usually hung on walls as decoration, being far too expensive to walk on or throw over the bed. Her designs come from all around the world, as well as the original ones she develops herself. Ms Throstle was doing quite nicely, thank you, until she made a rug for Mr Rahkshan. Now she is doing very well indeed.

Mr Rahkshan is a silversmith, and owns the shop next door. He is a Muslim. One day, in a period when Ms Throstle was beguiled by the geometric patterns of Islamic art and producing beautiful works under its heady influence, she made Mr Rahkshan a prayer mat. Her motives were not purely spiritual – she fancied him madly. The design was based on five lines, radiating from a point halfway along one side. Mr Rahkshan was captivated when she explained how it worked. You simply placed the mat on the floor, with the appropriate line pointing in the direction of the sun; then, as you knelt on the mat, you were automatically facing towards Mecca.

It was only accurate, of course, when within a few hundred miles of Oldfield. The design would have to be modified for use in other parts of the world. Mr Rahkshan proudly showed the mat to his friends. As well as having direction-finding capabilities it was also a thing of beauty, for Ms Throstle had invested her best efforts, plus a few prayers of her own, in it. One week later he gave her a firm order for twenty similar mats, at an extremely agreeable price, with promises of more to follow.

A month later they became partners – alas, only for business purposes – went mail-order and put the other looms into use. They were inundated.

'The secret of a good reputation,' Mr Rahkshan would say, 'is to produce a good-quality article and deliver it on time. Then you can charge what you want,' and he would give his tinkling laugh that entranced Ms Throstle. The trouble was, they had received so many orders they might have difficulty in achieving the second premise. Simply packing all the rugs for posting was a gargantuan undertaking. Fortunately a little factory that made cardboard cartons came to the rescue. They were in Welton, joined on to the back of ABC House, domicile of Aubrey Cakebread.

Business for them was desperate; they were rapidly coming unstuck at the flaps. When Mr Rahkshan asked them to make boxes for the mats, they gladly offered to pack, address and post them, at a small extra cost. It was a satisfactory arrangement all round. The grateful staff worked all weekend to process the latest order. They finished it late Sunday afternoon, and had just left the factory and were walking down the cobbled lane alongside ABC House, on their way home, when I burst into their midst.

There were about six of them. They were gathered around me, trying to comprehend my gibberings, when Cakebread appeared at the side door. He was brandishing the shotgun, no doubt with two fresh charges up the spouts, and looked intent on murder. The alley should have been deserted at that time of day. When Cakebread saw the crowd he panicked and fled back inside. I don't know if Penny Throstle's mats ever do any good for the people who pray on them, but there is no doubt that they saved my life.

Cakebread had killed Truscott with the second barrel. He jumped into the Rolls and fled through the front entrance. The poor gateman was dozing in his hut when the car smashed through the barrier. He hadn't even known that his boss was in the place. It was a long time, though, before I learnt all this.

I was in intensive care for three days, in hospital for three weeks and off work for three months. Who decided that a week should have seven days? All round the world, too. Bet you'd never get today's politicians to agree to it. Hospitalisation gives you the opportunity to ponder on questions like that.

I once went to the funeral of one of my more agreeable clients and I was the only mourner there. It occurred to me then that a measure of a man's life is the number of people who attend his funeral. OK, so nobody turned up at Mozart's, but there's always an exception. Another good indicator, I have since discovered, is how many visitors he gets when he's in hospital. Numerically I didn't do too badly, but they were all policemen or policemen's wives. I had no illusions – Gilbert organised a rota. There were still days when I felt that the hands of the clock were painted on, and I longed for a familiar face to come round the corner. There was nobody special, though.

Except just once. I'd had a bit of a relapse after they brought me to Heckley General and was lying with a tube up my nose and a drip in my arm. The nurse was smiling as she held the screen wide open and told me I had a visitor. Julie hobbled in on her new crutches. 'Hello,' she said, softly.

I tried to smile at her, but my throat felt as if I'd swallowed a chainsaw.

'My mum told me what happened to you. I hope you get well soon. I've brought you something to read.' She wobbled alarmingly on the crutches as she retrieved a magazine from the pocket of her dressing gown, and held up the latest copy of *Just Seventeen*.

I managed, to say 'Thanks' as she placed it on my cabinet.

After an awkward silence she said: 'Martin came to see me. And Claire and some girls from school. I think Claire fancies him. She says she's going to tell him some names of . . . you know . . . the drugs thing.'

I shook my head. 'It doesn't . . . matter,' I croaked.

'Are you in pain?' she asked with concern.

I gathered up my reserves of strength and courage and mumbled: 'Only . . . when . . . I laugh.'

She smiled at me. Her face really was bonny. As if an afterthought she dipped into her pocket again and produced the teddy bear. 'He's yours now,' she told me, as I reached out for him.

I held him up so I could see him without moving my head. One eye was missing and an arm was hanging on by a thread. 'What's he . . . called?' I asked.

Julie manoeuvred on her crutches and pointed herself towards the way out. 'Douglas,' she said, over her shoulder, 'Douglas Bearda.'

I watched her swing hesitantly away. You'll be all right, I thought. Then I drifted off into the best untroubled sleep I'd had for months, with Douglas watching over me from the bedside locker.

They'd removed a few feet of my intestine and a piece of liver, but it wasn't a problem. The doctor told me that I still had twenty-odd feet of gut left, and the liver is the only major organ we have that can regenerate itself. I was in nearly new condition and my warranty was still valid.

'Just go easy on the alcohol,' he told me, on the morning I was discharged, 'and lay off the fried food.'

'No problem, Doc. What about my sex life? Will that have been affected?'

'No, of course not,' he replied in his most reassuring manner.

'Pity,' I said. 'I was hoping it would have been.'

CHAPTER TWENTY-TWO

The waiter asked if we preferred our coffee and liqueurs where we were, or would we rather make ourselves comfortable in the lounge.

'In the lounge?' suggested Gilbert.

Annabelle and Molly nodded their acquiescence, so we all moved through and resettled ourselves in the easy chairs round a low table.

'You know,' said Molly to Annabelle, 'this is the first time Gilbert has ever told me about a case. Usually I have to be content with what I can glean from the papers.' She turned to her husband: 'Go on then, finish it off: what happened to this Cakebread man?'

The waiter appeared with the coffees. He placed them on the table and told me that my tea would be along in a moment, in the tone of voice he normally reserved for customers who'd asked for the ketchup.

When he'd gone Gilbert said: 'Well, the local police put out an APW – that's an all-ports warning – for Cakebread, but, frankly, they were a bit slow. He made it all the way to Blackpool airport, where his plane was. He'd flown it the day before and left instructions for it to be refuelled and serviced for use the following weekend. It hadn't been done though. He made an unauthorised take-off and headed south. The tower alerted us and the RAF and various tracking stations, and he was shadowed all the way. When it was obvious that he was making for foreign parts the RAF asked the Americans for assistance. Apparently our planes are too fast and the helicopters haven't the range. The Yanks had an IO stooging around somewhere . . .'

'What, an old BSA motorbike?' I interrupted. 'My father had one of those when I was a kid.'

'No, dumbo, it's an aeroplane. Weird thing with two big jet engines on the back. Apparently they can fly quite slowly if necessary. So this A10 tagged on to Cakebread's tail and followed him. Somewhere off the Channel Isles he ran out of fuel and ditched in the sea. It was dark by then. A fishing boat recovered his body next morning.'

We sat in silence for a few moments. Death, even the death of an enemy, always deserves a few private thoughts. I poured a cup of tea and sweetened it with half a sachet of sugar.

'Why did he shoot . . . Truscott, was it?' asked Molly.

Gilbert didn't volunteer a reply, so I did. 'We can't be sure,' I said. 'To begin with, Truscott was bearing down on him brandishing a gun. It may have flashed through his mind that the game was up and Truscott could turn Queen's evidence. Alternatively, he may have realised that Rudi had given the game away, and shot him in anger. Another possibility is that he'd intended to kill him all along, once he had no further use for him. We'll never know the truth.'

I looked at Annabelle and we exchanged smiles. She was wearing a navy-blue pinstriped suit with red blouse and accessories and looked incredibly beautiful. Her skirt was shorter than I would have expected, displaying a pair of elegant knees that gave me a pain in my operation. I wasn't complaining; I just wanted to sit there for ever, basking on the edge of her limelight.

'That's it,' announced Gilbert. 'No more shop talk. Have you seen the price of cauliflowers lately, Annabelle? That's what we ought to be doing: growing cauliflowers.'

She laughed at him. 'Could I just ask one more question?' she said.

'You, Annabelle, can ask as many questions as you like.'

I was going to have to watch Gilbert; he was as bewitched as I was.

'This Truscott man. Why did he approach Charles in the first place? What was he thinking of?'

'Good question,' replied Gilbert. 'I'll let my trusty lieutenant answer that one.'

I lowered my cup. 'Vanity,' I said. 'Truscott had a very desirable lifestyle. He'd stopped lecturing and lived by his paintings – his copies of other artists' works. He'd sell to dealers, at an inflated price, without making any claims or telling any lies. They'd show the pictures to gullible gallery owners, again being somewhat frugal with the truth. There's nobody easier to cheat than a greedy person who thinks he's pulling a fast one. The painting would find itself on somebody's wall, credited to one of the masters. Truscott wasn't satisfied with that, though. He wanted recognition for himself, and it was gnawing at his heart that he didn't get any. There's a popular belief that artists are only famous after death. When Cakebread came to him with this scheme he saw it as a way of making a million or two, then vanishing, presumed dead, after leaking the information that the Art Aid paintings were really his work. He wanted the best of both worlds. I was the stooge he chose to make the leak.'

'I see. Or I think I do. And the real paintings were traded for drugs in North Africa?'

'That's right.'

'Were any drugs recovered?'

'Yes, quite a haul. Mrs Cakebread spilt the beans to save her own skin.'

We said goodbye to Molly and Gilbert in the car park and I drove Annabelle back towards the Old Vicarage.

On the way she asked me about the Picasso. 'Will they be able to tell which is the real one?'

'No problem; they'll just X-ray them both.'

'Won't the canvas be different on the modern one?' she said.

'Not necessarily. There are thousands of cheap Victorian paintings about. Just about every house sale has a few. Truscott would buy them all, just for the canvas and the frames.'

'You're very knowledgeable about art.'

'Not really, and I did attend art college. Maybe it wasn't a complete waste of time after all.'

I let the car freewheel to a halt outside her gate. My hand was hovering on the ignition key, wondering whether to stop the engine, when she said: 'Do you mind if I don't ask you in, Charles? It is rather late and . . .'

'No, of course not,' I lied, comforting myself with the thought that bishops' widows have to keep up some sort of appearance.

'Thank you for inviting me out, I've really enjoyed myself. And I'm so pleased that you're recovered.'

'Thank you for coming. And . . . well . . . thanks for enquiring about me. That's what helped me through the long days.' And the endless nights. She pulled the handle to open the door.

'Annabelle . . .' I said, 'shall I try for those tickets for the next concert?'

'Yes, I'd like that,' she replied, and leant over and

kissed me on the cheek. Then she turned and got out, as my fingers trailed down the sleeve of her jacket.

On my first day back I arrived in the office bright and early, but everybody else was already there. They'd bought me a box of After Eight chocolates, a bottle of Albanian sherry and a rather nice bunch of carnations. They all said they were glad to have me back and one or two asked to see my scars.

'Sorry, private viewings only,' was my stock reply. I opened the box of chocolates and passed them to Maggie.

Nigel had moved on and was now a uniformed sergeant in Halifax. Tony Willis had been promoted to full inspector, and would be leaving now that I was back. I'd be sorry to lose him. There was a new face, though, hovering on the edge of the group.

'Who's the dishy blonde?' I whispered to Sparky.

'Helen Chatterton,' he replied. 'Just joined us this morning.'

'That's right, I remember her. She started at the same time as Nigel Newley. He said she had . . .' She certainly didn't look as if she had halitosis that could raise the dead.

'Said she had what?'

'Oh, nothing. I suppose I'd better have a word with her.'

Sparky introduced us. She was polite, with an air of efficiency that hid any nervousness she might be feeling. I gave her the latest printout of unsolved mysteries and told her that I'd see her after the morning meeting. People were starting to drift away. Somebody thrust the chocolate box into my hands; it was empty.

'Just a minute, please,' I shouted. Everybody turned to face me. I stood on a chair for greater effect. 'Before you all go I'd just like to say two words . . .' I held the After Eight box above my head and turned it over. The empty brown wrappers tumbled around my head and settled on my shoulders. 'Greedy sods!' I yelled.

Upstairs it was more of the same, for about a minute, then we got down to business. I was brought up to date with happenings in the division and told where to give priorities. The rustlers were still at their dirty deeds, but more so.

'It's not just someone knocking off the odd lamb for the deepfreeze,' Gilbert told me. 'It's on a commercial scale now. The hill farmers are already going through a bad time; this could break some of them. Put it higher up the list, will you, Charlie?'

When I went down to the office again Sergeant Jenks was waiting with Helen. He said: 'It's good to have you back, Mr Priest. I made a list of all the people who rang to see how you were. Thought that perhaps you might like to thank them. Mind you, most of 'em are villains. That lady – Mrs Wilberforce – she rang every day at first, when it was touch and go.'

'OK, I'll ring her, er, them. Thanks for the list.' He left and I turned to Helen. 'Right, Helen. It's your first day with us and my first day back. What have you decided we should concentrate on?'

She pursed her lips and tilted her head in a thoughtful manner. 'We could always go see Mrs Wilberforce,' she suggested.

'Er, no, that can wait. I was thinking more along the lines of . . . you know, crime.'

I was close to her now, as we pored over the printout. I took a long, deep inhalation. The ganglia along my nasal passages went on to red alert. Helen pointed at various offences, mainly burglaries, and spoke intelligently about them.

I took another slow breath. Airborne molecules reacted with receptors and sent impulses spinning to my brain. I could smell . . . summer breezes wafting across the meadows of Provence; the forest at Kielder after a rain shower; all the spices of Araby. Pheromones bombarded my senses, triggering reactions in other parts of my body. That bastard Newley had been winding me up.

'Yes,' I croaked, struggling to adhere to the company's guidelines, 'that's all good stuff. However, we've been instructed to give more priority to the sheep-stealing. It's getting out of hand. So far, we've concentrated on the sharp end of the crime: kept observations, looked for tyre tracks, that sort of thing. Maybe we ought to be investigating the disposal end of it.'

'Talk to the butchers, see if they've been offered cheap lamb chops,' she suggested.

'That's the idea. I'll show you where most of the offences were committed, to give you an inkling of what we're up against; introduce you to the farmers; then you can do the leg work. OK?'

'That's fine by me, sir.'

'Rule number one – and we don't have many – cut out the sir.' I pulled my jacket back on, curled the corner of my lip and said: 'OK, Frank. Let's go.'

Helen looked at me, nonplussed. 'Pardon?' she said.

I shrugged my shoulders. 'Steve McQueen,' I explained, 'He said that, in *Bullitt*.'

She thought about it. 'No he didn't. In the film he was called Frank – Frank Bullitt. He didn't say it to himself; his partner said it to him.'

'You're right.' I stabbed at her with a forefinger. 'OK – you can be Steve McQueen, I'll be the little Mexican. Let's go!'

If you enjoyed *The Picasso Scam*, read on to find
out about the other books in the
Charlie Priest series . . .

➤◆◄

To discover more great crime novels and to place an
order visit our website at
www.allisonandbusby.com
or call us on
020 7580 1080

The Mushroom Man

There's nothing Detective Inspector Charlie Priest hates more than a case involving children. When Georgina, the eight-year-old daughter of local businessman Miles Dewhurst, goes missing, Charlie and his colleagues soon start to fear the worst. Charlie's suspicions are focused on Dewhurst and, in a race against time to find Georgina, Charlie's life is further complicated when it seems a killer is targeting clergymen. Three have died suddenly, and a picture of a Destroying Angel mushroom has been left beside the body of the latest victim. But why would a serial killer focus on men of the cloth?

The Judas Sheep

Detective Inspector Charlie Priest is officially on sick leave, but this brief break from work comes to an abrupt end when Mrs Marina Norris's chauffeur is found dead from unnatural causes – namely a blast to the head from a Kalashnikov. Meanwhile, big-time drug smugglers on the Hull–Rotterdam run demand his attention. His contact, Kevin, is a lowly cog in the great smuggling wheel, and easily hoodwinked into believing that Charlie's line of business is similar to his own. But the real villains are not such pushovers, and when Charlie uncovers a connection with his previous enquiry he realises that he's on very dangerous territory indeed.

Last Reminder

Hartley Goodrich has been found dead in his armchair, right beside the flowerpot that caused the gaping gash in his head. There's little doubt that this was murder, and when Detective Inspector Charlie Priest discovers that Hartley's financial advice had lost his clients a small fortune, there's no shortage of murder suspects either. But is the case all it seems? The enquiry reopens an investigation that fizzled out years before, involving diamonds, drugs and stolen gold bullion . . . and plenty of danger to boot. But when everything he holds dear is threatened, Charlie knows he can't stop digging until he's found out exactly what's been going down on his patch . . .

Deadly Friends

When Dr Clive Jordan's dazzling career is brought to an abrupt end by a bullet, his colleagues are devastated – especially the female ones. If the doctor hadn't been as discreet as an undertaker's cough, Detective Inspector Charlie Priest would suspect a jealous husband. But it's not going to be that simple. Charlie knows for certain there's a killer on the loose – and almost certainly a rapist as well. The chances of bagging either of them seem slim, but Charlie's a lot tougher and smarter than his affable manner indicates, and that's bad news for the villains on his patch.

Some by Fire

Charlie Priest was a newly promoted sergeant on the Leeds force when he was called to the scene of a tragic fire, deliberately set. Now a DI in nearby Heckley, Charlie jumps at the chance to reopen the investigation when a message left by a suicide victim suggests a new lead. Meanwhile, Charlie's under pressure to apprehend the burglars who're playing a dangerous game with wealthy elderly couples. By a combination of luck, detective work and, Charlie would say, soaring flights of the investigative imagination, he is soon closing in on the perpetrators of both crimes. But a cornered villain can be dangerous for a copper who'll take every kind of risk in the hunt for justice.

Chill Factor

Super-salesman Tony Silkstone wreaks a terrible revenge when he comes home to discover his wife dead, apparently strangled by her lover after a sex game that went wrong. But Detective Inspector Charlie Priest is the investigating officer, and he cannot be convinced that this murder is as cut and dried as it seems. When a hitman comes to town, Charlie is more interested in identifying the proposed target than in arresting the hitman, a strategy that produces surprising results. And when links are found between Mrs Silkstone's killer and the murder of a young girl in another part of the country, Charlie follows the trail only to discover that he is suddenly faced with difficult questions about his friends and his feelings towards them.

Laughing Boy

Laura Heeley was just an average mother of two, but at the age of thirty-eight her life was swiftly taken from her, stabbed in the back on the way home from bingo. Colinette Jones was a popular, attractive and intelligent student, but she has been strangled, her body dumped on the roadside. What is the connection between the two victims? Detective Inspector Charlie Priest must solve the mystery, though with no clear motive and police movements restricted by foot-and-mouth disease this proves an increasingly frustrating task. As the number of victims mounts, it becomes clear to Priest that this could be his biggest challenge yet . . .

Limestone Cowboy

DI Charlie Priest is wise-cracking his way through his daily routine, but it's not long before the clouds roll in. Someone has been tampering with food tins in the local supermarket. A national scare ensues and if Charlie doesn't act fast he could be dealing with a murder inquiry. As if that wasn't enough, he learns that an organised dog-fighting ring has set up operations nearby. Charlie's relationship with Rosie has reached a rocky patch too. When Charlie gets to the bottom of her change of heart he is somewhat concerned, and offers his help. But, as he's about to learn, sometimes helping only makes things worse . . .

Over the Edge

Joe Crozier, a businessman with a decidedly shady past, is enjoying an evening of being wined and dined. But after refusing to sell his nightclub, the Painted Pony, he is bound and gagged, and takes a silent and deadly dip into the nearby river. Meanwhile, DI Charlie Priest is called to the murder scene of the famous mountaineer Tony Krabbe, who has been attacked with his own ice axe. Charlie's love-life then takes a turn for the worse. He is desperate to seek out the truth in the two murder cases, but can love and violent death ever make comfortable bedfellows . . . or will Charlie finally be pushed over the edge?

Shooting Elvis

Is selling your employer's confidential records enough to warrant a particularly sadistic murder? Acting DCI Charlie Priest asks himself when handed the file on a bizarre murder. Appearances deceive, and it transpires that the victim may have been chosen simply because of his physical appearance. And when another body turns up, Charlie begins to wonder if he himself is the catalyst that motivates the killer. Before long he is embroiled in much more than a hunt for a murderer – now it is personal.

Grief Encounters

The monthly superintendents' meetings never hold much excitement for DI Charlie Priest, but this time he is in for a surprise. DCS Colin Swainby is to resign, quietly and without fuss, because certain allegations have been made against him. Allegations involving a woman, and it's not his wife. When MP Edward Gross finds himself similarly compromised, he also opts for a quiet exit, but his has a far more permanent outcome. Priest knows there must be a connection – he has to prove it before the body count starts escalating.

A Very Private Murder

DI Charlie Priest is on gardening leave – the neighbours have complained about his weeds – when the call comes. Ghislaine Curzon, girlfriend of one of the royal princes, is in Heckley to open the Curzon Centre, a new shopping mall and conference facility. But as she reveals the commemorative plaque it looks like someone has got to it first, defacing it with a single obscene word in foot-high red letters. The visiting dignitaries are aghast and the chief constable insists on Charlie investigating the case. When the mayor of Heckley and driving force behind the construction of the controversial new mall is found murdered, killed by a single shot to the head, the investigation takes a deadly turn. It's going to take more than standard police procedure to crack this case.